PENGUIN METR~~O~~

WORLD'S ~~WORST~~ BEST GIR~~LFRIEND~~

Durjoy Datta was born in New Delhi and completed a degree in engineering and business management before embarking on a writing career. His first book, *Of Course I Love You . . .*, was published when he was twenty-one years old and was an instant bestseller. His successive novels—*Till the Last Breath, Hold My Hand, When Only Love Remains, World's ~~Worst~~ Best Boyfriend, The Girl of My Dreams, The Boy Who Loved, The Boy with a Broken Heart* and *The Perfect Us*—have also found prominence on various bestseller lists, making him one of the highest-selling authors in India. Durjoy also has to his credit eleven television shows, for which he has written over 1000 episodes. For more updates, you can follow him on Instagram (www.instagram.com/durjoydatta).

Celebrating 35 Years of
Penguin Random House India

ALSO BY THE SAME AUTHOR

World's ~~Worst~~ Best Girlfriend

DURJOY DATTA

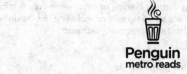

Penguin
metro reads

An imprint of Penguin Random House

PENGUIN METRO READS

USA | Canada | UK | Ireland | Australia
New Zealand | India | South Africa | China | Singapore

Penguin Metro Reads is part of the Penguin Random House group of companies
whose addresses can be found at global.penguinrandomhouse.com

Published by Penguin Random House India Pvt. Ltd
4th Floor, Capital Tower 1, MG Road,
Gurugram 122 002, Haryana, India

Penguin
Random House
India

First published in Penguin Metro Reads by Penguin Random House India 2023

ISBN 9780143448365

Typeset in Bembo STD by Manipal Digital Systems, Manipal
Printed at Gopsons Papers Pvt. Ltd., Noida
Text is Printed on Recycled Paper

www.penguin.co.in

To myself, who manages to write despite the cutest, most distracting buttons of all time

PART 1

1.

Aanchal Madan

'Why are they getting so angry?' asks Maa, pointing to the group of people talking loudly in the hotel lobby. 'It will just be a couple of hours more.'

'Why wouldn't they, Maa? They have paid for this holiday,' I tell her. 'They want things to be perfect.'

'Unlike us freeloaders, Didi,' whined my nervous brother, Gaurav.

'That's not true,' I argue. 'We also deserve to be here, okay? We won the lucky draw fair and square.'

And yet, I feel odd. The only reason we are at this seven-star, Rs 40,000-a-night resort, on an all-expenses-paid vacation is because, for the first time in our lives, we have been *lucky*.

Just then, a bright-eyed, tall, polished representative from Mahindra Vacations walks towards the crowd of twenty-odd weary, impatient, grumbling middle-aged people. Most of us have been waiting in the hotel lobby since seven in the morning for our rooms to be assigned. Every thirty minutes, the representative asks us to wait for another thirty minutes.

Other families are angry at the mismanagement, but not us. We have had the welcome drink thrice. We have clicked pictures near the pool, at the beach and at different spots in the lobby. We are sending pictures to our cousins who also can't believe our luck.

The representative addresses everyone brightly, 'Welcome to Westlife, Andamans! The check-in is at 12, but we are trying to get everyone into their beautiful rooms by 11 a.m.!' He checks his watch. 'It's 9.30 right now. So, we want all of you to wait around for just a couple of hours more in the lobby, have the welcome drink, enjoy the weather by the patio while the housekeeping staff makes sure your rooms are perfect! Thank you for your patience.'

The crowd raises its hands in exasperation and grumbles under its breath.

'This is what money does to you,' whispers Papa to us. 'Makes you ungrateful. Look at the Mahindra guy, talking so politely and they are not listening to him.' Papa turns to look at me. 'Tell me, had you not listened to that Mahindra person in the mall, would we have been here?'

Three months ago, a Mahindra Vacations employee had hounded me at Big Bazaar to fill up a contest form:

One Lucky Winner Gets a Fully Paid Vacation to the Andamans!

We, the Madans, never fill out contest forms because we are the exact opposite of lucky. Everything we touch turns to ashes. It's as if God didn't shuffle the card deck before dealing them to us. All we got were cards of humiliation, frustration, despair and hunger.

A year after I was born, Papa's new shop—Aanchal Stationery—closed down. A few months later, a tree fell on his scooter.

When I was three, Maa fell down while bathing me and has three crooked toes and a slightly unbalanced walk to remind her of that.

My younger brother's birth was supposed to change the tide. He, too, failed. When I was four, I stepped on my brother's hand and broke two of his fingers. He made it worse in the following months by getting sick too often and draining money on antibiotics, injections and visits to the emergency ward.

When I was eight, Papa's second store—now named Gaurav Stationery—shut shop.

Our family turned to religion. The pandits said, *Griha bhari hain*, once the stars align, we will bathe in milk and sleep in silk. Poojas and *havans,* rings on our fingers, lockets on our necks didn't change our fortunes.

When religion didn't work, we turned to academics. It was our last bastion: luck could be broken by the surety of mathematics, science, geography. For six years, I stood second in class and missed out on the school scholarship. Paying for education— Gaurav always came third so he used to miss the scholarship as well—meant smaller meals, faded clothes, and we grew up bony and sickly and the only medicines we could afford came in small homeopathy bottles we borrowed from our neighbours.

Maa's stitching business lost money.

Papa got beaten up after his tuition students failed.

We lost our savings in the bank scam.

Mobiles were snatched from our hands.

We never once won anything in a contest or on a scratch card.

Sometimes our luck would change, but soon after, the universe would balance it out by cracking our water tank or making our scooter's engine die on us.

Until this Mahindra Vacations holiday.

Only because I filled up that form. I saw the resort on the pamphlet. I saw the people in the images. It was everything I wanted.

Our conversation is cut short by a guy's compelling, booming voice.

'Amit, it's Daksh. This is my first experience with Mahindra Vacations, and I must say, I am sincerely . . . what can I say . . . touched to see your concern, your effort. It's just so heartwarming, it's almost like you're my best friend now,' he mocks in his gravelly, raspy voice. 'Having said that, we have some frail old people just moments away from fainting with low blood sugar. My own sister is very young and can't wait for so long.'

His voice is deep, like it's coming from inside a cave. It reverberates inside my rib cage even though he's ten yards away from me. I stand on my toes to get a good look at him, but all I can see is his floppy hair.

'I understand—'

'I'm not sure you do, Amit,' his voice now goes deeper, the rumble in it almost scary. 'Otherwise, your initial time estimate would have been more precise. Now, we're left with two potential scenarios. One, we have a long complimentary breakfast while you solve the room issue. Or collectively we'll paint a tragic picture of our ordeal with Mahindra Vacations online, complete with heartbreaking images of our elder members on the floor, writhing, eyes rolling. I'm sure we can find some good actors here. I will make my own sister lie down here, face down. The choice, Amit, is yours because your name is going in every one of those reviews.'

The confused crowd mumbles in agreement.

Amit's smile slowly disappears and a deep, scared frown settles in.

'I . . . I . . .' Amit stammers. 'There's no need to really do that.'

'Then what are our options here?'

A nervous, sweating Amit tells that he will talk to the management and get back to us in fifteen minutes. It doesn't take him that long.

'The restaurant is straight ahead and then right,' Amit informs us dryly, his voice devoid of any enthusiasm. 'Mahindra Vacations is always working to deliver your best vacation.'

'Of course they are,' I hear the guy say.

Free breakfast.

Maa squeezes my arm excitedly.

'That fellow is clever,' whispers Maa.

'Not clever,' I respond. 'Just rich. Had I paid for this vacation, I would have fought too.'

'You just said we deserve to be here, Didi,' taunts Gaurav. 'You had the chance to fight, instead, you were very happily having welcome drinks.'

'Shut up.'

'Maybe our luck's changing,' says Papa brightly.

I shake my head to warn him. Papa is the only optimist among the four of us, even though he has suffered from the legendary bad luck of the Madans the most. He should know better than anyone that whenever things seem to go our way, something goes wrong. Over the years, we have learnt not to laugh a lot, or allow ourselves to be very happy. The law of averages works against us.

We follow the hotel staff to the restaurant. That's when I see the guy for the first time. He's in a loose black T-shirt and a pair of black shorts. His hair is carefully messy, falling over his ears. He is the colour of wet sand, his jawline is jagged and he has a high forehead. When he turns, I see he's handsome in a way guys are when they are just turning into men. His voice belies his boyishness. He seems to be my age, but I would have guessed much older by his voice. The others in the group thank him. For everyone who's a lot older, he dips to touch their feet; for everyone who's only a little older, he gives them a warm smile and says something that makes them laugh. He has switched out of his terrifying, threat-wielding persona in a split second.

We enter the breakfast area. The waiter is walking us to our seats when I see him again with what seems like his family.

I first think he's carrying a bag over his shoulder. Then, I see it's a little girl—the sister. He's carrying her like a sack, and she's bobbing, giggling and squealing happily in his grip. He's carrying her as though she weighs nothing. When he turns, I see his eyes. There's a sense of surety in them, a sense of danger, a sense of entitlement and definitely, arrogance.

2.

Aanchal Madan

The waiter seats us right by the hotel pool, with a prime view melting into the sea. Girls and boys my age are prancing about the beach in their swimsuits. Large parts of their bodies are exposed to the sun. They splash about in the water, jostling in the sweltering sun without the fear of getting darker. Maa has never allowed me to have tea or coffee as she thinks that, with each cup, my skin will turn duller, darker, like a Glow and Lovely shade card in reverse.

The old and young are dressed alike at tables around us—beach shirts and shorts, and floral dresses.

Gaurav leans into me nervously. 'Everyone is looking at us. We look . . . different.'

He's right, we look *different*. Maa's wearing a new saree with a heavy gold necklace. Papa's wearing a crisp white half-sleeved shirt, trousers and office shoes. Gaurav's wearing Papa's old shirt, re-stitched to fit him. I'm sweating in the thick black formal outfit I bought for a family function. We are dressed for a wedding, not a beach. But these are our best clothes.

'Who cares how we look? We are probably smarter than anyone here. You stack their answer sheets and ours, and we would beat them straight out, okay?' I tell him, the pep talk partly for myself.

Gaurav rolls his eyes. 'Not all rich people are dumb.'

'Oye, our money situation is not our fault, okay?' I remind him. 'Our poverty is not our choice. We were born into it and we are clawing out of it. That's all that matters.'

Gaurav's not convinced.

I make a beeline for the buffet counters. I pick up a plate and start ladling it with food I would never be able to afford otherwise: salmon, croissants, packed yogurt, waffles, pasta. Gaurav flits around nervously next to the counters. People keep cutting lines and going past him. Gaurav needs to stop being a pushover. The path of the rich and successful is paved with people like him, like my parents, who got rolled over.

I pick up another plate to fill it with food I know Gaurav would like—cupcakes, French toast and ice cream cups in three flavours. He's a bit of an addict. Of sugar lately. And video games. He leans into something and then loses himself in it.

'Hey!' a voice calls out.

I wonder if it's the restaurant manager asking me to put back the food. I turn, constructing in my mind what I would say to him, 'Just because we look a certain way, you can't discriminate', 'We too have the right to be here', 'We won this holiday, check our vouchers, this behaviour is unacceptable!'

He's not the manager.

I recognize the hair immediately. That entitled guy from the reception.

Daksh. He's smiling at me, his perfect white teeth glinting. He's a few steps away, but I can smell him. He smells . . . *rich*. It's a swanky showroom smell, it's a nice restaurant smell. It's sea and flowers and comfort and money.

'That's the last in strawberry,' he says, pointing to the strawberry ice cream cup on my plate. 'Can my sister have it? She's right there. You know how kids are, so prone to tantrums.'

He then points to a little girl in a high chair a little distance away from us.

'Her name's Rabbu, Rabbani actually.'

'Strange name.'

'I agree,' he says.

'I don't like kids.'

'That's exactly what I used to say.'

'They do nothing, are useless and yet everyone gives everything to them,' I say, as I hand the ice cream to him. 'We shouldn't spoil them.'

'I agree. Most kids are only cute to their parents, an environmental burden on the planet, a waste of resources.'

He looks at the ice cream and then at me.

'But despite all of that, you can use them to get what you want.'

'So, you want the ice cream and not her?'

'We both do. It's encoded in our DNA. Our double helix looks like an ice cream cone. Our Covid tests show positive for milk.'

The guy's funny, but I don't want Maa to catch me laughing with a boy.

I point to the ice cream cup he's holding in front of me. 'You can keep it,' I tell him. 'By the way, Maa called you clever for what you did this morning. But . . . ummm . . .'

'That guy was irritating.'

'Why give that threat when you can afford the breakfast? If I had the money, I would have just gone in.'

He smiles. 'He could have just said, "We fucked up, guys, and we are trying to fix it." Instead, he was smiling and being irritatingly polite and whatnot. And honestly, we deserved the breakfast. No one starts a holiday like this. Anyway, I'm Daksh. Where are you from?'

'Where I'm from, I can't be seen talking to you for long. Maa must be watching. So, I'm going to frown like we had a disagreement and then I'm going to walk away. But thank you for this breakfast. It's . . . a lot for us.'

'Am I supposed to frown too, so that your mother really buys the story?'

I turn away from him and walk to my table. As expected, Maa warns me, 'Don't talk to him. You know how boys like him are!'

'Maa, we were just disagreeing on who should have the ice cream,' I answer. 'And what do you mean "boys like him"?'

'Rich boys.'

'Poor guys are okay?'

'Don't argue with me.'

I look at him from the corner of my eye. He's talking animatedly with his sister who giggles and hugs him. They both look uncannily similar as they scoop up the ice cream from the cup.

His parents are at the table, sipping coffee from tiny espresso cups. Like him, they are thin, tall and attractive. They look fresh, unhurried, relaxed. Unlike my own. Maa–Papa have smiles on their faces, but if one looks closely, they will find that every little wrinkle on their face tells a story of failure and humiliation. They have spent their entire lives worrying about rent, our fees, fixed deposits, broken-down refrigerators, cracked TVs and our future. Maa–Papa have done everything they can for us, and yet it has never been enough. Our luck has a way of grabbing us by the throat and dragging us underwater.

When I look at his parents and others around me, I realize being rich is not a large house, a car, nice clothes or a big TV. Being rich is a state of mind. It's like when a train breaks out from the dirty city into a wide open field of sunflowers and a light breeze. It's like you're finally at peace. Being rich is reaching a meditative state where your worries about your future, about making ends meet, vanish. It's not a number in the bank. It's when the anxiety about the weight of the future is lifted off your shoulders. It's that laugh without the slightest hint of tension.

That's what I see on his face. Daksh's face.

3.

Aanchal Madan

We have two adjoining rooms with a connecting door—one for my parents, the other for my brother and me. The bed's made, the curtains have been pulled back so that the sun bathes the room in its light. It smells of roses. There's a small bowl of fruit on the table. The bathroom has two sinks, a bathtub and a shower, tiny bottles of shampoo and conditioner, and electronic blinds so you can watch the sea while you shower. I sit by the window and look outside. The waves lap at the shore. I should be enjoying the view but it keeps reminding me of what we don't have, and can't afford.

The world's beauty has a price to it.

And all I want is enough money to pay that price.

I have often dreamt about the rich. I have stopped in front of big houses and wondered how they live. I have watched people outside airports drag expensive suitcases and fantasized about their travels. Today's the first time I am on the other side. The grass just doesn't look greener on this side. It *is* greener on the other side. This is how others live. This is what I want.

Maa–Papa roll the suitcases to their room and start to unpack.

I go to the bathroom. I turn the blinds down and call Vicky—saved as Neha in my contacts—whose calls I have missed.

'Hello?' I whisper into the phone.

'Where are you, *jaan*?'

'Hiding in the bathroom, which, by the way, is the size of our house. And I'm missing you so much. You should have been here. It's . . . beautiful.'

He responds, his voice soft as a warm blanket, 'Saw pictures of your room online. Once we are older, we will go on such holidays every month. I promise you, Aanchal.'

'We have to, Vicky, it's not an option,' I assert. 'We want this, for us. We have to be rich. It's . . . it's a different life these guys live.'

I take a deep breath and start dreaming with open eyes. Vicky, my parents, Gaurav and this life of abundance and luxury.

And just as my heart starts to visualize it, my mind tramples on the dream, splintering it. Minds don't allow hearts to dream. The mind reminds us of fear and failure. Of hunger, dust, ashes, humiliation.

'I'm nervous, Vicky. What if—'

He cuts me like he has so many times before. 'Don't spoil your vacation, jaan. There's still a week to go. An *entire* week for the results to be announced.'

There's a knock at the door. It's Maa.

'ATE TOO MUCH! Two minutes!' I shout.

I wait for Maa to leave. A moment of silence passes between us.

'I love you, Vicky,' I confess. I have been repeating these words for the past two years. They still make me feel warm inside. But for the last two months, they come with a heavy sense of guilt. 'I love you so, so much.'

'Love you too, jaan,' he responds. 'I hope you sleep well tonight.'

I haven't slept for more than two hours since the last of my twelfth board examinations. The nightmares of not scoring enough to get into SRCC keep me awake.

But one nightmare haunted me more than the others.

In the nightmare, Vicky is inside the gates of SRCC, and the gates are closed in my face. I keep standing there clutching my marksheet, my future in tatters.

It seemed so real, I cut a deal with God.

I drew a small swastika on my palm in deep red. I promised I wouldn't let it wear out till the results were announced. But in return for a small favour. If one of us had to get into SRCC, it should be me, not Vicky.

Vicky, of course, doesn't know that.

'I will try to sleep,' I tell Vicky. 'You're my jaan, you're my everything. I need to go now, jaan. Everyone is waiting.'

'No.'

His words have a vice-like grip over me. He knows if he asks me to stay, I will stay. My body, my heart, surrender to his will. But every time I talk to him, I wonder if God will manipulate the results to favour me. Or if hearing my prayers would make him act the way he hadn't thought of earlier. Every time I darken the swastika in my hand, I feel like the world's worst girlfriend.

'You can go,' he allows me.

'Thank you, jaan. I love you.'

'Same, jaan, same.'

He disconnects the call. Then I delete the call records.

Later, we order room service after confirming twice that it was complimentary. Two pizzas, two portions of biryani, two chicken burgers and one daal-khichdi. We start watching a movie on the big flat-screen TV—a movie we have watched before, but here in this room, with the quiet air conditioner blasting cold air, the movie feels different. Gaurav orders dessert, popcorn and cold drinks in quick succession. Don't be vulgar, Papa warns Gaurav but orders another helping of gulab jamun. Maa sends pictures she has clicked during the day to her neighbourhood friends. Papa burps intermittently because he has overeaten again. All of our worries are wiped clean. There are instances I have been truly happy but none of them beats what I feel in this moment.

What would I not give for every afternoon of ours to be like this? On a soft bed, with the TV on, with a smile on my parents' faces?

I would give *everything*. I would give everything for this.

4.

Daksh Dey

I'm alone on this mile-long beach the resort has carved out for itself. I have been up and down the beach multiple times, staring at my phone, waiting for Sameeksha's text. The network is four bars, but I still wave my phone in the air from time to time just in case. I call her again. There's no answer. My thumbs hover over the keypad, never touching it, as if once I start typing, I wouldn't be able to stop and I'd send her something stupid and desperate like *'I will die without you, please text me back'*. I put the phone in my pocket. The water of the ocean washes up to my feet. It was warm and inviting in the morning, but now in the dark, the cold, gurgling ocean looks terrifying.

I hear feet splashing in the water and a boy's bickering voice. I turn and I recognize their faces immediately. It's the girl and her brother from the morning.

They were the only ones in the lobby who were laughing and giggling despite the unprofessionalism of the guy from Mahindra Vacations. After the breakfast buffet, I saw them on the bus to the Cellular Jail, the first stop on our itinerary. Her mother must have clicked a hundred pictures from the bus itself. The girl and her brother kept arguing and I wondered if Rabbani and I would have been the same had our age difference not been sixteen years. Now Rabbani will think of me as a God-like figure, an elder brother who knows all about the ways of the world. I prefer this. A little later, the girl went on darkening the swastika in her palm. The boy's father gave him his phone and he shut up for the rest of the ride.

Then I spotted the sister in one of the little cells, listening to the tour guide, anger and pity dripping from her eyes. She held up the group, kept lobbying questions at the tour guide, and despite the fury in her eyes, spit flying in the air, flailing hands, she looked stunning. When I first saw her at breakfast, I had brushed off her prettiness, thinking it was Sameeksha's absence that was making me search for nice faces, consoling myself that, in the worst case, if she does leave, the world has enough beauty. But I knew the moment the light fell on her from the little window of the cell that I would never forget her face. She wore a white *salwar* suit with self-work on it, and the fact that I remember what she wore in the afternoon surprises me, and she glowed. Her face reminded me of an article I once read, which said the right ratios, angles and mathematics is what makes beautiful people, beautiful. I imagined her God and creator immersed in their art, carving out her bones, slicing her skin. His palette crowded with bloody scalpels, torn veins, skin drafts; his mind obsessed dangerously with getting those ratios right to the point of madness. Her face sliced and sewn to reach perfection. She's about 5'6", slender and has a heart-shaped face that ends in a sharp chin. A slight shadow of acne on her face only heightens her beauty. Her lips are full and chapped and every time I have seen her, she's making them worse by touching them. I knew at that precise moment what this warm, gooey feeling in the pit of one's stomach is. This feeling of wanting to out-focus everything but that face. A crush. A pointless somersault of the heart based purely on how someone looks. But how someone looks isn't a trivial detail. Right now, she's in a frayed T-shirt, pyjamas, and I wonder how she can still look like she's taken care to dress.

'Hey.'

They don't hear me and keep on walking.

We are only three in the entire Mahindra Vacations group who are in the same age bracket. The others are too old, or too young. Old parents, new parents: that's the target segment of holiday packages. I have been on enough of these holiday packages to know that eventually the parents band together and the younger people stick together. If I don't make friends with them, it's going to be an extremely long week.

'Hey!' I say, trotting alongside them. 'Hi. I met you guys in the morning. I was the guy with the ice cream. Daksh. Are you guys going kayaking tomorrow?'

The brother stops and looks at me with an icy stare. 'She has a boyfriend. Vicky.'

'I hope he's treating you well,' I say to her.

She catches my gaze and I can't place her expression, a mix of curiosity and scepticism.

'I'm Aanchal,' she says. 'And yes, he is, Vicky's the best. There's no one like him.'

That's a bit of an overcompensation, but I don't point it out.

'Good for you. I'm a boyfriend too, but unfortunately, I can't say the same about me. That, of all the boyfriends in the world, I'm the best one.'

'I can't say the same about me too. I'm a fairly average girlfriend.'

Aanchal. I say the name aloud in my head.

Nice name, but too average for her.

It's hard to look away from her. Silvery moonlight reflects off her face in ways that remind me of how stages are lit, how spotlights are arranged just to accentuate the art. I notice Aanchal's eyes—a shade of light brown Sameeksha would know. Sameeksha's make-up kit has brown but it's not brown, it's always something different—almond, burnt ember, coffee, tan— and she loves to tell me why 'it's not brown, okay!' I wonder what Sameeksha would say if I texted her about my new-found crush. In the three months we have been together, Sameeksha has used the word 'cute' for three guys—two in her college, one a Bollywood star—and in my head, I have flayed them alive, fed them their eyeballs and quartered them.

I turn to Gaurav. 'And what's your name? Rabbani, my sister, wanted to know who gave up their ice cream for her.'

'Gaurav,' the brother answers gruffly.

'The jail was heartbreaking, right? I saw you guys there.'

'It was boring,' he answers impatiently.

It's cute that Gaurav thinks I'm interested in his opinion.

Aanchal shakes her head. 'It made me furious,' she replies.

'Why are you talking to him?' Gaurav protests.

'Because your mother is not here so we can talk and choose not to be bored,' I answer Gaurav. I turn to her. 'Furious? Why did it make you furious?'

She digs her toes into the sand and turns her gaze towards it. 'It seemed so . . . pointless. So much pain and suffering for independence. And for what? The best-case scenario for any Indian is to get settled in the country that ruled us. It seems like we wasted all those lives.'

'Happiness comes from freedom of choice too. Now, we are free to go to the country of the *gora* even if it's on illegal boats or whatever. Is that what you plan to do? Move abroad?'

She and her brother look at each other and share a soft chuckle. She turns back to me. 'We can't afford it,' she confesses. 'We can't even afford this resort. We are only here because we won a lucky draw.'

'We should go, Didi,' urges Gaurav, pulling at his sister's arm. Gaurav, half-scared, half-angry, looks towards the resort building as if someone has trained binoculars on us. He then looks at me with a creepy smile and says, 'If you want to stay, give me your phone.'

'No,' Aanchal warns Gaurav. 'You have played enough games.'

'You can talk to a random guy who's trying to hit on you, but I can't even play a game? How's that—'

I interrupt him. 'I'm not trying to hit on your sister, Gaurav.'

'Of course you will say that!'

'I have a girlfriend back in Dubai. I mean, I did before I came on this trip. Now I'm not too sure where we are at,' I answer and, just to poke him, I add sincerely, 'You would know, right, how tricky relationships are? You look like someone who's a bit of a . . . playboy?'

Aanchal turns to me. 'You live in Dubai?'

'Who cares!' whines Gaurav. He tugs at her arm. 'Didi, please, can I have your phone? What's the point of a vacation if I can't have fun? I will play just one game and give it back to you!'

'The point of a vacation is also so you can meet new people,' I offer an answer. 'Did you guys notice there's literally no one young in our group except the three of us?'

Gaurav stares at me blankly. 'New people aren't more interesting than *Call of Duty*.'

'You're not entirely wrong,' I concur. 'The guns in the new version are legit. The new camo skins are a little expensive, though.'

Aanchal gives her phone to Gaurav. 'Five minutes,' she warns him. 'And don't hold the phone too close to your eyes. And not 100 per cent brightness, okay?'

He takes the phone, walks gleefully to the nearest sunbed and sits down. I hear the faint sounds of *Call of Duty: Mobile*.

'You're right about the young people . . . everyone's old,' says Aanchal.

'Your brother's cute in that annoying way that boys are. Never wanted a brother, though,' I lie.

Her brother's not cute. He's skinny and shrieky and nervous-y, and the way he leapt at the phone reminded me of Gollum. But the new *Call of Duty* has been making boys of all ages behave that way.

I continue, 'To be honest, I never wanted a sister too. But it's cool now. So, you like it here?'

'I've never been to a place like this,' she remarks. 'When I read about the Cellular Jail, I never thought one day I would get to see it. All this is new . . . exciting. And I have definitely not met anyone who lives in Dubai.'

'Do you want to have coconut water? They have the ones with malai in it.'

'No.'

I stop the coconut water cart and order two coconuts. When I tell her it's free, she gets one for herself and one for her brother.

'That's the thing about places like these. Now that you have been here once, you will feel significantly less excited the next time. All resorts look the same.'

'I don't think I will ever have a free coconut and say, no, this doesn't make me happy,' she says. 'What happened with you and your girlfriend?'

'You know, teething issues. We had just started dating,' I explain to Aanchal. 'You know how the beginnings of early relationships are, right? Like a minefield. Every text, every touch, every phone call, everything we say or don't say has the potential to ruin everything. I'm just wondering what I did wrong. But I don't want to text her and come across like . . . desperate.'

She frowns. 'Love is not a game. You should text your girlfriend what you honestly feel. You should be able to say what you feel like.'

'If that's the case, honestly, I feel like asking her why she's being an asshole when we are so perfect together. She just went off to her Nani's house in Hyderabad for the holidays without even telling me. Went off the radar just like that. Kept me on seen, no replies, nothing. Anyway, I don't know why I started moaning about her. So, you're from Delhi, right? I was in Delhi till about thirteen, then we moved to Dubai. Where in Delhi are you from?'

We finish our coconuts and dump them in the dustbin.

'Paschim Vihar. I just gave the board exams,' she says.

'Oh, nice. When are the results out?'

'Next week. I'm aiming to go to SRCC.'

'SRCC?! Doesn't SRCC require like a 100 per cent best of four? That's impossible.'

She shrugs. 'Not impossible for everyone who gets into SRCC every year. Anyway, I have to do it. They have the best placements at Delhi University.'

'Yeah, I have heard. But tell me something. A 100 per cent best of four means you can't get even one question wrong in all four subjects combined, right?'

She nods. 'I'm only nervous about English. Math, accountancy and business I will score 100. The results are the only thing that's like . . . not ideal in this holiday. Which college are you from?'

'Way worse, way worse, it will make me sound like a loser,' I tell her with a laugh. 'BITS, Pilani, First year, environmental engineering, Dubai campus.'

'But then you're rich. You don't have to be great in studies.'

'Umm . . . okay. But, you know, college is not just a placement agency. You make friends, network, there are extra-curriculars, festivals and all of that. Like I manage my college magazine and that's a lot of fun. I like reading so I thought that would be a fun thing to do.'

She doesn't look convinced. 'If you're good at English, you should give GMAT or CAT a try.'

'You just reduced an entire history of thousands of years of writing and reading to a tool to crack MBA entrance examinations.'

'So, you don't want to do an MBA?'

'It's far too early for me to decide,' I answer. 'You know what it feels like? Like I'm the frog pinned to a table and you're a high-school student dissecting my choices. But now it's my turn—you're dating someone called Vicky? Is it like his real name?'

'A lot of people are named Vicky.'

'I mean . . . sure.' Curiosity gets the better of me and I ask, 'Do you have a picture of Vicky?'

'Why do you want to see that?'

'I want to see who gathered the courage to ask someone like you out.'

She stops walking. She turns towards me, the pools of her big brown eyes flickering. I try to guess if she's angry or shocked. Then, she smiles and looks even prettier. I didn't think that was possible.

'You were just telling my brother you weren't hitting on me,' she says.

'That's true, and I am not hitting on you,' I explain. The great part of talking to anyone on these trips is that whatever happens, it happens here and you don't take it back to your normal life. So I continue. 'I'm telling you that I have a crush on you. My crush is based on the way you look, and looks are a genetic lottery, a roll of the dice, not an achievement. You could be a horrible person, I'm not saying that you are . . . but you could be. But yes, your face looks like someone took a scale and made it perfectly proportionate. It's weird. Don't people tell you that?'

'No, and you can't have crushes on people if you're already in love with someone,' she says. 'Anyway, I don't have a picture of Vicky. I just know if I keep even one picture, my parents will find it. My luck's super bad. I'm the unluckiest girl I know.'

'Unluckiest? That sounds like an exaggeration.'

'Pandits say my *kundli* is a bloodbath. My terrible luck will last four more years. That's why I'm wearing this ring. My parents . . . we . . . we are a bit superstitious.'

'Not one picture? Not even in hidden folders? Or on social media?'

She shakes her head. 'We can't afford to be on social media. It's a distraction. We will make our profiles once we get to SRCC.'

'That's the strangest condition to make a profile. Is your guy trying to get into SRCC too? 100 per cent in all four subjects?'

She nods, her eyes glinting. 'He wants it more than me. You have no idea how bad I was at accountancy. He taught me everything. Without him, I wouldn't have dreamt of getting into this college.'

'And what if you don't? What's your Plan B?'

Her eyes flicker. I see horror in her eyes. 'That's not an option. The second-best college is not good enough for us. If we want this life . . . the one you're living, second-best won't make the cut.'

'But some people will argue that being rich isn't the answer to happiness.'

'Rich people and extremely poor people say that. We are in the middle. I will be a rich, unhappy girl, married to a rich, unhappy boy, and we will be jealous about others who have bought bungalows and worried if our imported cars will be scratched by drivers.'

'Is that what you think rich people do?' I ask. 'By the way, I'm not rich. I'm upper middle class.'

'Another rich-person thing to say.'

Just then, Gaurav comes running to us, waving the phone.

'DIDI!' he shouts. 'Maa is calling!'

5.

Daksh Dey

There are no messages from Sameeksha. It's unfair that my longing for Sameeksha is a physical pain—I can feel it in my chest. All morning I have been going back to the messages we had sent each other. The first four weeks of our relationship were a mix of pure passion and love. We couldn't keep our hands off each other. She used to joke that I'm in a very serious relationship with her breasts, and she with my dick. It was like our relationship was on overdrive, we were skipping stages. We would look at other couples and go, like, poor them, they don't know what a relationship looks like.

I keep my phone back in my pocket and turn to Rabbani. She's digging into the wet sand with her toys.

'Dig deeper, Rabbu. Who knows, maybe you will find some dino bones,' I tell her.

A squeal cuts the through the air. 'My *chhota* baby!'

I turn to see Mumma walk towards us. Rabbani turns and sprints towards Mumma on her cute, unsteady feet. She clings to Mumma like a little chimpanzee.

I feel a pang of envy in my heart.

I'm no longer Mumma's favourite child because well, I'm no longer a child, and I don't get the unconditional, all-consuming love Rabbani gets from Maa. When Maa got pregnant with Rabbani when I was seventeen, I was almost immediately expected to assume the role of a responsible older brother. I love being Rabbani's brother, but it would have been nice to continue to be a child as well. With Baba, nothing changed. Our relationship has always been a three-step loop. 1. Baba suggests. 2. I accept/reject the suggestion. 3. Baba is proud/disappointed.

Mumma turns to me. 'What are you thinking of doing today? You were saying you will go kayaking—are you?'

She points at the people congregating at the beach side for the activity.

'I'm thinking about it.'

'Don't waste the vacation because of a girl.'

'Mumma, *yaar*—'

'Maybe it's good that it ended.'

'It's not ended.'

'We told you earlier only. Anyway, how long could she have hidden it from her parents? Sooner or later, this had to happen. I'm just surprised it lasted three months.'

Sameeksha is the first girl I told Mumma about. I felt as though I was finally on to something, as though she was the one. Now I know telling her was a mistake.

Mumma realizes the conversation is a dead pursuit.

'Daksh?' She points to the distance. 'Isn't that the girl you were talking to yesterday morning?'

Standing in the serpentine queue on the beach, I see Aanchal and Gaurav with life jackets strapped on, getting ready for kayaking.

'The girl's beautiful,' Mumma observes.

'Mumma, yaar.'

'What? She is beautiful, look at her face!'

'Everything is not about looks, Mumma.'

'If everything is not about looks, what did you see in Sameeksha?'

'She's a good person,' I tell Mumma.

'If she was that good, she would tell her parents and not hide you,' argues Mumma. 'Make-up videos she can share all day on social media but not a single picture of you. Why?'

'Mumma, yaar . . . I am leaving!' I get up.

I hear Mumma grumble how Sameeksha was a mistake from the get-go, a vixen, a siren who ensnared her son with her large breasts. I won't lie: her large breasts were a part of the equation. I run towards the line of people now being led towards their kayaks. Gaurav and Aanchal are clicking pictures of each other.

'Hey, Gaurav!' I call out. 'Give me the phone. I will take a picture of you guys together.'

He looks at Aanchal for permission and when she nods, gives the phone to me. I frame them against the water.

'Guys, you need to do something. The kayak looks like a dead body you're posing with. Do something fun.'

'Like this?' asks Aanchal, raising a V sign.

'Something more fun. Okay, so Aanchal, you can pretend that you're hitting him with the oar, and Gaurav you can, like, jump backwards as if you're trying to escape. I will try to capture it when you're in mid-air.'

'No,' moans the joyless Gaurav.

'Do it!' exhorts Aanchal excitedly. Her bright eyes and open smile are more summery than summer itself. When I look at her through the screen of the phone I feel sad for her because no camera will catch the depth of her eyes, the poetic fall of her eyelashes and her gentle movements.

Gaurav is as stiff as a plank in the beginning but slowly loosens up and does better.

'One more time,' I exhort him. 'You're doing great. One more, just to be safe. Oh c'mon, your eyes are closed. Great, one video too. Yep, yep, done. Here.'

Once I'm done, Aanchal swipes through the pictures. 'Thank you,' she says, '. . . and thank you for putting some joy in my brother. Are you joining us?'

'The young have to stick together, don't they?' I say and pick up an oar.

'Life jacket!' the instructor warns me.

'I can swim.'

'You won't be the first swimmer to die,' says Aanchal.

'Fair point,' I say and put on my life jacket.

The instructors and his helpers make us sit and push our kayaks into the water. Gaurav puts all his strength into rowing and is leading the group. He thinks it's a competition. Cute. Aanchal and I lag behind.

'I did this in the Maldives once, but the kayaks were transparent and the water was so clear so you could literally see the ocean bed,' I say.

She looks at me with a mock frown. 'Unless we can paddle to the Maldives from here, you're showing off. This is the best day of my life, so don't spoil it.'

'Do you want me to take videos of you?' I offer. 'The light's just right and not taking any would be a waste of good lighting.'

'Can you take them from your phone? Mine's not very good.'

For the next fifteen minutes, she paddles and I shoot videos and pictures of her. The shadows of the mangrove branches dance off her face, playing hide-and-seek with different facets of her. And every time I check the picture I click of her, I am disappointed at the camera and my ineptness to capture the perfect shot of her.

'Thank you,' she says shyly. 'Vicky hates taking pictures of me, keeps saying people are looking, people are looking. I keep telling him that people will judge you no matter what you do. But he doesn't understand. Do you want me to click yours?'

'I'm good.'

'Of course, why would you? You have pictures from the Maldives.'

'Wait till you crack SRCC and become a hotshot C-suite executive somewhere. Then you will have pictures everywhere.'

Aanchal slows down. Everyone else—even the very old in two-person kayaks—pass by us. She paddles towards the mangrove bushes. The instructor has warned us not to do that. She turns to look at me.

'You might get these chances every year in places like the Maldives, not me. I will have to pay for my own holiday and that's going to take time,' she says as an explanation.

'Ouch.'

She stops paddling. 'I'm so envious of you guys. You people have everything.'

'There are people far richer in my college—ones with three cars, two house helps, a villa to live in. They are all vacationing in

Europe, not here. I don't want to come across as an asshole by telling you that a three-bedroom house and one car and the ability to afford one vacation to a resort a year isn't the exact definition of rich.'

'It is for me,' she says. 'Tell me what your father does and how much money you guys have, then I will tell you if you're rich or not.'

'Ummm . . . Baba's an engineer. We have things that we need, and we have savings to tide us through tough times.'

'So, if your Baba stops working, how many years of savings do you have, to maintain the same lifestyle before you have zero money?'

I never thought of it like that. 'Ten years maybe.'

'That's rich,' she says.

Her kayak gets dangerously close to the overhanging bushes. And, like a devotee of a cult leader, I follow. She reaches out, breaks off two small branches and keeps them in her kayak. She hands out a branch when she paddles close to me.

'For Sameeksha, who couldn't be here.'

I look at the branch. 'She's still missing, though.'

'What did you do?'

'Why do you assume I did something?'

She laughs. And despite the pain, her laughter fills me up with joy. It's not even a balm for my heartbreak. A balm's ineffective. Her laugh is like open-heart surgery, like installing a pacemaker, as if my pain's non-existent, a memory. Her laugh reminds me of a question I have been asked often by others who don't read fiction, why do I waste time with it? Since they won't read, I want them to meet Aanchal instead and realize what power art holds. Is my judgement of her through the narrow lens of what I consider beautiful and arty? Yes. But do I care? No. I want to keep looking at her.

She says, 'It's just that, whenever I think of a rich guy, it just feels like they can't be in the right. Okay, what did she do?'

'It was me.'

'Knew it.'

'She was hiding our relationship from her parents,' I explain. 'Like you are. But one day, I think I just felt a lot of love for her, and I posted a picture of us online. She lost it completely. And then, she stopped talking to me. In my defence, it was for just a couple of minutes and then I took it off. There was no caption too.'

She looks at me.

'C'mon. It was for just a couple of minutes! Okay, whatever. We are not talking about that any more. I'm sure she will come around. No one saw that picture. She can't make it that big of a deal.'

The instructor waves at us from a distance, asking us to slow down—it's a tricky passage. I navigate through with my mind elsewhere.

'Daksh?' she says.

'Was it bad?'

'What?'

'When your mother got pregnant? Was it bad in school? You must have been like sixteen, seventeen?'

She's the first person who has asked me that. Most people just can't get over the fact that my parents had a kid in their mid-forties.

'The range of their jokes was impressive. Really cruel, hurtful stuff. I was ashamed till I realized my parents were different but in a good way.'

'How did you handle the bullying?'

'That part was easy. I told those boys that their mothers were untouched by their fathers, their vaginas were slowly drying up and their only resort was delivery men taking their mothers in stairwells while their fathers were at work.'

'In my school, they would have opened up your skull with hockey sticks.'

I hold out my arms to show her the thirteen stitches on the right, seven on the left.

'Weren't you angry with your parents?' she asks.

Our kayaks float idly and bump into each other under the overhang of the mangroves. I'm miles away from the school, from my college, and even from Rabbani. No one can ever know what I say here, to her. Something I haven't allowed to tell even myself.

'Should I tell you what I want to tell you?'

She doesn't answer. It's the safest place I can share this. She has no connection to my world.

'For all those nine months Mumma carried her, I prayed for Mumma to have a miscarriage. I wished for death,' I confess.

'Okay.'

'Mumma was already old when she had her, so it was a real probability. And not just when she was a foetus, just a wiggly little thing in an ultrasound, but into the last few weeks too—when she was a complete child, with arms, and legs, a beating heart, movement, anger, hunger—I wished she would die. Right until the moment of her birth, I wished for Mumma's umbilical cord to strangle her.'

My breath becomes heavy, like a viscous fluid in my windpipe.

In a small voice, I continue. 'Just saying these words out loud feels like someone's jammed their arm down my throat and is crushing my heart.'

'She wasn't a part of your future. It was okay to feel like that,' she says matter-of-factly. 'When did it change? You seem quite involved with her now.'

'It's kind of a cliché. Those dark, crazy thoughts just vanished, turned to dust the first time I saw Rabbani squirming in Mumma's arms. She wasn't even cute then. She was positively rat-like, with tiny claw-like hands and hair all over her forehead. She was primed for me to hate. She wasn't like a cute newborn, she was a frowning, angry newborn. But I found myself at the epicentre of love. I looked at her and I was like, I should hate you, but all I did was take her from Mumma and coo to her like I was a fucking midwife. I didn't sleep that night. Like some creep, I stood over her crib and kept staring at her.'

'Because of love? Or were you scared that God would listen to you and take her away?'

'Both. I kept staring at her chest, watching it go up and down, making sure she was breathing. For months after, I would drag my mattress to my parents' room and sleep on the floor. I wouldn't sleep till either Baba or Mumma went off to sleep. It was like, if I closed my eyes, she would drift away. If I left her alone, she would leave us, die.'

'When did it get better?'

'It never got better.'

'We all ask things from God in our desperate times,' she says unsurely and falls silent. '. . . it's not who we . . . are.'

'What did you ask?'

Her eyes flit to the little smudged swastika that she's drawn in her palm. She shakes her head and says a silent *'Nothing.'* It's, of course, not nothing, and I wonder what it has to do with the swastika in her palm.

The rest of the kayaking group comes into view. Their kayaks are being pulled to the shore. A few are taking off their life jackets.

'Were you serious earlier about not liking kids?' I ask.

She nods. 'When Gaurav was younger, I saw him as competition for resources around the house. It was either his new school uniform or mine. His shoes or mine. To be fair to my parents, they never discriminated. We were both equally deprived. I only started to like my brother when he started doing well in school. The first time I felt true love for him was when he won a quiz competition and got a thousand-rupee prize.'

'I feel my crush on you slowly evaporating. But . . . three years ago, we could have bonded on our collective dislike of children. I keep telling Rabbani that she'd better be super intelligent because I'm not dividing Baba's FDs with her.'

'At least you have FDs.' She laughs and her face lights up.

I paddle towards Gaurav's canoe and poke my oar into him. 'Your sister thinks you're a drain.'

'Didi? Maa–Papa,' he points to them. 'Ask him not to talk to us.'

Their parents are waiting at the beach. They are looking elsewhere.

'Don't talk to us,' says Aanchal as she passes by me and joins her brother.

'We will be strangers again.'

'We aren't strangers any more,' she says.

The instructors pull our kayaks offshore.

6.

Aanchal Madan

I first watched *Mahabharat* when I was in the eighth standard. It was a bewildering experience. A brilliant story but with one very strange moment. Five men, closer to gods than men, stake their wife on a game of dice. I remember wondering if this was a dream sequence. That the god–like men would wake up and give up gambling for the rest of their lives in this realm. It wasn't.

But now, it makes sense.

What was a game of dice to the Pandavas, is FIFA for the boys of today: a hypnotic, relationship-destroying juggernaut of distraction.

Gaurav is playing FIFA on Daksh's PlayStation that's hooked on to the TV in the resort's TV room. His eyes are plastered unblinkingly to the screen. His fingers seem to be slowly melding into the plastic of the controller and soon there would be nothing to differentiate between him and the game. He's in a little world of his own. I wonder if Gaurav will refuse to play if I tell him that Daksh confessed he has a crush on me. I think like the god-like men, he, too, would choose FIFA.

When Daksh came to talk to us while our parents went for the cooking class, I should have made an excuse instead of encouraging a guy who had just told me he had a crush on me. But my resistance disintegrated in front of the sincerity with which he said, 'I'm bored. Do you want to hang out?'

And when Daksh told Gaurav about the PS he was carrying, it felt like Gaurav had a crush on Daksh. He was blushing. And it wasn't just him. Daksh has a way with people. I saw even uncles and aunties talk breezily, laugh easily around him. I have tried to step around it, not think about it, and I have tried to deny it. But he's charming, and not just to me. I had felt it on that beach where he was right—I was dissecting him—but his openness was so inviting. And then during the kayaking, he was so easy to be with.

Before this trip, one of my biggest fears was that I would feel out of place. In my mind, I had ready quips for everyone who would even hint that we didn't belong. But that night on the beach, it was like he broke down all the imaginary walls I had built around myself. I had imagined that everyone would be mean to us, but here he was, smiling, wanting to spend time with us, even indulging my irritating brother.

Now Daksh is sitting on the beanbag next to me and is impressed with how quickly Gaurav picked up the game.

'Beginners don't get these tricks so easily. You saw what Gaurav did there? It's Elastico, takes very quick reflexes,' Daksh tells me.

'My brother's stupid. Anything that he can do, I respect it less.'

'C'mon,' Daksh protests. 'There's an entire industry being built around e-sports. Many seventeen-year-olds in the West have earned a fortune playing games. In India, it's going to be huge in the coming years.'

'My parents will gouge his eyes out before they let him play a video game,' I counter. 'Both he and I are meant to become fat rats in the rat race. Alternative careers and passions are not for us.'

'And SRCC is the first hurdle in the rat race?'

'Exactly,' I answer. 'The placements will ensure we don't have money problems again. If you compare it, the average placement at SRCC is far better than even the good ones in any other college. If Vicky and I fail to get into SRCC, it would be another three years of slogging to clear the next hurdle. The struggle will go on.'

He nods, but I don't think he gets it. I don't expect a guy who thinks playing video games is a legitimate career choice would know what difference the right college can make in the lives of people like us.

Daksh checks his phone—the third time in the past twenty minutes. I would like to live in a world where my biggest concern is that my girlfriend is not texting me back, where my sister's not getting the right flavour of ice cream and where my parents are getting mocked for having sex. But despite all this, I don't resent Daksh. It's quite the opposite. Never had I imagined that someone would tell me he had a crush on me and I wouldn't find it creepy. I have wondered if it's because he's handsome . . . or because he has a sister who he dotes on . . . or because he's nice. I can't place it.

Over the years, I have received chits in my bags with scribbled love confessions, I have been told of crushes, my name's written along with other girls' names in boys' washrooms . . . but no one has ever told me to my face they have a crush on me as respectfully as Daksh did.

He's the opposite of creepy. When he trains his eyes on me, it's like standing on the beach, the warmth of the morning sun slowly bathing you. He's rich but not obnoxious, just the kind of rich I want to be. And every now and then, my mind reminds me of his razor-sharp nose or his defined jawline or the softness of his eyes. And then, sometimes, I inspect Daksh's confession of his crush in my mind. It warms my insides. There's a way he talks that makes me feel looked at, like I'm important, like I matter. It's the spotlight he shines on me. And it makes me feel horrible. It reminds me of what Vicky says about other girls in our school. The ones with short skirts. The ones who used to hang out with boys near the washrooms.

'That kind of girl.'

'Still no text?' I ask him, wondering how he must make Sameeksha feel if he can make me, a random stranger, so wanted. And then I wonder how I would feel if Vicky went ahead and told a girl he had a crush on her. Not nice.

He shakes his head. 'She will . . . sooner or later.'

'She's in college?'

'First year, Philosophy Honours. But she wants to move to the UK to study English. She's trying, let's see.'

'How cute that you guys can do courses like English and philosophy without worrying about the jobs you will get after them.'

He frowns. I worry if my constant haranguing about his richness would put him off.

He says, 'Yaar, what can I say? It's true that our future plans will not implode if we get one question wrong. To get 100 per cent in all four subjects to get into a college . . . it's just . . . crazy . . . it's a bad education system.'

'I'm not blaming you, by the way,' I clarify. 'It's strange that most of our lives is just chance. It's luck. Must be fun, though, living in Dubai.'

He laughs, some of the colour coming back to his face. 'Ummm .... I was about to say it's okay, it's not special, but you will judge me, so let me recalibrate. Umm .... so . . . it's amazing compared to India. Less traffic, no bribes, things work, no one cheats, everything is air-conditioned, it's super safe. It's like a shopping mall. You hardly ever complain in a shopping mall.'

'But?'

'I never said there was a but.'

'It felt like there was a but . . .'.

He gives in. 'But Mumma says there's no culture. Everything is man-made, artificial.'

I roll my eyes. 'Give me comfort over culture any day. Anyway, everything is man-made, artificial. The oldest temples and mosques in India are man-made. Two hundred years later, they will call Burj Khalifa a monument. It's a matter of time.'

He looks at his phone again.

'I need to go to the market real quick,' he says. 'Do you want to come?'

I want to go wherever he goes. It's absolutely wrong. A part of me tells me that this is what the holiday is about: to experience new things. So what if the experience is to be in the company of this charming guy who thinks gaming is cool, that Philosophy Honours is a legitimate career path and talks about how education systems should be fair. But another part of them reminds me of the slippery slope. Vicky doesn't know of Daksh's existence. Not that there's anything to tell him. I have not lied to him, not explicitly, just not told him. But telling him isn't smart. Vicky doesn't like me talking to other guys, like I don't like him talking to other girls. And this is literally the worst time to fight over something that's nothing. Daksh has a crush on me, not vice versa. To me . . . he's . . . in Daksh's words, a frog pinned on the table to be dissected. Just that he's not a frog, but a prince, a naïve prince who's gorgeous to look at and adds to the scenery of the holiday. My internal monologue makes me . . . not like myself.

'*That kind of girl.*'

'I can't come with you, Daksh,' I refuse.

'Your parents are at the cooking workshop. They aren't going to be free for the next . . . at least an hour.'

'I know, but it will be one more lie I will have to tell Vicky. The list's getting longer and I don't like it.'

'It's going to the market, it's not a date.'

'It's going to the market alone with a guy who has told me he has a crush on me. There is a considerable difference,' I correct him. 'I can't even tell him I met you.'

He frowns.

'He doesn't like it when I talk to other guys,' I explain.

'And what's one more lie when you have told him one? Come, I will get bored without you.'

Fifteen minutes later, I'm riding on his rented scooter to the market nearby. For a few split seconds every few minutes, he puts my hand on his waist to steady himself. I'm not cheating on Vicky, but he would call it that. Guilt washes over me in small waves. It happens more when I let my eyes linger on the little stubble on his face, the angle his jaw makes with his neck, his thick eyebrows.

'*That kind of girl.*'

We stop at a chemist, and he orders lens solutions, a pack of diapers, a strip of Flexon and two Cornetto ice cream cones. We eat our Cornettos and he asks me how Vicky and I met.

'We didn't meet frivolously at a party where our *vibes* matched.'

'I sense a slight mocking tone in your voice,' he smirks. 'But go on.'

'We were in the eleventh standard. I found him outside the vice principal's office, furious, absolutely enraged. A few people had cheated on an exam. They would have scored more than him. He was there to complain.'

'I think I can guess who was the most unpopular kid in your school.'

'I was there for the same reason,' I inform Daksh.

'Now I can guess who were the top two unpopular kids,' he chuckles.

As I tell him more about Vicky and he tells me more about Sameeksha, the contrast between us becomes clear to me. His is like a puppy in love, an unplanned relationship of two people who want to do nice things together, such as going to movies and parties—harmless but overall pretty empty. Mine's what a relationship should be like—a path for growth for both, a future to build. A relationship that can obviously withstand the confession of a crush from a random guy.

'I'm eventually going to tell Vicky about you . . . just have to find the right time.'

'There's nothing to tell,' he says.

I bite into the ice cream. 'It's the first time I'm doing something like this.'

'That's literally the rule number one of vacations. You do things you haven't done before. Normal rules don't apply. We are just hanging out. And you won't even remember this holiday, or me, in a few months from now. So chill.'

He pats me. His touch is so casual. It doesn't mean anything, of course. But it goes to my list of things I can't tell Vicky about. The list of things that signify we were nothing.

'I'm chilling. This is the most chill I have been in the last two months. The stress of the results . . .' I say. 'It felt like I had taken a huge breath and I couldn't let it out till my results were announced. But this holiday . . . it's brought some of my breath back. It's a good distraction.'

'Good to be a part of the distraction,' he says with a warm smile.

'I can't believe Gaurav didn't stop me from going with you,' I remark.

'FIFA—'

My phone ringing interrupts him. It's Vicky. My stomach churns with guilt. I collect myself and receive the call.

'Good morning, jaan.'

'The integration question, the last one,' he stutters. 'What was your answer?'

'Why?'

'I checked the answer keys. What was the answer, Aanchal?' he barks.

We had decided we wouldn't check the keys. We had decided we would live in the confidence that we wouldn't get anything wrong.

'Aanchal?' he grumbles.

I recall the question. It wasn't a tough one. It was one of the five questions I had tackled in the first thirty minutes. '42.'

'No,' he says.

His words are like a tight slap. My heart beats against my chest.

'No?' I mumble. 'But I had revised . . .'

'It's 42,' he chokes. '42 is the answer. In all the answer keys, 42 is the answer. But how can it be 42?'

A flood of relief courses through my entire body.

'It was a six-mark question,' he continues, his voice feeling farther away than it is.

I feel the air shift.

'Vicky?'

I hear him breathe heavily into the phone.

'The answer is 42,' he says, his voice that of a broken man.

'So we got it right, then?' I ask, knowing it's a lie.

'21, I got 21 . . . Aanchal. Six marks . . .'

His voice trails.

He speaks again, this time with anger in his voice, 'SRCC is out of the question. I won't make it . . .'

'Jaan—'

'. . . you will.'

He disconnects the call.

I stand there, looking at the phone in my hand. I call him back. His phone's switched off.

'Overconfidence,' I say to Daksh. My head spins.

I sit on the sofa to settle myself. My blood boils. This is what I feared Vicky would do. I kept telling him to go easy, not make silly mistakes and that's exactly what he has done now. I can almost picture him smirking at the easiness of the question and then skipping the last two steps. That's where he made the mistake. My head feels heavy.

My voice comes out in an angry rant, 'We had done similar questions hundreds of times. Hundreds! He shouldn't have got it wrong. He used to solve the question but did not put the values in. Why? "It's so easy!" he'd say. Then he'd look at me as if I'm some dumb little girl. I had warned him, I had warned him so many times. I kept saying, "Vicky, complete the answer, Vicky, complete the answer," but no, he didn't listen.'

'It's one question, Aanchal.'

'One question?' I sneered. 'Where does this leave Vicky and me? If I get through and he . . .'

'In the same university? Still in a relationship?'

'You won't understand. You're just a Dubai kid,' I snap. 'Why am I even talking to you about this?'

He raises his hands in surrender and speaks calmly. 'Look, I know you're angry. But one of you still has a chance to get through. If not, you will be together for the next hurdle.'

'Just . . . don't talk about this.'

'Are you angry about him? Or are you scared about your result?'

'Can't I be both?' I growl. 'If he was in SRCC, I could have told my parents about him next year. He could have told his parents about me. How do you think his mother will react when I get a higher placement than her *raja beta* does? He's an only son. Aunty is obsessed with him.'

'And I'm assuming his parents won't understand even if you guys tried to make them understand?'

'You think Vicky himself will understand? Because of him, I have a chance to get into SRCC. He taught me . . .' I can barely breathe. Now if I get in and he doesn't . . . . it's . . . let's go back to the hotel.'

I fight my tears all the way back.

In the eight years that we have been in the same school, Vicky scored less than me only twice; once in mathematics, once in economics. The first time he called it 'too embarrassing' to lose to me. The second time he called our economics teacher a pervert who favoured me over him. Both times, he had been furious with himself—and at me.

After that time, every time our answer sheets were distributed, I wished that he'd score as much as I did to avoid the unpleasantness afterwards. Our names meant I was always roll number one and he was the last. My answer sheet the first one to be distributed, his the last. It also meant that if I scored a 99, I would hold my breath and pray till his roll number came, that he scored at least 99 as well.

Vicky didn't like losing to me—his student. And I didn't want him to lose to me. Partly because I feared how he would behave. And partly because of what his father would do to him. Maa–Papa expect Gaurav and me to do well; they scold us, withhold love, but they never raise their hand. But Vicky's father—a mathematics teacher—strips him and canes his back for every mark he loses. Uncle doesn't stop until he draws blood. Sometimes Vicky would come to school with blood seeping out of his school shirt. I shudder to think what his father would do when he misses SRCC by one question, and that too in mathematics.

Back in the TV room, Gaurav's still on the PlayStation.

'Gaurav, let's go,' I call out to him.

'Five minutes, Didi.'

'I'm not going to say it again, let's go,' I warn him.

He doesn't listen. I yank the wires out. The screen goes blank.

'DIDI!' he screams.

'You scream one more time and I am going to slap you. And if I see you playing video games once more, then see what I will do,' I warn him. 'Maa–Papa do so much for us and all you do is play games. One slap and you will understand.'

He's about to argue, but he looks at my face and decides otherwise. We walk silently to our room. He bristles but dares not say anything to me. My fury starts to peter out.

'Vicky got a question wrong,' I tell Gaurav. 'He won't clear the cut-off.'

He first shrugs to ignore me. Two steps later, he hisses, 'As if you care, Didi.'

'What does that mean?'

'You only care about yourself. Who cares what happens to Vicky?'

'What do you mean, Gaurav? I don't—'

He cuts me. 'Remember Geetika and Kanika? They were your friends till the tenth standard. But the minute you met Vicky and realized the two of you could make it to SRCC or something, you forgot them. It will be the same with Vicky. You will find someone else. He will be left behind. Don't worry about it.'

I feel as if my body was on fire. *How could my brother say this about me?*

'You mean I don't care about you? About Maa–Papa? How can you say this? Do I not do anything for you?'

Gaurav smiles. 'Didi,' he says softly. 'You obviously care about us, your own family . . .' He looks at me. '. . . but not about anyone else. Be it Vicky or anyone.

'Shut up, Gaurav.'

'You also know you're not the world's most caring girlfriend. You're the worst—'

'You're wrong.'

'Oh please, Didi, you're already talking to this guy. I'm sure you have a crush on him!'

'Oye!'

'What's that on your hand, then?' he points. 'If one person gets through, shouldn't it be you?'

I look at my hand.

'Whatever, Didi,' he says.

7.

Daksh Dey

Hi Daksh

> Where were you? Couldn't you send me one text all this while?

Been thinking . . .

> You don't have to go round in circles. You're breaking up, I know. You could have just told me rather than going missing for a week.

Had to think Daksh. Not a decision I have taken easily.

> You could have texted that you're thinking about our relationship. We could have discussed it. Is that too much to do?

If I had said anything, you would have influenced my decision.

We were together. How can I not influence the decision about us?

This is about me

Can I call you?

No

So we are breaking up and I don't even get to call you? Nice.

U will change my mind. It's much easier to do it over text

Easier for whom?

I'm sorry Daksh

Do I get a reason? Or are you looking to make it even easier for you?

Moving to London. I got admission. Got the news last week

Congratulations!

Sarcastic?

Absolutely not.

Thanks

So you didn't want to have a long-distance relationship. Is that why we are breaking up?

Among other things

Things? Good to know there is a list of things that are wrong with me.

Don't be like that

Like what? Hurt? I have spent almost every waking moment thinking of you and I shouldn't be hurt?

I'm sorry. I shouldn't have said that. I'm hurting too

It must be killing you to move to London and start an exciting new life there.

Daksh

Sorry, I'm just pissed. What are the other things on the list?

The past few months were great, Daksh. I don't want to end it with telling you things like this

> I deserve to know.

U're very nice

> No one has ever accused me of being nice.

You try to behave like you're a clever, haraami boy, but you're nice. Too nice

> This is a very strange reason to get dumped.

But I want something more in my partner

> What more?

Ambition Daksh. You don't want to do anything. You just read books play v games and watch shows. It's a little . . . sad

> Everyone should have their life figured out by the time they are 19?

They should at least try. I don't see that in U

> So my professional choices pushed me away from you. That's a bit weird.

You spent time with me

> That's a bad thing?

Its clingy

> Wow.

I can't be your everything. When you put up that picture, I knew we had to break up

> It's silly that you think you were my everything. You were a lot, but not everything. Don't overestimate your importance. I just liked your boobs.

Daksh.

> It was a joke.

Im sorry baby

I don't know what to say to you. This seems silly. It was just a picture.

It wasnt the picture. It was what it represented. I wish I had more to say

Why didn't you tell people about us?

I wasnt sure about us

You waited to get through to your college. Had you not got admission, would we still be together?

y r you asking me these questions? They dnt mean anything any more

Why did you keep me hanging?

Its hard to let you go

Lol.

I'm serious

Doesn't look like it.

Daksh. u're an addiction. It's hard, trust me

Whatever. This is just nonsense.

It is what it is

Nonsense.

Sorry Daksh

Can I call you?

u will ask us to get bck and you will convince me. I don't want that to happen

I won't.

Then why do you want to talk?

Because I love your voice.

Daksh. Dnt do that

It felt real.

It ws real

If it were, I don't think we would be talking like this.

I wish u were exactly what people told me you wud be like

What's that?

Flirt

I'm that.

No, you're not. u're a pit bull, a Rottweiler on the outside, but with the loyalty of an old Labrador

Good to know I'm a dog.

Honstly, I thought u would leave. Or I would hear you're cheating on me with a few more women

As evidence suggests, I get dumped.

Dnt be like that

What I'm like is none of your concern.

Sorry

It is what it is.

Daksh

?

Daksh?

It's fine. Take care.

How's Andamans

Don't be interested in my life. If it's not love, it's nothing for us.

Daksh yaar

I have a crush on someone though. She thinks I'm a dumb Dubai kid too. Some kind of streak I'm on.

Hope it works out with her

She's dating. Anyway. Got to go.

Bye. I'm sorry

I'm sorry too for not being enough for you. Should have never trusted a girl who doesn't end her sentences with a full stop. Learn some fucking English.

8.

Aanchal Madan

'Do you like the church?' Maa asks over the phone.

'It's so boring. I should have come with you,' I reply.

'It's okay, Aanchal. Be thankful. And don't separate from the group, okay? Keep wearing the hat they gave you. We will see you at the restaurant. And just see Gaurav doesn't jump around too much.'

Maa–Papa had chosen to skip the Ross Island Tour and instead visit the flea market with others from the group. They have been calling every five minutes to check on us.

'Okay, Maa, bye, bye.'

Be thankful.

Over the past few years, our stationery shop has seen a rise in the sale of a certain type of item: gratitude journals. It serves to remind people of things they should be thankful for. We never get repeat customers for gratitude journals. Because we take things for granted. For how many days can you keep writing, 'I'm thankful for my health' in a journal? Right now, I'm finding it hard to feel gratitude about this disappointing Ross Island tour. The guide's showing us around a dilapidated church. The ruins are just like any other ruins. Moss-covered bricks lying on the ground. There's no way one can picture what the actual church looked like. Should I feel gratitude that others can't experience this non-experience?

'Why did you say I don't care about Vicky?' I complain to Gaurav.

Gaurav's careless comment has kept me up all night. I feel I'm a rotten person because I feel gratitude and relief that it happened to Vicky and not me.

'Don't say things like that,' I warn Gaurav, who doesn't care.

Vicky's still not responding to me. Every few hours, he sends me a text before switching off his phone again.

Vicky please talk to me.

                                         need tym.

It can happen to anyone.

                            dun kno how i got it wrong

Vicky, please pick up once.

                                         Dun cal me.

I love you.

                        dis shouldn't hve happened to me

We will have other options.

                      dun know what I wil do. Stop calng me

Have you told Uncle?

                                              no

I miss him, but more than that, every time I read his text, a little voice inside me whispers, *Thank God it's not you.*

At a distance, I see Rabbani and Daksh.

Today, Rabbani's dressed in a cute dinosaur onesie with horns running down her back. Daksh is in a black sleeveless T-shirt and shorts. Sweat is trickling down the rippled muscles of his arms and he seems to have gone browner. Daksh is running behind Rabbani with a camera in hand. Both sister and brother can't stop giggling. I envy the naïve, dumb simplicity of their lives. Even Daksh's relationship is just that. Naïve, simple puppy love. Three months and he's calling what he has with Sameeksha love.

Rabbani then turns and looks at me. She starts to run towards me. I turn around to see if there's something behind me that she's running for. She stops just in front of me and picks up a small, shiny rock.

'Hey,' says Daksh. 'Rabbu, say hi to Aanchal Aunty, my crush on this vacation. Isn't she pretty?'

'Don't say that!' I protest.

'She doesn't understand that,' he chuckles.

My comment was not directed towards Rabbani but towards Daksh. He shouldn't call me pretty. He just . . . shouldn't.

'And I'm not an aunty to anyone,' I protest.

Rabbani's too absorbed in her rock to look up at me.

Daksh laughs. 'This church is such a scam, right? There's nothing here. I can get construction bricks from anywhere and call them historical ruins.'

'But it's all targeted to NRIs like you. They will sell you anything in the name of history and culture. And you guys will pay for it.'

He laughs. 'Your parents are at the flea market?'

I nod.

'Where's Gaurav? Oh, there . . . GAURAV!' he shouts and gestures to Gaurav to come over. He turns to me. 'I got something for him. And don't pluck his eyes out, okay?'

'What?' says Gaurav.

Daksh pulls out what looks like a gaming device from his pocket and gives it to Gaurav. 'It's the new Nintendo. You can play. Give it back when you're done.'

Gaurav looks at me and then at him. 'Is this a prank?'

'Why would it be a prank?'

'Why are you doing this?' I ask Daksh.

'Because he's the only one who can help me. I challenged my friend back in Dubai I would beat his score at Mario Kart. Clearly, I can't do that, but he's good at this.'

'No,' I refuse. 'He's not playing any games.'

'DIDI!' protests Gaurav.

'Gaurav, no,' I refuse.

'Didi, but this is so boring. I have nothing to do!'

'Gaurav—'

'Let him, it's just for the vacation,' Daksh interjects. 'And it's not for him, he's just helping me out.'

'Fine, whatever,' I concede.

Gaurav takes the Nintendo from Daksh. 'Thank you, Bhaiya!'

'No, thank you. And beat the score, okay? Don't waste time on the other games,' Daksh warns him.

Gaurav runs and finds a corner. I have never seen him happier.

'What?'

'You're strange, Daksh.'

'I know. According to Sameeksha, I'm also clingy, a loser, someone who has no aim in life and doesn't have anything figured out. Clearly, I don't have anything figured out or I wouldn't be giving a sixteen-year-old my video game so I beat my friend's score.'

'She broke up?'

Daksh looks at his feet, smiles sadly and nods. The grief that clouds his face doesn't match the length of his relationship. He looks at me with his sad, droopy eyes and says, 'How can a person's ambition make a relationship better? Such a strange thing to say. I don't love you any more because your career is not important to you. It's so fucked up.'

After measuring whether I should say it or not, I decide he deserves the truth. 'It's not, Daksh. I'm sorry about the break-up but maybe she wants someone with whom she can imagine a definite future.'

Rabbani shows him another rock. He smiles at her.

'It doesn't work like that,' he argues. 'People change, circumstances change. How can you have control over it? Love is not mathematics where you can get it right. There are no keys, no answer sheets.'

He looks at me suddenly remembering something. 'Vicky? Is he doing better?'

I shake my head. 'He's blaming me.'

'Why would he blame you?'

'I don't know. He's talking to everyone but me. I feel like he's punishing me.'

'I'm sorry.'

'Remember that night we met? You said you have a crush on me because of my genetic lottery or something? But I could be a horrible person? Do you still think that?'

'That you're a horrible person?' he asks. 'No, not at all.'

'What makes you say so?'

'Are you fishing for compliments? Because that's what it sounds like.'

'I am trying to feel okay about myself because I spent last night feeling like I only care about myself.'

'I have seen you care about your brother; I have seen you making sure your parents are comfortable around here, and you have been honest about your hate for my sister—'

I gasp. 'I don't hate her!'

'I'm joking,' he says with a smile. 'You're nice, Aanchal. You're not horrible. And anyway, everyone's allowed to be a little horrible.'

Just then the tour guide waves from a distance. As I walk back to the bus, I repeat to myself that I'm not horrible. I push out of my mind the thoughts of what Vicky's father will do to him. I try to convince myself that it's okay for me to have asked God to spare me instead of him.

'You okay?' asks Daksh.

I nod.

9.

Aanchal Madan

I'm alone in the room. Gaurav is in the game room trying to better the highest score on Daksh's gaming console.

Maa–Papa have gone on the food tour of the island. With every passing day, they feel freer to enjoy themselves. There's nothing more I like than seeing them without the burdens of every day weighing them down. It seems like this vacation has made them younger by two decades. Gaurav and I just have to work hard for a few more years and we could give them this experience repeatedly.

I'm staring at my open suitcase. In it, there's a black swimming costume. When we were buying clothes for this trip, Maa asked me if I wanted a swimming costume because the hotel had three swimming pools. I told her what I told Vicky: 'I don't know how to swim.'

'You don't go to a hotel pool to swim, you do it to pass the time. They are shallow pools,' Vicky said later, giving me a package. 'This is what you will wear.'

He had got me a black swimming costume, a sharp one, the one that swimmers wear, where their thighs are visible, not the frock type I have seen on a lot of women. I had refused. And yet here I am, carrying the swimming costume gifted by Vicky, hidden in one small compartment of my suitcase.

But I'm thankful I packed it. This swimming costume will be how Vicky replies to my texts.

I put it on. And even though I'm alone in the room, I feel exposed, naked. I wear the bathrobe over it.

I text Vicky.

I'm wearing the costume, do you want to see it? I can send you a picture.

He's online but doesn't reply.

Vicky?

                                        dun care Aanchal.

Vicky, please, you wanted me to wear it, and I want you to see it.

He goes offline.

For thirty minutes, I sit by the window of my room, wearing the bathrobe over the costume, waiting for his text, watching people of all ages, shapes and sizes at the pool.

He comes online again.

Vicky, I will only wear this for you, if you don't see it jaan, what's the point.

pls do watevr u feel like.

The guests are walking to the poolside in their shirts and shorts or dresses, with their pool bags. Then they take off their shirts, their dresses and gingerly step into the pool. They wade around without swimming. Some order drinks. That's when I see Daksh at the poolside. He's slathering sunscreen on Rabbani's face and arms. She runs to the shallow end of the kids' pool and starts splashing.

I text Vicky.

You were right about the pool, no one swims.

He reads but he doesn't reply.

I care about you, Vicky.

Send me 1 pic.

His text makes my heart jump.

Vicky and I have kissed. We have watched two movies where we have fondled each other, and we have talked dirty at times. But the rest, we thought we would do after our boards were out of the way. He has never seen me this way, nor have I seen him.

Are you sure?

Watever Aanchal.

I take off the bathrobe and look at myself in the mirror. I take a picture. It comes out strange. I feel it's sexy but also imperfect, but also perfect; wrong, but also totally right. I click a few more. The more my gallery fills up, the more I love the pictures.

My phone beeps. It's Vicky.

R you sending?

Yes.

Face flushed, my heart pounding against my chest, I send him one picture. The few seconds of waiting feel like hours.

Nyc. Send me another one.

Are you sure?

Pls.

I feel risqué. This time I pull a strap down. I really like the picture.

Wow, more?

This time I pull both straps down till a little cleavage shows. I have never felt this sexy.

Nyc.

I can imagine Vicky's face light up. It turns me on to think my body makes him happy. I send him more pictures, play risqué with the straps of the swimsuit, with varying degrees of skin showing.

More?

Latr. maa's coming. thank you. ☺

I love you.

I'm happy, flushed. My body feels like it's on fire.

I can't sit still. I'm too happy. If I can do this, why can't I go down to the pool and do what the others are doing? Of course I can. I will send more pictures to Vicky. I make my way down to the pool. My heart's beating like Friday morning's school march drum.

At the pool, I take off my nightsuit's pyjamas that I wore over my swimsuit confidently. I had imagined everyone would look at me and I'd feel ashamed, but everyone's in their own little worlds, having fun. The water's inviting. I feel it with my toes and then slowly dip my leg in. I feel lighter.

I feel *happy*. I keep going through Vicky's texts in my mind. And every time my heart does a little somersault.

I wade towards the other side of the pool. And like everyone else, I ask for a drink. The bartender pours me Pepsi in a tall glass filled with ice. I feel like *them*, like everyone else in the pool. I settle in one corner of the pool, with my phone on a towel near the edge. I can't wait to send Vicky more pictures. I like the possibilities of where this can go.

If I had known that this was what Vicky needed, I would have done it yesterday!

My reverie is broken when I see a guy slicing through the water at a considerable pace. He reaches the far end of the pool, does a flip and swims towards me. His arms move with grace and strength. His face lifts from the surface of the water. He wades next to me.

Daksh.

I always took him to be athletic but lightly built. But when he emerges, I see that he is athletic, his chest muscles are strictly separated. The veins of his arms crisscross and his biceps look strained. When he shakes off the water from his face, it drips down his chest, forcing me to look away.

'That kind of girl.'

His nakedness makes me conscious of my nakedness. He's too close even though he's not. When his eyes linger on my bare shoulder, I feel as if the water has suddenly gone cold. I don't want to feel this, but I do. I'm conscious of my eyes settling on various parts of his body. I want to look away, look at his eyes or something, but I can't. It roves on his body like I'm a roadside *mawali*.

'Did Vicky pick up?' he asks and then catches my gaze. He pauses and then says, 'From your face, it looks like he did. Didn't he?'

I nod.

'Did you send him a picture of you in your swimsuit?' he asks, looking at me. His eyes wander over my body and then come right back to mine. In that short while, I feel a strange excitement in my belly.

'How . . . how did you know?'

'. . . guessed. But good move. I don't think he's going anywhere now. I wouldn't if I were him.'

What does he mean by that? Why would he say something like this? I want to be angry at his objectification of me, but I . . . like it. I want to change the subject. His looking at me is discomfiting in the nicest way possible and I don't want to feel that, so I ask him, 'Sameeksha?'

He laughs. 'That's history, ancient history. Like she never existed.'

But it's a sad laugh from him, not one of those I have seen him do when he's with Rabbani. It's been only five days and I feel like I know the crinkles of his nose, his little tics, how his face is when he's happy as opposed to when he's just pretending.

'You deserve someone better,' I tell him.

'That's just something people say. I don't believe deserving someone better is a problem. What she said is true. The more I think about it, the truer it seems.'

'Then you will get someone who will like you the way you are.'

'For that, I will have to figure out who exactly I am. Look at you, or Vicky, or even Sameeksha. You guys have it all figured out. And I'm not like, filthy rich. Baba is just an engineer, it's been seven years he has been there. We have savings and all, but it's not like I can throw my life away.'

It's the first time I've seen him agitated.

'You're not—'

'I know I'm not throwing my life away. Not doing drugs or spending like crazy, but you guys are making me feel like I am.' He takes a deep breath and says, 'It's fine.'

We stay at the poolside for a little while. He orders a Pepsi too and a plate of French fries. I'm hungry and we both finish it swiftly. Every now and then my mind throws up an impossibility, a strange thing that I don't want: me and him. It's probably just the rush of a new place.

'What's that tattoo?' I ask of the little date that's scribbled under his shoulder on his chest.

'Rabbani's birthday,' he answers. 'The date that changed my life.'

'How did it change your life?'

'It's like I was meant to be a brother. I didn't know it, of course. And the day I became one, I knew, yes, this is what I want to be. I wanted a little sister. It was pretty cool.'

'Would you tattoo the date you met Sameeksha next to it?'

He frowns.

'See?' I tell him. 'You weren't meant to be with Sameeksha.'

'That's questionable logic but thank you for trying,' he smiles—a genuine smile, not his 'polite' smile. 'Hey? Your phone's ringing.'

Vicky calling.

I wipe my hands and pick up the phone.

As Daksh swims away from me, an idea gathers strength in my mind. It's stupid, irrational. But the more I try to push it away, the harder it pushes back. It takes shape. It gathers critical mass.

I wonder.

I wonder if . . .

. . . Daksh is lucky for me?

Whenever he's around, good things seem to happen to me. Breakfast, 42 and now Vicky's call.

'Hello, jaan.'

10.

Daksh Dey

It's taken me the entire morning.

I have deleted Sameeksha's picture. I have deleted the call records. The messages I sent her. I have removed all the likes

I posted on her pictures. It is dramatic because the end of relationships is meant to be dramatic. You have to end them in this fashion so there's a definite timeline to your relationship.

For the past two days, I have been turning over the relationship in my mind and wondering why I am not as sad as I should be. I should be wrecked. I should be crying. But no, none of that. On top of it, I feel like a bit of an asshole, because I do miss her breasts.

I knew why I chased Sameeksha apart from the obviously attractive physical features. I latched on to Sameeksha because the last two years had been a whirlwind of helping Mumma with chores, diaper-changing and doctor visits, and Sameeksha was one of the first few people who showed an interest in me. Sameeksha, with her seven-year-old sister, was also the only person around with a young sibling.

The more I analyse my lack of sadness, the more one reason stands out as to why I'm not as devastated as I thought I would be.

Aanchal Madan.

If I can have an all-consuming crush on someone while mourning the abandonment of a girlfriend, was it love in the first place?

The phone in my room rings.

'Hello?'

'Daksh?' says a voice from the other side. 'I'm at the business centre. Come.'

'Aanchal?'

'Come quickly.'

I cut the call and jump out the bed.

When I get there, she's bunched up in a corner in the empty business centre with the computer in front of her, sitting with her legs folded close as if hiding from a captor. She's chewing her nails. Her face is ashen. She's leaking her life force. Her knees are shaking. The room is absolutely cold and yet there are beads of sweat on her temples.

I rush to her. 'What happened?'

She looks annoyed. 'The results.'

'What? Oh!' It strikes me. 'It's today. Oh. Shit. So you're hiding here.'

She lets out a long breath. 'Gaurav and Maa–Papa were irritating me. They kept telling me that it's not the end of the world if I don't score well. They think I will kill myself or something.'

'You give that impression by the way you look right now.'

'They also know how important today is. They are just acting, trying to play it cool.'

She turns and stares at her computer.

I look at my watch. 'It's not 10 a.m. yet.'

'Sometimes, the results come quicker,' she says. 'But they haven't or I would've started getting messages.'

Her fingers are trembling. She closes her eyes and mumbles a prayer.

To distract her, I say, 'It was pretty unremarkable for me, the day my results were announced.'

'Were your parents angry?' she asks.

'Again, presumptuous of you to think I scored badly, but yes, I scored a 73 aggregate. No, they weren't angry.'

'They should have been.'

'Mumma hugged me. Baba went into a long-winded rehearsed speech about how no one remembers marks after a while. I remember we went out and had biryani. Right next to us, there were parents celebrating 90s, and there I was with a 73.'

'And you? How did you feel about 73?'

'I . . . . I was disappointed to know that I wasn't smart. I expected more, but the 73 sort of told me that I wasn't one of the smart kids. It was the final confirmation.'

She nods.

She turns to the screen and swivels it towards me. 'Can you check, please? I'm too nervous.'

I refresh the page. The results are still not out. I open a new browser. Sometimes, it shows the old cache if you keep trying to visit the same website. No change. So, instead, I take out my phone and I type in the website in my phone's browser. It takes time to load. But it does.

'Aanchal?' I say.

'What?'

'The results are out.'

Her face turns red. I dangle the phone in front of her. She looks at me, eyes piercing mine and orders me, 'You're going to check my result.'

'Wha—'

'Do it, Daksh,' she says, her voice barely a whisper. '3455883.'

'Are you sure?'

'You have to do it, you just have to,' she says.

I type in the number. The page takes time to load. I say a silent prayer. She stares at the smudged swastika on her palm and closes her fist. Her scoresheet opens incredibly slowly. I find myself praying again. *Please help her, help, her, help her, help her, help her, help her, help her.* I want to hold her and tell her that everything is going to be fine.

My heart begins to race. The numbers start appearing. I don't see twos, or threes, or even sevens.

100.

99.

99.

100.

100.

Those were a lot of 9s and 0s.

That's two marks lost.

Only two marks.

'Those are SRCC marks,' I mutter.

I turn to see her frozen. Her mouth is parted, stuck in a surprised expression. She's not moving.

My body's flushed with adrenaline. It's like someone exploded a happiness grenade in my mind. I have known her for only four days, yet I'm joyous in her joy. I look at her, waiting for her to move, react, exult, run from the room to scream that she has done it. But she does nothing. Slowly, she becomes like those Christian statues that are reported to cry. Tiny tears streak down her cheeks.

'Aanchal?'

'3455902,' she says finally.

'But that's your name. These are your marks. See? Aanchal Madan,' I confirm.

'Vicky,' she explains.

I put in the roll number. This time the page opens quickly.

100. 100. 99. 94. 94.

'98.25,' she whispers.

These are not SRCC marks. All that separates Aanchal's success and Vicky's failure is one question.

'Vicky's not going to make it,' she mumbles.

She opens her palm. The swastika is smudged because of the sweat.

Her phone starts to beep. She picks it up. And switches it off.

'Who is it?' I ask.

'Classmates.'

She takes a few deep breaths—a sense of calm descends on her. And probably for the first time, I see how she really looks. It's like watching a flower bloom in a time-lapse. It isn't the Aanchal of fifteen minutes ago. It isn't the Aanchal I kayaked with. It isn't the beautiful, moonlit Aanchal of that night at the beach.

This Aanchal is *different*.

A different kind of beautiful. This Aanchal has a smile on her face. A smile that emanates not from her lips but from her heart. Her eyebrows have smoothened. There's a glow on her face. Her eyes have widened. There's a blush on her cheeks. It's as if she was a perfect sculpture but now the right words have been chanted and she's coming to life. She's transformed from a mortal to a goddess. I have shrunk and she has grown and what's between us is not friendship but something bordering on devotion. She can order me to walk to the window and jump and I would, with a smile on my face. She could ask me to kill, and I would.

'I should go,' she tells me.

My heart breaks in slow motion. Each little fragment shredding my insides. Just three words—'I should go.' And yet, my mind can't convince my body not to feel the pain.

I don't want her to go anywhere. I want her to stay, and I want to keep looking at her. 'You should go.' It's the biggest lie I have ever said.

'Thank you,' she squeals.

'For what?'

'You turned my luck, Daksh,' she says. 'Don't you see it?'

'No.'

'You're my lucky charm. That's why I called you here. I have to go, okay? I will see you in a while.'

As she leaves the business centre, I feel alone. I don't feel lucky, I feel lonely. I feel like the loneliest fucking guy in the whole world.

11.

Daksh Dey

I feel like my heart's spasming like a lizard's tail that's been cut off. I don't want to leave the Andamans. The reason's becoming clearer and clearer as the time to leave nears. And the clearer it gets, the more my heart shrinks.

In the afternoon, I see the Madans at the restaurant. Aanchal waves at me and calls me over. She has told her parents about me being lucky for her. Her parents ask me to join them for lunch but I decline. It's their moment to enjoy, I tell them and leave. Later, I see her near the pool talking on the phone. The way she's smiling, her tone, I'm sure it's Vicky. Her giggles, the thought of more pictures being exchanged between the two, feels like someone has plunged a knife into my heart and is twisting it.

In the evening, I decide it's enough. It's a crush and there's no way I'm going to make it seem more than that. I remind myself that Sameeksha dumping me is making my heart believe in things that don't exist. I decide to see Aanchal, talk to her and let my heart settle.

The opposite happens.

It's the last night so all the guests are invited for a cocktail hour. Aanchal wears a dress that looks like it was bought just today. It's a short, black, shimmering dress and she looks painfully gorgeous. Not that she looked any less beautiful in her suits.

I pretended to be busy on my phone the entire time because there was no way a conversation is going to make it better.

I don't sleep the entire night. I think of her so incessantly my head hurts. I feel like a hypocrite because didn't I just confess how broken I was to Sameeksha less than seventy-two hours ago? Crushes are supposed to be cute, not damaging. Aanchal whirls around in my head like a raging tornado, eviscerating everything in its path.

The sadness I felt for Sameeksha isn't a patch on what I feel now. It's as if it wasn't even real. That sadness was made up, as was the love. Now I know. I know.

Now, we are at the Marine Museum. A drab place for the last day of our trip. I should have been excited to go back but now I want this little island to be cordoned off from the rest of the world by mile-long waves. Aanchal and I stuck on this island for all of eternity.

'Don't you like the museum? We thought you would like it,' says Mumma.

'It's nice,' I say. 'Just a little tired, maybe.'

'Is it about Sameeksha?'

'Mummy yaar, no,' I respond. 'I'm over it already.'

'It's her loss totally,' she says and runs her hand over my head. 'Where can anyone get a boy like you?'

'There are plenty of people like me.' I spot the Madans in the distance. I point at them and tell Mumma, 'Can you believe it? 100 in four subjects. You remember mine?'

'It's not important to me how much you scored. I remember we went out on your results day. We had biryani at Karama. Do you remember that?'

'I scored 73 per cent.'

Mumma shrugs. 'It's just numbers.'

'Two people in the past week have called me aimless, a drifter. Like some kind of loser.'

'Whoever said that doesn't know a single thing about life.'

'Why weren't you angry? There were other kids who scored in the 90s. Our neighbour's daughter, Baba's colleagues' sons. Why did you two never sort of . . . push me?' I probed.

Mumma rubs my back. Maybe they are to blame for my aimlessness. They should have been harder on me. Maybe people like Aanchal will win at life and I will be some guy living off the leftover savings of his parents.

Mumma takes a deep breath, then smiles at me.

'You were always a good child,' she says. 'Do you know that? Other kids used to run around, break things, do all kinds of nonsense. But not you. You were such a well-behaved child we kept thinking you'd get the *nazar*. You listened to everything we said, ate your food without a fuss, never cried for toys. Some parents know how to raise children. Your Baba and I didn't need to learn. You were so easy.'

Mumma's eyes are slightly glazed over. She's looking at me but it feels as if she's elsewhere. Somewhere in the past.

She continues, 'All you didn't do was score marks. Not because you didn't sit with books, you would—'

'I was just dumb.'

'Not everyone does well in school, Daksh. You were sincere. What could we have scolded you about? Nothing.'

'You could have pushed me during the boards. I would have . . .'

Mumma starts to laugh. She wipes her tears. She holds my hand like she used to before Rabbani was born. It used to be embarrassing, but now I realize how much I miss it.

'You were in the eleventh grade when Rabbani was born,' she says. 'You were there whenever I needed you. You stayed up so many nights. One cough and you would come running from your room. You scored 73, it was a miracle. How many students in your class can match that? Not one. Your Baba and I kept feeling guilty about the timing. Baba, especially. Kept saying we destroyed your career. I kept telling him there's more to life than a career. We got to see how you were, how you would be as a man. That means a lot more to me, to your Baba. You're a nice boy, Daksh. Who cares about these little things? Who cares if you're not ambitious or you don't know what you want to do in life? For me, the way you are, you're already winning in life.'

I look away. The last thing I want to do is cry in the middle of a damned museum.

So I say, 'Fine, I will add that to my CV.'

'Look there,' Mumma says and points at Baba.

He's struggling to keep Rabbani from knocking over artefacts. She continues, 'You got a 100 long before your results were announced. You were with us. That's all that matters. What are marks? Nothing. Here today, forgotten tomorrow. We will always be around.'

12.

Aanchal Madan

Our bus waits for us at the main gate of the hotel to take us to the airport. We had been excited and nervous about this trip for months. I had dreamt about it, and it's been life-changing. I feel like I'm a different person from the one who walked in. Gaurav tells me it's because now I'm at the precipice of my dreams, my family's dreams, coming true. I'm close to the finish line.

Which is true. Ever since my results, I feel like I have gained a few inches, walking a little taller. I lied to Gaurav when I told him that I feel like I deserve to be here. But now I believe it. Now, I will be in the top 0.1 per cent in India. SRCC will open those doors for me. I'm three years away from the top placement on the campus and earning my own money. And who knows? I might even choose to do an MBA and leapfrog into more success. What difference would there be between these people and me? I will be paying for my flights, have an American Express card in my purse and complain about faulty air conditioning in my hotel room.

All that I dreamt of is now within my grasp. It's sweeter because I earned it—I have fought and clawed for every inch and it's mine.

Maa told me yesterday to keep being humble. Baba had nodded too. I think they are just scared. We are entering the unknown. I have caught them staring at the marks. As if they will change. I have told them, this is for life, the marks are etched in stone and so is the trajectory of my future. Maa said a prayer, to be humble on my behalf. I told Maa I will tattoo the swastika permanently to thank God.

When I board the bus, Daksh is already there. He's sitting on the last seat, staring blankly out of the window. I see him unshaven for the first time. He looks tired, unkempt. The fresh summeriness I associated with him is gone.

I cough to get his attention. He looks at me. He forces a smile and then goes back to staring at the hotel staff loading our suitcases in the belly of the bus. Every now and then, I turn back to check on Daksh. Now he has headphones clamped over his ears, his head resting on the window sill. It seemed like he had handled his break-up pretty well, but now that I see him going back, maybe I had read him wrong.

He looks sad.

The bus leaves the hotel.

I know I will never forget Daksh.

When I look back at the moment of my board results years from now, I'd remember he was the person who checked my results. I will remember the joy on his face as if it wasn't my result but his. It was just pure joy and celebration. He looked at me like I had won over the world. He had no concept of struggle, of achievement, and yet he was happy for me. Between that morning and now, I have shared my results with many people, and many have said they are happy for me. But, apart from my family, his celebration, his reaction was the purest of them all. His one-person audience applause made me feel like a rock star. Not even Vicky, who kept talking about his options, matched it.

I will never forget it.

Daksh feels like a friend now—my first one after Vicky.

At the airport, I lose him.

I load the suitcases on to the conveyor belt. I give our identification documents to the airline staff. I do it like I have done it a million times before. None of the nervousness of the first time.

We all settle down wherever we can find seats. All this while, Gaurav hasn't looked up from Daksh's Nintendo Switch once.

'Don't forget to return it to him,' I say.

He doesn't listen. He's transfixed.

I look around. I can't find Daksh.

I kill time by replying to all the congratulatory messages.

Every now and then, I look around the airport to find Daksh.

'His flight is to Hyderabad from where he will fly off to Dubai,' says Gaurav, when he sees me crane my neck.

'So?'

'He's on the other side of the security check.'

I get back to answering calls. We clear security after a while. The airport's small but I still can't spot Daksh anywhere near the boarding gates.

'Probably at the lounge,' says Gaurav, pointing to the business-class lounge.

'Give me the game, I will go and give it to him.'

'Absolutely not. I will give it to him when he boards the flight.'

'It doesn't look good, Gaurav. Just give—'

I try to take it from him, but he pulls it closer to himself. 'You take it, and I will tell Maa about Vicky.'

It's a threat he often gives me. He never means to do it.

'You won't,' I say sternly. 'One more game. I'm going to the washroom. Once I come back, you're going to return the game.'

'You're going to see him,' says Gaurav. 'I knew you had a crush on him!'

'Play your game, don't be oversmart. One more game,' I warn him.

I tell the man at the business-class counter that I need to see a friend. He thinks for a moment and lets me go when I tell him I just need to say goodbye.

The lounge is almost empty. I spot him immediately. Rabbani is watching a video on Daksh's phone and he's feeding her some kind of purée.

'Hey.'

'Oh, hi,' he says, looking up.

Rabbani waves at me. I wave back. I don't know what to say to Rabbani or what to do with her. I want to tell Daksh his sister's cute because I know he would like hearing that, but it would be an outright lie.

'I wanted to say bye,' I tell him. 'Gaurav told me your flight is to Hyderabad. It's before our flight so . . .'

He smiles at me. It's one of his fake smiles.

'It was nice meeting you,' he says, while putting another spoonful of bland-looking paste in Rabbani's mouth. 'If you ever come to Dubai, let me know. I will show you around.'

I know it's just a thing to say. He obviously doesn't expect me to come to Dubai. I return the formality.

'And if you come to Delhi, I will show you around. You have a friend in Delhi.'

'Are we friends now?'

'You know what I mean,' I say. 'Daksh? Should we exchange numbers?'

'Are you assuming I'm going to make international calls to you?' He chuckles. 'Give me your number.' He gives me his phone. I type my number in.

As he stops smiling and I stop smiling, the air shifts.

It happens in an instant.

Our lives are going to begin again.

This island was a common meeting ground, where new rules applied, where new feelings could be felt, stilly futures imagined, but now we are going back into the real world, where we have nothing in common. He has his own life, his own circle of friends, an ex-girlfriend, and I have my own life. What would we mail each other about? If we had exchanged numbers, what would we even talk about?

'Gaurav will return the Nintendo when you board.'

'He's quite good at it.'

'I should go.'

He gets up. He wipes his hands with a tissue. 'Bye,' he says. He steps forward towards me and pulls me into a hug.

My body stiffens up.

I have never hugged a guy other than Vicky.

This is my first hug. With my first proper friend. Who's also my lucky charm.

Slowly, my muscles relax and I feel his warmth against mine, the intention of truly saying goodbye and of telling me that the past seven days meant something. It's not an empty hug. This hug means something, it says words that might be too odd, or too forward to say.

Then we let go.

'I will see you around,' I say sadly. And then I turn to Rabbani and say, 'I will see you too.'

Daksh laughs. 'It's okay. You don't like kids, it's fine.'

'Sorry.'

'Bye, Aanchal.'

'Daksh?'

'I know it's hard going back but trust me, things are going to be fine.'

'Fingers crossed.'

I walk out of the lounge feeling strange. Like I had gained something in the course of seven days and now I was leaving it behind. On the flight back to Delhi, I start thinking of what I could mail him. But then I think, *what's the point?* We lose friendships even when they are right in front of us.

When I land, I check my phone for his message. I check the time. He would have landed in Hyderabad an hour ago.

When I get back home, I check my phone again for a message from him.

The next day, I wait for his message.

Three days go by; I wait for his message.

A week later, I learn that Gaurav lied to me. I find the Nintendo hidden in the cupboard. He never returned it.

'I couldn't find him in the lounge,' he admits.

'You stole it.'

'Please don't tell Maa,' he begs.

'I won't.'

'Are you angry?'

'No, not really. He can buy another one.'

Months go by, and he still doesn't send me a message.

PART 2
FOUR YEARS LATER

PART 2
FOUR YEARS LATER

1.

Aanchal Madan

The airport announcement board blinks. Mumbai's check-in is in Aisle G. Maa–Papa stare at me from the other side of the glass walls of the airport departure terminal.

'You can go, Maa! I will be fine,' I say into the phone.

I see tears in Maa's eyes. She mumbles, 'Aanchal, your brother—'

I cut her short because it's already a priority on my list. 'I will find Gaurav and talk to him. Don't worry. Now, I'm going. Go, now, Maa.'

'Don't go here and there too much, stay in the hotel only. And keep sending us locations,' says Papa, worried.

The light's dying from their eyes. For the first time since I was born, they would go to bed without any children in the house. I don't share their sadness. I'm excited! My first business trip, my first solo trip. I slept for barely two hours last night. My colleagues at DeliverFood had been so envious for the past month. I told them they should have worked harder!

'Keep eating. And keep calling Vicky,' adds Maa.

'As if that's a choice, Maa,' I answer dryly.

'And his mother too,' reminds Maa again. 'She will also be worried. You know she loves you.'

Vicky's mother loves only one person—Vicky. If it were up to her, she would sew strings into Vicky's flesh and make him dance like a puppet. His mother had stopped eating for three days when Vicky moved out of the house to an apartment closer to his office.

'I will call her once I'm in the hotel.'

'Get them something from Mumbai,' Maa requests.

'Maa, you get everything in Delhi. I will be busy at the conference, what will I get them? Don't just say anything.'

'*Achcha, achcha*, okay, don't, but please call them. Don't give them a chance to be angry.'

'Okay now, go,' I tell them.

I wave at them and cut the call. Their shoulders droop.

At the aisle, sleepy, tired mothers cradle screaming, tired babies. Their husbands check in on airline apps. There's a group of boys and girls—younger than me—on their way to Goa. Envy engulfs me when a boy in the Goa line kisses his girlfriend.

I miss feeling loved.

It's been months since Vicky has meaningfully kissed me. Kissing him is like kissing a dying fish. His eyes are open, the irises moving about. The stench of our rotten relationship makes me gag. I wonder how he still stands me. Had I been him, I would have dumped me years ago. I'm literally the world's worst girlfriend. He has said so a bunch of times during our screaming matches, of which there are many.

After the security check, I buy myself a coffee. *Look at me*, I tell myself. *At an airport, alone, on a business trip, buying myself a coffee*. I feel important! I take a sip. The coffee's scalding and breaks me out of my reverie. *Shit*. I pat my trousers. My phone's not there. I left my phone at security. I run back. The lady who frisked me hands me my phone with a shake of her head as if to say, *today's youth, totally irresponsible*.

There are thirteen missed calls from Vicky. His name makes me bristle with anger. I call him.

'Jaan,' he answers, his voice dripping with concern. 'Did you leave your phone at security?'

'Why are you calling?'

His tone shifts. 'What do you mean, why am I calling?'

'I called you so many times last night. Couldn't you send me one reply? Where were you?'

'Nowhere,' he answers irritably. 'Just office and then home. Why are you shouting?'

'When did you come back to the apartment?'

'I didn't see the time. I was too sleepy. Why is this an interrogation?'

'You're lying to me again.'

'I'm not lying! I genuinely didn't see the time. Why would I—'

'You could be with anyone, Vicky! Who knows who you sleep with behind my back!'

'WHY THE HELL WOULD I DO THAT?' he shouts.

'See, you're getting defensive,' I shoot back. 'Of course you can sleep with someone. To punish me because you don't even like me any more!'

'Calm down, Aanchal.'

'Fine!'

'What fine?'

'I can't say fine now, Vicky? You have a problem with that too?'

'Am I making everything a problem?' he snaps.

'No, I am making everything a problem. I am the one who came back late and didn't message. Come back at whatever time you want! Do whatever you want to do all night! Why should I care? Don't message me. Don't call me. FUCK WHOEVER YOU WANT TO!'

He breathes heavily into the phone. 'We can't argue about the same thing again. Every time we talk—'

'Who dropped you home, Vicky?'

'C'mon, Aanchal. Get over it, it was one time!' he thunders.

'It's one time I saw. Who knows how many times Sanya drops you home? Who knows if she's still with you and you guys are laughing at me?'

'Yaar! Can we stop arguing about it!'

I keep up the harassment, my voice dripping venom. 'You're making me argue about it, Vicky! I'm not crazy that I stay up worrying about you. First, you don't text, and then, you start lying to my face! Am I stupid?'

'Don't create a scene for no reason.'

'All of this is my fault, true, true. You not texting me at night is my fault. Right! I'm the crazy one!'

'Yes, *kuttiya*! You're the crazy one! God knows what you want from me.'

'Don't swear at me, Vicky. I will tell your mother.'

'Go, tell her what you want to! She knows what you are,' he yells. 'And you know what, Aanchal? Whoever thinks all of this and has these crazy doubts, that person is the first to go and fuck other people. You also know that!'

'Why do I even bother talking to you!' I lament. 'No matter what I do, you will always turn it around on me. Always. Like I'm the worst person in the universe!'

It pushes him over the edge. '*Madarchod*! Is there any point talking to you?'

'Yes, yes, everything is wrong with me only. You're perfect. Everything about Vicky is just perfect!'

He sighs heavily. 'Every time there's some new drama. I call in the morning, there's drama, in the evening, there's some new drama . . .'

He lets out a huge sigh. I know what he's doing. He's trying to put an end to this fight. He likes to torture me like this. He makes me feel like he's going to leave me and then never does. It's a jail I can never leave.

'Aanchal.'

I don't answer him. I want to fight. I want this to go on.

'Jaan,' he says softly. 'I just wanted to tell you I will miss you.'

I have no choice. 'I will miss you too,' I respond dryly.

'Love you,' he says. 'I love you so much. You know that, don't you?'

Those words, which once held immense power, mean nothing to me now. It's dirt.

'Same.'

'Will you call Mummy?'

If I don't call, Vicky's mother will call Maa and I will have to talk to them over a conference call.

'Once I land,' I tell Vicky.

I cut the call. I find a place to sit and enjoy the rest of my coffee.

2.

Daksh Dey

I park the scooter at the side of the road.

'Stop moving, Rabbu! The scooter will fall. How many times do I have to repeat the same thing?'

'It's not me, Dada, it's the holes in the road!'

Rabbani's large, watery, hypnotic eyes make me want to believe her. I have read parenting books, listened to podcasts on how to effectively raise children without losing your shit. They are fucking useless when you're in it. Only Amrita Thakur, my favourite podcaster, says it like it is. In the truly testing moment, you go back to the basics. And while raising kids, the basics are to shame them!

'Rabbani, do you want to be late? Your teacher will say what a useless brother you have. Do you want her to say that?'

She touches my face lovingly. 'You're not useless, Dada. You're the best. Dada is amazing! Dada is the best!'

It's something I made her learn and repeat even before she knew what the words meant. Now she uses it like a drug to uplift my mood even if she doesn't mean it all the time.

'Don't move, okay? Jump everywhere but not when you're on the scooter.'

She pinches her throat. 'Promise.'

I turn the ignition and the scooter comes back to life. Rabbani clutches the display panel with both hands to keep herself steady. Outside her school, I weave my scooter between the mass of spluttering, stuttering cars that stretch for over a kilometre of traffic jam.

'When will we get a car?' she asks.

'Probably never,' I answer. 'Why would you want to be a loser like them?' I point to the cars, honking.

Her classmates, six years of age, have already started comparing cars. A couple of boys make fun of Rabbani because her Dada drives a scooter. I try to see the positive, hoping Rabbani is traumatized by those boys and boys in general, grows up hating boys and dates girls instead when she's of age. That would work best for everyone.

Amrita Thakur talks in her podcast that despite good sense, she likes to brainwash her children. And so I tell Rabbani every day that young boys are pig shit.

Rabbani hugs me at the school gate.

'I love you, Dada,' she says.

'I love you, too,' I say, but of course I'm lying. Love's too small a word compared to what I feel. 'You're a *cutu* button,' I tell Rabbani.

'No, Dada, you're a cutu button.'

'That's also true,' I say.

Rabbani's class teacher, Archana Kotak, is waiting for her outside. She smiles at me.

Archana Kotak and I went on a date a few months ago. At the end of the date, a drunk Archana wrapped her arms around my neck. Then she rejected me by saying, 'I am not ready to be with someone who has a lot of baggage.'

'As far as baggage goes, I have been a hoarder over the past few years,' I answered. 'I have a conveyor belt of different sizes and weights.'

She ran her fingers over my face and slurred, 'But just because we can't date doesn't mean you can't take me home, because you totally can.'

'I live in a one-room kitchen,' I answered. 'Rabbani would be there, and so would my father. Might get awkward if they wake up and find the nursery teacher in a reverse cowgirl.'

'I will have to go back home and google "reverse cowgirl",' she chuckled. And then, with lips upturned in mock sadness, she added, 'I would have taken you home but I live with my parents. They will self-immolate.'

Neither of us wanted to spend on renting a room for the night. Our desire wasn't worth that much. That was the end of the date.

Archana takes Rabbani by her hand.

'How have you been?' she asks me with a smile.

'Hanging in there,' I respond.

On her right hand, a gold band glistens. This is her last month at the school. She's getting married and moving to Chandigarh next month. It's ironic that she's getting married to a farmer who might or might not know what a reverse cowgirl is.

3.

Aanchal Madan

The aircraft lurches. I spot the dark, endless ocean from my window seat. We touch down. The network comes back on. There are missed call notifications from Vanita Pen.

Vanita Pen is Vanita Iyer, my best friend. Four years ago, Vanita Iyer asked me for a pen during registration day at SRCC and then promptly lost it. She insisted I save her number and remind her to return a pen. I never changed the name. She never returned the pen.

Vanita walked into SRCC as if she had always been there. Despite being too tall at 6'1", too lanky and shaped like a stick figure made by a child, she walked with the grace and surety of a dancer, the pace of an athlete.

On the first day, when a professor told her her skirt should be longer, she cried and then reported him. On the second day, she wore a shorter skirt. On the third day, she got through dramatics, dance, music and debate societies, and didn't join any. On the fourth day, two guys asked her out. While I was taking my first, small steps at SRCC, keeping my voice down, existing, she had been gliding through the corridors, laughing, announcing her arrival. I liked Vanita. Everyone liked Vanita. She would talk to you as if you had known each other for years. 'She's an army kid,' people would whisper. 'Army kids can talk to anyone.' There were many army kids in our college. None like her. Throughout that first week, I would go back home and daydream about talking to Vanita, of being friends with her, walking the corridors like her, being exactly like her.

'Do you have my pen?' I asked her on the seventh day.

'No,' she replied with a crinkled nose.

'I want to be friends with you,' I told her.

She laughed with her face, her body and her eyes. 'Aren't we already?' she said and put her arm around me. 'Do I still have to give you the pen back?'

And that was that. By the end of the first month, we were thicker than sisters.

Since then, we have lied to each other's parents. We have got caught marking proxies for each other. I have cursed all her boyfriends, nursed her through the break-ups. We have pushed each other out of the way of rampaging DTC buses.

She told me about her struggles with her body, her hate for her own dark skin, her rage against her tiny breasts, the depth of her sadness, the intensity of her grudges, the sharpness of the blades she had once considered as a child.

I told her about my anger with the world, the water in my milk, being touched by an uncle, the extent of my ambition, the shame of being poor, the loneliness of not fitting in.

I told her she was the hottest girl in the college. She told me I was the prettiest girl in the college. Sometimes, she would just look at me and say, 'Why the fuck are you so beautiful, Aanchal? It's not fair.' I might have loved Vicky, but Vanita was my favourite person in the world. I could have died for Vicky, but I wanted to live with Vanita.

* * *

Vicky Garg hated Vanita Iyer at first sight.

Vicky hated everyone in those first few months of college. Including me, especially me. While I went to SRCC, he went to Ramjas. Despite how much he tried to hide his displeasure, it always bubbled to the surface. He would take out his anger on me, call me a parasite. He would tell me he was the only reason I was sitting in SRCC. He would scream, grip me harshly and then fall to my feet, cry and apologize.

'You can't keep taking his bullshit,' Vanita would tell me in those days.

'Without him, I would be sitting at Saraswati College,' I would answer.

After the first couple of months, he forgave me for taking his place at SRCC. We cried and had sex for the first time. Our first time was horrid, but we slowly taught ourselves and it got better. Then we had sex a lot. He would send me horny texts throughout the day, and I would respond with hornier texts. It was as if our intimacy temporarily erased all our problems. But that's all that it was: *temporary*.

And things became better till they got worse.

Our lives, once entangled, started disentangling. Our worlds, once the same, were now different. Ramjas College and Shri Ram College of Commerce are just four minutes away from each other. Yet it seemed as if we were in different universes. I wanted to dance in the college choreography group. He wanted me to join his group of guys on a drive to Murthal for paranthas. I wanted to earn money from economics tuitions for CAT. He wanted to shift his focus to the UPSC exams like his new best friend, Sanjog. We were fighting every day—shouting, screaming. He would call Vanita a slut. I would call his friends hooligans and Sanjog a pervert. He would call my college snooty. I would call Ramjas a college for losers. He would shout at me for wearing clothes he didn't like, and I would scream at him for drinking with his friends. He would call Papa a failed man. I would call his mother a *chudail* (witch). He would accuse me of being a wannabe. He would fight, call me names, but then spend the night outside my apartment building to apologize. He would delete the numbers of any guy in my calling list. And every call waiting meant a three-hour argument. I would call him *ganwar* (uncouth), he would say he wanted to break up, I would say I wanted to break up too.

Some relationships end. One big incident and everything's ashes. Some relationships decay. You can't tell anything's changing. But it starts to smell, rot and corrode from the inside. Our decay was slow.

His friends thought he deserved better, my friends thought I deserved better.

We told each other, you have changed. You're not the old Vicky. You're not the old Aanchal. We said these words so many times, we forgot who the old Vicky and Aanchal were. I didn't remember a Vicky who wasn't angry, who wasn't just a moment away from slapping me. He couldn't recall an Aanchal who didn't snap and lie at the drop of the hat. We couldn't understand each other, or see each other's point of view.

Before I went to SRCC, we had the same dream.

We were in the same team.

And now things are unravelling.

'It's like that cave,' Vanita told me. 'Socrates' Cave! So see, imagine you're in a safe cave. So Vicky and you were in a safe cave when you were in school. That's all you know exists. Both of you know nothing about the outside world. But then one day, you leave the cave and go outside into the forest.'

'The forest is SRCC?'

'Yes, also Delhi University, the college experience, being the best here on campus, etc.,' she said. 'So there are great things to see, experiences to be had, sights to admire, rivers to swim in, but also dangerous animals that can rip you to shreds. What do you do? Stay safe in the cave? Or take a risk and experiences everything? Stay in the cave with Vicky? Or just be outside . . .'

I wish I had stayed in that cave. I wish I had never ventured out. I wish I had never met Rajat. I wish I had never let Rajat touch me.

* * *

I call Vanita as soon as I reach the conveyor belt.

'WHERE THE HELL ARE YOU?' Vanita screams.

'I'M SO CLOSE TO YOU!' I shriek.

Happiness courses through me like waves crashing on a shore.

'Listen, I'm going to class right now. I will see you in a couple of days. Got a couple of exams to wrap up,' she says. 'And then we will go find your asshole brother.'

'I'm so excited!'

'See you, baby.'

We disconnect the call. A year ago, Vanita joined Symbiosis, Pune, even though I had asked her to work for a couple of years, take the CAT again and try for the IIMs. *Stupid choice.*

A car's waiting for me outside the airport, which takes me to the hotel where the conference is taking place. The Marriott at Bandra-Kurla Complex is packed with people like me—young guys and girls on behalf of their companies. I close my eyes and say a small prayer of gratitude for being here. God's fickle-minded, better to be safe than sorry. I click pictures of my room and send them to Papa, Maa and Vicky's mother.

Vicky's mother calls me.

'Beta, very nice room,' she says sweetly. 'Flight *theek thi*?'

'Yes, Mummy,' I answer. Calling her Mummy feels like running my tongue over a grater.

'But remember, beta, you're there for work. So go for the conference and then back to the room. Okay? And keep calling Vicky.'

'I call him, Mummy, but he doesn't pick up.'

'I will ask him to call you back,' she says.

A few minutes later, I call Vicky a bunch of times. He doesn't answer the calls. I hope he's with Sanya. I hope he falls in love with Sanya. I hope he sleeps with her, and I can get proof of him cheating on me. But most of all, I hope he hates me enough one day to dump me. I hope I can get rid of him.

4.

Daksh Dey

I park the scooter a stone's throw away from Rabbani's school, Star International, and directly opposite the Marriott, whose parking lot is teeming with cabs today.

Satbir, who's on a morning shift this month, salutes me as I approach him. He looks hassled today.

'Good morning, Sirji. How's it going?' I ask and point to the waves of cars honking in the drop-off area.

'Busy,' he replies as he waves his metal detector half-heartedly, pretending to frisk me. 'Some sales conference is happening. Full capacity. New floor manager. Don't get caught.'

The ground floor is packed. There is a line outside the breakfast restaurant. Men in formal trousers and ties, women in skirts carrying laptops, talking urgently over phones.

I turn towards the mezzanine floor.

The washroom, as usual, is empty.

The Marriott, which also houses the offices of three firms on seven of its floors, installed showers in all the washrooms. It was for executives who cycle, take the local or just get sweaty during their daily commute to take a quick shower before starting work. After the initial enthusiasm, they lie unused.

But I use the shower.

Back home, the water never gets warm enough. And heating water on the gas takes too much time. And is a shower really a shower if the water's not hot? Here, the pressure is great, the temperature is just right, and my office is just a ten-minute drive away.

Satbir, Kiran, Sameer—the guard, floor manager and housekeeping head—have all caught me doing it. They are now friends and turn a blind eye. 'Just don't get caught,' they warn.

I shower, slip into my clothes, fix my hair and get ready for another day of defeat and disappointment.

I work at Cloud Inc., a cloud service provider company that is in direct competition with Amazon and Microsoft. When I say 'competition', I mean we are being pushed into extinction. The office is like a virus-infected wasteland where one person goes missing every day. There will come a day when I reach the office and find the shutters closed. But till then, it pays for sundry bills, Rabbani's fees and Baba's treatment.

I'm usually the first one in the office, but today I have decided to be late. I turn towards the Starbucks on the ground floor, which is spilling with people. I get into the line to get my free birthday-week drink. I take out my birthday gift to myself from my bag, a hardback, *The Stalker*, a 450-page dumb slasher thriller.

'Daksh?' I hear a voice from behind me.

I turn.

The woman is staring at me.

I know this face. But my mind doesn't bother to sift through the faces to remind me who she is. I had read somewhere that the mind is an attention-focusing tool. Right now, it focuses on her and nothing else. *Who's she?* This internal question gets no answer from my brain. Instead of where I have seen her before, it fixates on the shape of her nose, the glint of her eyes, the fruity smell of her shampoo. I keep staring stupidly. The woman's *beautiful. Who's she?* The question echoes inside me again. No response. It's like when a strong electromagnetic pulse fries all microprocessors.

'Aanchal,' the woman says.

'Oh,' I say. My mind whirrs back into the present. 'Of course!'

It's not obvious that it's her. She has *changed*. She was beautiful then, beautiful now, but . . . she has *changed*. She's taller, straighter. Her shoulders are pulled back. She looks stronger. She's clutching a laptop bag, the taut muscles inside her shirt are unmistakable. My mind switches to portrait mode, everything blurs around her. She takes up a lot of space, like a beautiful giant. Like a warrior princess in formal clothes. No longer a girl but now a woman, not a princess but a queen, not a student secretary but a politician. People around me are buying their drinks unmindful of this most beautiful woman standing in their midst. Her cheeks are now higher and sunken. The white shirt's tight against her breasts, her trousers are creaseless against her thighs, and I notice she has gained muscle tone. I may sound shallow, but screw morality. Is gasping at a waterfall, a verdant forest, a canyon, a mountain, shallow? Her beauty is an objective truth.

Now my mind starts to rev and stutter to life.

The beaches of the Andamans, the hotel pool, the history tours. I took her number and never called her. Her brother, Gaurav, stole my Nintendo.

'Daksh! I can't believe it's you! Wow, oh my God, it is really you. Isn't it?' she says brightly. She's smiling from ear to ear, her eyes wide.

Now, I'm smiling too. 'This is insane, isn't it? Aanchal Madan, never thought I will see you again.'

'How much time has it been? Three—'

'Four years.'

'Four years! You're here for the conference?' she asks. 'I still can't believe it's you!'

She touches my arm for a brief second. It feels . . . nice.

I notice the change in her voice and diction. It matches the corporate-ness of her clothes, her straight back, her unwavering gaze, the strong grip she has over the leather laptop bag she's carrying. Four years ago, there was an aura of nervousness about her. Right now, she exudes confidence. She was out of place then, but now she belongs. It looks like she's not here to attend a conference but to conduct it.

'I'm here for the coffee,' I tell her, my senses coming back to me. My heart beats so fast I can hear it. I step out of the line to allow others to order their triple-shot Americanos and chai lattes. 'And Rabbani's school is right opposite.'

'You live in Mumbai now? Have you moved here?' she asks.

'Yeah, we got tired of driving around in our Lamborghinis and living the habibi life in Dubai. It's been around two years since we came here.'

We in the present doesn't include Mumma.

She laughs in the sweetest way possible. Then she grows silent as her eyes rest on me.

Unlike her, who's dressed like she's here to conduct a board meeting, I'm in an old black T-shirt and black jeans. I wonder if she notices the sadness that has settled like dust on my body and ossified around my eyes.

Can she read the history of the past four years on my face?

The heaviness of my heart?

Does she know how many times I have fantasized about my own death?

Can she see in my eyes that true, lasting happiness seems unachievable?

That in these four years I have gone through a lifetime's misery?

A moment of silence passes.

I wonder what has changed in her life. She flips her wrist and looks at the time on her gleaming Tissot watch.

'Can I see you later?' she asks. 'I have a session I need to attend right now. But I will see you, right? You won't go missing again for four years?'

I want to see her again. I don't know if I can. Between the project deck that's pending, Baba's physiotherapy and Rabbani's classes, and the time for the nurses . . .

She touches my arm and interrupts my schedule-juggling.

'I will, of course, see you,' she commands. 'I need to say sorry for Gaurav stealing your Nintendo. Before you say anything, I would have returned it had you called me, but you didn't. So, you need to say sorry for that.'

'I was hoping you had forgotten all about it.'

'Forget? Me? Daksh, I waited by the window with my phone in my hand, waiting for your call. I cried and cried and cried,' she replies with a laugh. 'Will you drop me a message? Do you even have my number any more?'

I don't tell Aanchal that I know her number by heart.
4049494979.

That's her number.

Unknown to her, these ten digits have been a safe shelter, a reason to smile and an escape for me.

And she can't know. It would be weird. Where would I even begin without sounding like a serial killer with drills and knives locked up in a basement with blood stains on the skirtings?

Four years ago, her number had helped me tide over a terrible jolt to my male ego. Within days of landing in London, Sameeksha started dating someone rather publicly. There were Instagram posts all over—kissing, holding hands, stupid fucking videos.

Shattered, I nursed my ego thinking about Aanchal, staring at her phone number. Aanchal reminded me that what I had for Sameeksha couldn't be love—since my crush on Aanchal was so much stronger than what I felt for Sameeksha. I wanted to call Aanchal. But I couldn't have called her. If I did, I would have to tell her that thoughts of her had completely invaded my mind. I would have to tell her that I had started daydreaming about her like a fucking schoolkid.

And so, I waited for my stupid crush on her to weaken.

Then one day, I got a notification that she had just made a social-media account. It was locked, she used just her first name, and in the display picture, she was with a guy. *Vicky*. I wanted to, but didn't send her a request because a) what did I expect would happen and b) what would she tell Vicky, the possessive guy in her display picture, about me?

However, despite choosing not to add her, every now and then over the course of a year, I would search for her profile using her number, see if her display picture was still the same, zoom in on her and feel my heart brim with awe, joy and jealousy.

Till the day she deleted her profile.

Three years ago, when my life turned to shit, her number changed from being a source of joy and daydreams to being an escape.

On the darkest of nights, when giving up seemed to be the only option, I would look at her number. I would imagine dialling it. I would imagine her picking up the phone and telling me that she had been waiting for my call.

Two years ago, I sat down to delete the phone numbers of friends, relatives and acquaintances from my contact list. People who had abandoned us. Industrial-grade assholes, every last one of them. I kept scrolling and deleting. With angry, trembling fingers, I deleted Ashish Uncle, Baba's colleague—he stopped taking my calls. Athavale Uncle, our neighbour, who told us they were under financial pressure and couldn't loan us any money. I deleted Atul Uncle, that bastard to whom Baba had loaned money multiple times, whose extended family had stayed with us for a month a few years ago.

My fingers had hovered over Aanchal's number. I didn't delete it.

When we moved to Mumbai, it coincided with her creating a new LinkedIn account. The display picture came first: a white shirt, chin high, success and determination in her eyes. Then came the details.

Aanchal Madan, third-year student, SRCC
Aanchal Madan won the inter-collegiate debate competition
Summer intern at Coca-Cola

Last year, she added another bullet point.

Aanchal Madan joins DeliverFood

The girl who had nothing, wanted everything and got everything.

On the lowest of days, I would find her on LinkedIn and tell myself that I couldn't allow destiny to define my life. That I could fight, just as she did. She was a flicker of hope, of light.

So do I remember her number? Yes, I do. If they rip open my heart, they will find the numbers floating in it like little cereal alphabets float in Rabbani's milk every morning.

'My number is 4049494979,' she says.

I fake-type it on my phone.

She smiles. 'I will wait. This time I hope you do call.'

She waves me goodbye, turns and joins the stream of people leaving Starbucks. A few men notice her as she waltzes past. They all turn to look at her.

5.

Aanchal Madan

I can't concentrate on what the panellists are saying about customer lifecycle and brand architecture. My mind wanders off towards Daksh. I could hardly believe my eyes when I saw him at the coffee shop. I was only looking in his direction because he stood out. While others were hunched over and buried in their phones, he stood upright, his head slightly bent, lost in his book. In a sea of men and women in light shirts and stuffy trousers, he was an island in a black T-shirt, a pair of black jeans and dirty white sneakers. Unlike others, there was no sense of urgency in his movements, no looking over his shoulders to see how far the line had moved.

My heart jumped when I looked closely.

Daksh!

My lucky charm.

Waves of memories crash over me. The guy whose Nintendo Gaurav had stolen. The one who took my number and never called. The one who checked my board results on his phone. The one with whom I had shared a Cornetto, the first person I lied to Vicky about. He had grown up, now a guy with deep eyes, a sharper nose, rougher skin, the calmness of someone . . . I don't want to say wiser because that's old, but he is . . . mature? Quieter? I can't place it. But I know exactly what he made me feel. Comfortable.

That has remained the same, though.

He smiled at me and talked to me with the same politeness and grace that I'd found so charming all those years ago.

Daksh was eighteen when I first met him. At the time, I thought everyone in college spoke with the humility and openness that he did. Four years have passed, I have talked to countless people, and none of their conversations are etched in my mind like his are. I still remember how he made me feel during those conversations.

Today, after all those years, he reminded me of that feeling of being seen, of being important. Of what it's like to have an audience of one and yet feel as if an army of people are hanging on to your every word. Once again, he made me feel as though everything I said should be carved in stone. I could have read a grocery list and he would have still listened to it intently.

Though this time, an air of heaviness clung to him.

Throughout the day, I keep looking at my phone, hoping he would text or call. That, too, hasn't changed about him. He made me wait then, too. As the day progresses, I push thoughts of him away. Maybe this is what guys as charming and handsome as Daksh do—make girls feel like they are the centre of their universe and then leave them just like that.

At the end of day one of the conference, the organizers tell us they are throwing a party for all participants at Opa, a bar a few kilometres away. When I tell Maa–Papa about it, they beg me to take permission from Vicky's mother.

'I'm not going then. I would rather wrestle a snake than take her permission,' I tell them, which is an apt analogy, but she's the one Vicky has wrapped around my neck to slowly wring the life out of me.

'Why do you say these things, beta?' asks Maa, horrified.

So, I sit in my room and try to ignore the chatter outside in the corridors of people leaving for the party. An hour later, I bite the bullet and call the *kutti*.

'Mummy, can I please go?' I ask Vicky's mother in a coy tone.

The disgusting woman grumbles over the phone. I picture a frothing bulldog. 'Did Vicky ask you to take my permission? If he has, then my answer is no.'

'He's not picking up, Mummy. He has a review meeting till late tonight. But I have dropped him a message. He has not replied but I thought I'd ask you.'

'When did you text him?'

'An hour ago.'

'Vicky messaged me fifteen minutes ago. If he was okay with you going, he would have told me. And beta, you know he doesn't like all this. Why do you want to go? All the people will do there is drink. You shouldn't go,' she says with a sense of finality.

'Mummy, I won't drink—'

She interrupts me rudely. '*Beti*, I told you what we wish, the rest is up to you,' she says sharply. 'Don't ask us if you don't want to listen.'

I know if I push her, she will twist it and use it against me.

'Okay, I'm sleepy anyway, Mummy. I will go and sleep instead.'

'Good girl.'

Angry tears spring up in my eyes.

I'm angry with Vicky, his mother and, most of all, with myself.

I wrote my death sentence the day I started cheating on Vicky. The day I walked into Rajat Bopanna's IIT Delhi hostel for the first time and let him do whatever he wanted with me.

After my first time with Rajat, he whispered his questions as he planted kisses on my neck.

'Why are we doing this? Aren't you happy with Vicky?'

'Each one of your kisses is like a tiny revenge for every time Vicky has made me cry.'

'Does he still make you cry?'

'I cry, but the tears are fake.'

My tears had dried, my spirit was dead, long before Rajat. He walked into my life with a different purpose. It made me realize I didn't want love from Vicky but cleansing, revenge and distance.

Vicky and I were unfixable.

We had tried to fix our relationship multiple times. Naïvely, we thought that with enough love and affection, it could be fixed.

In the first year of SRCC, Vicky and I were in the worst phase of our lives. We couldn't talk for a minute without it devolving into a screaming match. All that was left was resentment and hate. When the first-year results were announced, Vicky was nineteenth in his class, I was twenty-second in mine. This was not the future we'd seen for ourselves.

'You should break up with him,' Vanita had advised. 'Does he even want you?'

It was a question that haunted me. So, I went and told Vicky I wanted out. I got the answer swiftly. He slapped me and then broke down in tears immediately. He sobbed and told me that if the relationship didn't mean the world to him, he wouldn't be begging and crying. He said that the only person who mattered was me. He loved me so much that it made him angry, vindictive, broken. Without me, he would walk into the traffic, take a knife to his wrists, jump into a canal.

I believed him. Every word of it.

'There's so much history, Aanchal,' he had fallen at my feet and sobbed. 'We've been through so much together. I can't just let it go. You can't walk away just because it's become tough.

We both got caught up. We both made mistakes. We should try again. I really want us to try again.'

I believed every damned word he said in his hurt, quivering voice.

'We can't let this go to waste,' I told him in tears. 'We've given it so much. Will we let our colleges come between us?'

'I will be better,' he promised.

I took it to be the gospel truth, the word of God, etched in stone.

We started to rebuild our relationship.

We spent more time together. We began studying together again. Our scores improved. After college, we would go on long walks and recalibrate our thoughts about our future. He asked me to reconsider the CAT and start thinking about the UPSC. We were spending hours at coffee shops watching TV serials, finding empty movie halls where we would touch each other and sitting around on college lawns completing assignments. And every Friday afternoon, his friends and mine would organize a house party and get drunk. Despite Vanita not liking any of his friends, even she would hang out with Vicky and his gang.

Vanita admitted she was impressed we could find it in ourselves to love each other again.

I would say Vanita even started hating Vicky a little less.

And just when things seemed to settle, at one Friday house party, Vicky's best friend, Sanjog, tried to slip his hand into Vanita's dress and caress her breasts.

Vanita pushed his hand away.

But he became more aggressive and tore a part of her top. Vanita shattered his nose with a swift uppercut. She then asked a bleeding Sanjog to apologize. Sanjog claimed a drunk Vanita had come on to him.

'You think I would touch an ugly girl like her?!' Sanjog had screamed like a rabid dog.

'You're dead,' Vanita had answered in the coldest tone I had ever heard from anyone.

Half an hour later, at a police station, a constable and Vanita's mom slapped Sanjog in quick succession. Sanjog was made to strip down to his boxers and apologize to Vanita. Vanita's mother clicked pictures and warned Sanjog that if she heard anything more about him, she would paste posters of him all over the university.

'CHOOSE HER OR ME!' Vicky had screamed at me the next day in full view of his friends, including Sanjog. Vicky's hand squeezed mine. 'HE'S MY BROTHER! DO YOU KNOW WHAT HE HAS DONE FOR ME?'

'But Vicky—'

Vicky ground his teeth and spoke through a clenched jaw. 'Vanita is a slut, everyone knows that. That *randi* (prostitute) was drunk. We have all seen her grind with random men in clubs,' he seethed. 'Just because her parents have contacts in the police, she got away with this.'

'She was not the one—'

'You also know what kind of girl she is. You will also end up being a randi like her! Mark my words,' he barked, his face inches from mine.

'Let's go, bhai,' growled Sanjog and pulled at Vicky's arm.

Sanjog looked at me with spiteful eyes. He stepped close to me. I could smell alcohol on his breath.

'Vanita will pay for her mistake,' he said. 'One rod, a bottle of acid, two men on a motorcycle with their faces masked, that's all it takes. Tell that to your friend. She can suck all the dicks she wants once she's strapped to a hospital bed.'

Sanjog didn't know that Vanita wasn't talking to me. She wouldn't talk to me till the time I broke up with Vicky.

'Why are you asking me to break up with Vicky?' I argued with Vanita. 'It's not Vicky, it's Sanjog. Vicky's just standing up for his friend!'

'Why is it even a choice?! Are you even listening to yourself?' Vanita had screamed at me in tears.

I begged Vicky to talk to me.

'*Oye behen ki laudi*, we are over,' he would say to me. 'If you're talking to Vanita still, then go to hell. You and your liar friend can go fuck whoever you want to. Go, get fucked by the entire college, but don't you dare call me!'

'Why would she lie?'

'Why would Sanjog lie? Why would he even want to touch the small, black, raisin-like breasts of your friend? My dick's fairer than her face!'

Both Vanita and Vicky distanced themselves from me.

Vanita wouldn't even sit in my line of sight. I would spend hours outside Vicky's college, waiting for him. I naïvely believed that if only he would talk to me, I could set things right. I was blocked, cast away. I spent a month crying, waiting, hoping things would go back to the way they were before. My loneliness consumed me.

That was when I slipped.

I found Rajat, a fourth-year student from IIT Delhi, on a dating app. I didn't even know if he was funny, considerate or nice. But I know that he was present. I know that he listened. In those days, that was kindness enough. I repaid his kindness by going to his hostel, walking down that corridor with multiple pairs of eyes staring at me, and then getting naked with him on his reeking bedsheet, bottles of Blender's Pride rolling about the foot of the bed.

I allowed him to fuck me.

Over the next few weeks, Rajat helped me tide over the storm of sadness Vicky and Vanita had pushed me through. He introduced me to shots of Old Monk chased down by small gulps of orange juice, Maggi cooked over steam irons, and learning to ignore the leery cheers of his friends outside. I would spend multiple afternoons drunk and hungover, watching him and his friends pass around a foul-smelling joint.

'You need to let Vicky go,' he told me one day. 'Vanita seems to be a nice person.'

'Leave him and move in here? Make a little tent with your unwashed bedsheet and stay here?'

'You deserve someone much better than me. Literally, the entire hostel is wondering which animal I sacrificed to make you decide to be here with me,' Rajat replied with a chuckle. 'I am not a fool to think that this is anything more than your rebound relationship. I'm not stupid. But I also know that Vicky doesn't have a place in your life. You should tell him it's over.'

There are times I wonder what would have happened if I had listened to Rajat, found the courage and told Vicky that it was over from my side as well.

If only . . .

But before I could make up my mind, Vicky saw me with Rajat at Safdarjung Market and all hell broke loose. Vicky, Sanjog and his friends came at Rajat with bricks, belts and rods. Even with three hairline fractures and being surrounded by six angry men, Rajat maintained that he was just a friend. Not even a friend, he insisted, more like a brother. But the damage was done.

That day, I gave Vicky the right to call me randi, whore, kuttiya all my life.

* * *

Outside, I hear the corridors of the Marriott fall silent. Everyone's left for the party. I blink away my tears. A familiar feeling of wanting to hurt Vicky crops up in my heart. I put my phone on airplane mode. I let Vicky and Vicky's mother believe that I defied them and went to the party. This is what my life's reduced to—these games. Hoping for hate.

6.

Daksh Dey

'If the building crumbles down someday, it will be because of the weight of your books,' warns Jagath, my neighbour and best friend, seeing me keep *The Stalker* on the top of the tall stack of books in the corner of the room.

'Give some of them away. It's not like you will ever read them again,' he repeats.

'He would rather die,' remarks Zeenath, my other neighbour and other best friend. She recognizes her mistake immediately. She mumbles, 'Sorry.'

Mortality is a topic that we tread lightly on in our house. As if on cue, Baba groans in the background. The scarred stump of his amputated leg juts out from beneath the blanket. I'm about to get up, but Jagath is quicker. He pulls the blanket over what remains of Baba's leg.

'Keep sleeping, Uncle,' he says to Baba, who groans some more and goes back to sleep.

* * *

'You're very lucky we could save your knee,' the doctor at Dubai Prime Hospital had told Baba. 'That's quite fortunate.'

'Why just lucky, doctor?' Baba mocked the doctor. 'Am I not the luckiest man in the world? Why don't you exchange places with me? Come, come, you lie down in this bed, let me cut off one leg of yours, then I will tell you what happened to your family. Come . . .'

The doctor tried to calm him down. 'I understand what you have gone through, Mr Dey. What I'm trying to say is that the prosthetics will be . . .'

By then, Baba had crumpled into tears.

* * *

Jagath comes and sits at the table.

'Thank you,' I tell Jagath and he waves it off.

Jagath and Zeenath start serving themselves the bhindi and daal that I've made this evening. Jagath and Zeenath, entry-level techies at Wipro, had been living in one-room-kitchens at Dhumketu Apartments long before I moved in with three cardboard boxes, four-year-old Rabbani and my depressed, partly sedated Baba hobbling on a crutch.

Jagath had noted our lack of luggage as we moved into the one-room-kitchen next to his and had said, 'Minimalist? Nice, bro.'

My minimalism was forced upon me.

The customs officer at the cargo terminal in Mumbai stared at the contents of the twenty huge cartons in which we had packed our life in Dubai. Clothes, toys, books, shoes, electronics, TV, utensils, blankets.

'45,000 rupees', he told us.

'But this is just . . . stuff,' I said, my voice barely audible.

Rabbani got down from my lap. She picked up a unicorn pillow from the pile of toys. She hugged it and came back to me. 'I want only this,' she said.

'This is just . . . stuff,' I found myself repeating.

But it wasn't long before Jagath and Zeenath figured out the real reason behind our minimalism. They say they first talked to me because they saw a potential friend in me.

They lie, of course.

They saw me struggle with Rabbani, with Baba's disability and with my grief. They knew I would crumble.

They saw the truth behind the smiles I gave them every morning. They noticed me on the roof of our building, where I went on the worst of the nights and closed my eyes so hard hoping that when I opened them, things would be different. On weekends, they saw me sleeping on the benches while Rabbani played with the other kids.

Then one day, to help me—and help themselves, which they claim is true but was another lie—they suggested that we should split the tasks of our respective houses to make life easier.

'Why?' I had asked them.

'Who wants to spend the entire day doing chores?' Zeenath had answered.

'We should work together as a team, make our lives easier,' Jagath had added.

I resisted but Jagath and Zeenath can be persuasive if they want to. I didn't ask why they hadn't gone to the other young people in the building with the same offer. Because I probably knew the answer.

I needed help.

Zeenath chose to do all our laundry barring Jagath's and my boxers. Jagath, who stays up nights hunting for deals, chose grocery shopping. They knew I could cook.

They persisted with the arrangement for a few days. But after that, they said they should come over and eat at my place. They could help me wash the dishes too, after. My resistance was broken down swiftly. I, too, realized I needed help or it would break me. I could only mumble a soft 'hmmm'. And from that night, they started coming over every night. We would eat at the small fold-out table at my place, one of us would wash the dishes, the other would entertain Rabbani.

I have never told them, but those first few quiet dinners saved my life.

I don't where I would have been without them.

'Stop looking at your phone, Daksh. You're not calling Aanchal. She's here today, she will be gone tomorrow. Why do you want to get into this? I forbid you!' Zeenath warns me.

'Bhai, we should do a toss. Let fate and the universe decide,' advises Jagath.

'Fate's not been particularly kind to him. Don't say such nonsensical things. Fate and the universe, my foot,' retorts Zeenath.

'Change your perspective,' offers Jagath. 'He's sitting with us. Uncle is slowly recovering. Rabbani is turning out to be an oversmart teacher's pet. I would say fate's turning.' He tears a big piece of a chapatti, dips it in the daal and eats it. 'This is so tasty.'

'The chapatti is too thick,' complains Zeenath.

Jagath turns towards me and in his usual calm, soothing tone fit for a Kannada Hindu godman asks, 'Why do you want to call her?'

Zeenath doesn't let me think. 'He asked you something . . .' harangues Zeenath.

'Let me fucking collect my thoughts,' I protest.

'Collect my thoughts?' scoffs Zeenath. 'Your phone doesn't have a single number of a person who's not important to you and it has hers?' snarls Zeenath.

'Why is Aanchal important?' asks Jagath.

I sigh. 'It's weird,' I confess. 'Aanchal . . . she's been a source of, like, strength. She's like . . . the world wasn't kind to her family and look at her now . . . she fought on, soldiered on . . . and, you know, gave her family all that they needed. If only I can—'

'A lot of people do that. Just open Humans of Bombay, it's filled with such stories,' scoffs Zeenath. 'Your case is different—'

'Don't compare two kinds of suffering, Zeenath,' interrupts Jagath. He gives me the phone. 'Call her.'

'Whatever,' shrugs Zeenath. 'This is a mistake.'

I dial the number. It's switched off.

'See, this is good,' says Zeenath.

7.

Aanchal Madan

It's 11 p.m. My stomach hurts from a full portion of butter chicken that I just finished. I cradle a cup of chai and my phone.

The airplane mode is still on.

Vicky would have called incessantly for the last couple of hours. My phone would have been unreachable.

In these two hours, I have clicked a picture every few minutes. The chicken. A selfie in the mirror. The tea. The hotel room. The show I'm watching on my laptop. A selfie in the restaurant mirror.

I switch off the airplane mode.

The phone pings to life.

I wait.

I wait for Vicky's anger to start to show up on my phone.

I revel in the anticipation. To know that Vicky would have tortured himself wondering where had I gone. Whose jokes was I laughing at? Did I smile at someone? Did someone brush themselves against me? How angry would he have got? Sometimes, I think about my shackled future and fantasize about how I would eventually kill Vicky slowly. Through trans-fats, through stress, through constant nagging, through liver failure brought on by his mounting consumption of alcohol.

I check my phone.

48 notifications.
32 unread messages.

All the messages are from Vicky. He walked right into the trap. I feel myself smiling reading the very first message. Like a writhing, dying fish.

Aanchal?
09:54 pm

R u thr?
09:54 pm

Where r u?
09:55 pm

Did u go to the party?
09:58 pm

Didn't maa ask u not to go?
10:02 pm

Where r u?
10:03 pm

Switch on your phon
10:04 pm

How cud u go without our permission?
10:05 pm

Saali, randi, where r u?
10:06 pm

Jaa, jiske saath sona hai
10:06 pm

U just see wat I do to u
10:06 pm

Fucking u can nevr change
10:07 pm

Behen ki laudi, kiska chus rahi hai. Tu fon utha.
10:08 pm

Now u see. It will be fun to see uncle aunty cry at my feet. U
just c
10:08 pm

Oye randi
10:08 pm

Yaad dilau kya tere baap ka tatte mere haath mein kyu hai?
Should I remind u y your family would have to beg me?
10:09

Then there's an image he has attached. It's the one of me in a
black swimming costume. I am pulling down one strap, baring
my cleavage.

Randi I hv a mor of dese. M sure a lot of ppl will like
seein these
10:09 pm

Wat did Vanita say? She will put Sanjog's poster? Ask her to
stop me from putting these posters
10:09 pm

Where r u?
10:10 pm

U call me n I promise I wun do it. I wil forgive u
10:10 pm

I am only stupid I believed u cud change
10:11 pm

Ur dead Aanchal
10:12 pm

Ur gone, whore
10:13 pm

Everyone will spit on u. ur own family too
10:14 pm

Then there are more pictures of me. In different states of undress. Most of them are in a black swimming costume. Some of them are from the time we were trying to repair our relationship and the only time he would talk to me is when I would send him these pictures.

There are more texts.

BHEN KI LAUDI!
10:15 pm

Jaa maa chuda
10:16 pm

Tune dil tod diya. U broke my heart. I tried everything but now
ur responsible.
10:17 pm

That's the last text, but there are plenty of missed-call alerts after that.

Now I text him.

My internet wasn't working. I was at the hotel.
10:30 pm

Then I send him the pictures of me in the hotel, alone, with the time stamps to prove it. I never left the hotel. But I have to admit, this is better than a party could have been. He would have harassed me anyway even after giving me permission, so in the battle of worsts, this is better.

Sorry, Aanchal
10:33 pm

Sorry, I didn't mean all dat
10:34 pm

Whatever, Vicky.
10:35 pm

This is my life.

I'm about to sleep when I get a bunch of missed call alerts from an unknown number. I punch the number into Truecaller.

Daksh Dey Home.

The phone asks me if I want to save the number. I save his number as *Lucky Charm*. I tuck myself in with a rare smile on my face. When I close my eyes, I'm back at that coffee shop, he's there with a book, and he's looking at me like I'm the most interesting person in the whole world.

8.

Daksh Dey

Jagath, a legitimate monk in a software engineer's body, forced meditation on me a year ago.

'You're slipping away, bro. You have to do it!' he insisted.

I wasn't slipping away. I was doing whatever was asked of me. Working a dead-end job, raising Rabbani, feeding everyone, making sure Baba got his medicines on time, kept the Activa and the house in running order. I was at the opposite end of slipping away.

'Do something for yourself, for your heart, for what's inside of you,' he repeated to me.

I did plenty for myself. I binge-watched shows and read books.

'For your mind, bro,' he had argued passionately. 'How long can you weather the storm in a weak raft? Make your mind a battleship. Because on the deck of the raft, there's a little girl and your father. If it comes loose, the sea will swallow you whole. You can't slip away, Daksh. You don't have that luxury.'

I had brushed him away.

But one night, I saw his analogy in a dream. A hastily-put-together raft. Rain pouring like silver bullets. Baba crouched in the corner, screaming from the pain in his leg. A terrified Rabbani mumbling about a brother who left them alone.

In the crackling lightning, I saw Mumma's face.

The next day, I was up at 5 a.m.

Since that day, we are on this roof every morning.

'Good job, bro,' says Jagath softly. 'Let go of all thoughts. Don't judge them. Just look at them and let them go.'

The thoughts are many.

Anger against Baba for his inability to break through the storm of his depression.

I let it go.

Irritation with Rabbani for speaking so much, for taking so much of my energy, for having to pack her lunch, something that others my age don't have to do.

I let it go.

Hate and resentment with Baba for being ungrateful for what I do for him. Is it too much to ask him to look at me once and say thank you?

I let the thought go.

Rage against Maa for leaving us.

I let it go.

A fantasy of Rabbani at boarding school, away from me. We are rich, I'm free of responsibilities. Baba's fine.

I let it go.

I let it go.

I let it go.

When I open my eyes, Jagath, with his calm, creaseless forehead, asks me, 'Better?'

I nod.

My alarm beeps. The first set of reminders blows up on my phone.

Breakfast + lunch

Rabbani's picnic form

Lunch pack

Reminder for Baba to take a shower

'See you at breakfast,' I tell Jagath who leaves for his morning run and to do things that people my age should be doing.

9.

Aanchal Madan

The blaring sirens cut through the afternoon sky.

The fire trucks haven't reached yet. People from the hotels and office buildings within a kilometre's radius have spilled out on to the narrow street, blocking all exit and entry points. There's smoke coming out in puffs from the sixteenth floor of the TheyWork building next to us. By the time the fire trucks reach, and the firemen hop off and uncoil their hoses, the fire is all but out. Mumbai feels like it's one good fire away from the apocalypse.

Durjoy Datta

'Must be for insurance. These guys have a high cash burn rate,' Ramneek, the girl from a grocery-delivery start-up, remarks.

The firemen announce that we are not to go inside the buildings for the next hour or so.

'We have jobs to go back to,' complains Ravinder Singh, a credit-card marketer, who has no idea whose job is supposed to be more important, to the firemen who went into the smouldering remains.

The air smells of burnt plastic, sweat and panic. On the other side of the road, frantic teachers are trying to herd children into lines.

Unlike some of the other people around, these little children don't evoke smiles in me. I don't feel like rushing to hold them, talk to them.

But then I see her face . . . she's no longer a baby . . . I join the dots instantly. The resemblance is uncanny.

She's the spitting image of her brother.

Rabbani.

Her hair is perfectly plaited, there are ink marks on her shirt, her laces are open and she's animatedly talking to her classmates. She's holding an audience with the other kids who are hanging on to her every word.

The nervous teachers scurry about, taking headcounts, checking the IDs of parents and handing the children over. Slowly, the group around Rabbani thins, as everyone's parents collect their children.

Rabbani scans the crowd for Daksh or her parents, I'm guessing.

And then, a bright smile leaps to her face. I follow her line of sight and spot Daksh. He's parking his scooter. I never thought I would see Daksh riding a rundown scooter. But then again, Daksh has always been weird.

Daksh waves at the teacher. I follow Rabbani as she runs towards Daksh. Daksh picks Rabbani up and buries his face excitedly into her neck, sending her into splits of laughter. That's when he notices me.

'They evacuated the hotel too,' I explain my presence. '. . . and I saw her, she's ditto like you. Like a photocopy, isn't it?'

'Called you last night. Your phone was off.' He sounds concerned. 'Was everything all right? You shouldn't switch off your phone in a new city.'

Rabbani pulls at my sleeve excitedly. 'Jagath Dada and Zeenath Didi were talking about you,' she chirps.

'Rabbu?' says Daksh, surprised. He turns towards me. 'They are my friends. They wanted to know whose number I was trying. They know about my crush.'

My face goes warm. How easily he says it. How innocently, but also how seriously.

'What's a crush?' asks Rabbani.

Daksh starts laughing. 'When you really like someone's face,' he answers. 'I told you this the last time we met Aunty, but you were too young. Look at her. Isn't she beautiful?'

'Ummm . . .'

'Rabbani,' I say and catch her attention. 'I'm your Didi, not Aunty, okay?' I turn to Daksh. 'You called quite a few times yesterday.'

'How could I have not? It was a crazy coincidence seeing you,' he responds. 'Anyway, my friends were over, we were up till late so I thought you could join us too.' He pauses, then catches my eye. 'If you're free today, you can come to my birthday party.'

'It's your birthday today?'

'I turn twenty-two. Legitimate adult now, a whisker away from the mid-twenties. Pretty soon, I'll be complaining about arthritis and all that. So, will you come?'

His eyes are soft, like a Labrador's. In the past couple of minutes, he has gone from being concerned about me to being happy about his birthday, then calling me home excitedly.

'Of course I will come. Send me your location and the time,' I say.

His face lights up. 'I will text you,' he says. His eyes catch mine. 'See you tonight?'

I nod. He smiles one of those charming smiles of which he has plenty. He makes me feel something I haven't felt in a long time: a nervous kind of joy.

Daksh drives away with Rabbani clutching on to him like a little chimp.

My phone pings. It's Daksh's message with a location and an address.

1223, Dhumketu Apartments, Kandivali, next to the under-construction petrol pump.

Once back in my room, I google Dhumketu Apartments. The pictures show it's a crumbling, moss-covered, four-storey building with only one-room-kitchen layouts. As I zoom in, I see a bunch of scooters lined up in front of the entrance. One of them is Daksh's. He made his invitation sound personal, at his house. But now seeing Dhumketu Apartments, it feels like it's his bachelor pad. Wait, he did say *home*. Though Dhumketu does look too rundown for Daksh and his family.

I will find out tonight. But before that, I must figure out a lie for Vicky.

10.

Daksh Dey

We are making biryani for my birthday—the only dish that can carry a party on its own. Jagath and I are on kitchen duty. Rabbani's helping Zeenath clean the house.

'Does she know?' asks Jagath as he chops up the onions.

I shake my head.

Zeenath frowns. 'She saw you drive a scooter and didn't ask? This location, the address, the scooter, they should have all been dead giveaways. That's a sign, Daksh. You should never fall for someone who's not interested in your story.'

'Stop sounding like an Instagram caption,' I respond. 'And no one's falling for anyone here. I have just invited her to my party, that's it.'

'You're not falling, you're already in love, bro,' Jagath tells me, as if it's a matter of fact. 'And this is not a party, it's your family. You're calling her to your inside circle.'

'Vicky's still around,' I remind the both of them. 'And look around yourself, Jagath. What do you think will happen? I'm not trying to imagine something with her. I know it's impossible.'

'I look around and I see that the house looks beautiful, that's all I see,' he notes.

'You know what I mean.'

Jagath lowers his voice to a whisper. 'She's going to ask about Uncle.'

Baba is sleeping with his face towards the wall. I had forced him to take a bath today. Every day, it becomes easier to help him towards the bathroom. He gets lighter and lighter. Every day he becomes more bones than flesh. And every day, it becomes harder and harder to shave him. With his skin drying, cheeks sinking in, some hair escapes the blade. Sometimes I cut him. His flinches are sometimes the only expression I get out of him.

After Maa, different doctors had different diagnoses for Baba. One said it was prolonged grief disorder, others said it was depression. Some advised grief counselling, others prescribed antidepressants.

Nothing worked.

I watched him lose weight, suffer from insomnia, cry or not react at all, and go through extreme bouts of sadness. Sometimes he would ask to see Mumma. Every few nights, he would sit up and start crying and blaming everything on Mumma. It helps to blame everything on Mumma. It's an easy trap to fall into: to blame it on Mumma. It's because of her that Rabbani is growing up without a mother, and with a father who simultaneously hates and loves her absent mother. It's because of her that the three of us are living in this ramshackle one-room apartment, three beds lined against three walls of the room. It's because of her that every month Jagath and Zeenath have to loan me money to tide me over the last week.

In our one-room-kitchen, Baba gets the longest wall. His bed is lined up against the 10-foot-long wall. Next to the bed is a cabinet with his medicines, documents, certificates, medical reports. There's a small chest of drawers with his clothes: five T-shirts, five pairs of trousers, three pairs of shoes. Out of all the pairs, the left shoe is mint-new. Right opposite Baba's wall is the smaller wall for Rabbani. But it's big enough for her to have her little bed; an easel for painting, and drawing, scribbling; a rack for her books, school bag, shoes and her clothes. My side of the room has a window, beneath which there's a fold-out table that doubles as a desk and the dining table. Right next to it is a makeshift floor-to-ceiling bookshelf. We don't have a lot of stuff: there are only so many things you can stuff in one room.

'You're the first guy I have seen who makes a big deal out of his birthday,' says Zeenath, scrubbing the wall.

'A birthday is a big deal,' I tell Zeenath.

'VERY BIG,' squeals Rabbani. 'BIGGEST DEAL IN THE ENTIRE HISTORY OF THE PLANET OF THE UNIVERSE!'

11.

Aanchal Madan

I tell Vicky that Vanita has reached the hotel and will stay over. He believes me when he hears her in the background—it's a conference call instead.

Vanita's coming tomorrow morning.

'It's laughable he falls for this,' says Vanita and adds after a pause, 'What do you think will happen tonight? And don't you dare say nothing because if he's as good-looking as you keep telling me he is, you'd better do something!'

'Nothing,' I answer. 'I don't want to add another lie to my stack of lies.'

'Vicky deserves every lie and more that you tell him,' Vanita says. 'He deserves the worst in the world, and most of all, he needs to die. Slowly. A little arsenic in his food every day will do the trick.'

'I wish he had really killed himself,' I say.

'He's a coward. He would never have done that.'

'I actively dream about him having slit his wrists properly and his mother finding him in a pool of blood.'

'He would leak tar, not blood, his soul's so black.'

'We are bad people, Vanita.'

'No, he is. I always told you that.'

Had I not been blinded by love or whatever it was I felt for Vicky, I would have picked Vanita the day Sanjog had assaulted her. Girls often forget that other girls are their soulmates, guys are just accessories. Had I listened to Vanita, I wouldn't still be running after Vicky, I wouldn't have found myself in Rajat's hostel room, and Vicky wouldn't have found Rajat and me in that market and beaten him black and blue.

That day, he had left the market with a warning, 'Now you see what I do with you.'

The next day, he was at my home with his parents.

On the table, there were printouts. I still marvel at Vicky's vileness. He had taken printouts of the swimsuit pictures I had sent four years ago along with the others I had sent him over time. There were other printouts of our rather graphic sexts, our promises and then of my confession that Rajat and I had been physical. His mother was crying, his father was livid, and there

were little slits on his wrists. His mother had caught him with a
knife in the bathroom.

His parents looked at me and said, 'Fix him.'

My parents watched, dumbfounded, heartbroken. Every last
speck of respect I had earned, I lost in that moment. I agreed to
fix him. What else was I supposed to do? With those pictures on
the table? With those slit wrists? With Maa–Papa looking at me
wondering whether the pictures would cause more damage or
the fact that I drove a guy to suicide?

I kept staring at the tiny cuts. Not a knife, I knew. A dull
paper cutter. Not with the intention to kill, but to be effective
enough to be threatening. But could I have told all of them that
Vicky, who prepared for everything so rigorously, did such a
bad job of trying to kill himself? Had he wanted, he would have
completed the job.

'If you don't fix him,' his mother said and looked at my
parents, 'we will destroy your daughter too. We have all the
pictures.'

With my nod of agreeing to fix Vicky, I laid the reins of my
life in Vicky's mother's hands.

Since then, I have been University Rank 3, got placed
in DeliverFood as a senior analyst at a salary twice the college
average, made my parents move to a three-bedroom apartment
and started two systematic investment plans. And yet, my history
with Vicky and my relationship with Rajat (which Vicky calls
cheating and his mother calls an affair) is what defines my life.

Everyone—Maa, Papa, Vicky's parents, Vicky—lied that
they would put what I did behind them. His parents kept
hugging mine in public, taunting them in private. Soon, our
extended families started asking us if we would get married soon.
His relatives added me on Facebook. His cousins met me. I kept
getting more entangled in the web of his family, slowly choking,
their furry tentacles closing in on me.

It's been close to two years that I have been going over the details of my relationship with Rajat, with Vicky. The questions remain the same. My answers remain the same lies.

'We only met thrice.'

We met seven times.

'We have only kissed.'

We have had sex twice.

'I was thinking about you. I was too sad.'

I was glad it was over with Vicky, and I felt relieved.

'I told him we had broken up. He thought we had broken up.'

I told Rajat that Vicky wasn't talking to me and even if he was, it would have made no difference.

'I didn't enjoy it.'

I did.

'I didn't touch his penis. I didn't give him a blowjob. I didn't let him touch me.'

I did.

Even now, we have these conversations every week. He asks the questions, I give him the same answers, and he tells me I'm lying. We will have them till the end of time.

Vanita continues, 'You didn't listen to me then, but listen to me now. You should get rid of him, no matter what the cost.'

'It's a matter of time. He will hate me enough one day to leave me. I will be free of him then,' I tell Vanita. 'Okay, I need to go now!'

12.

Aanchal Madan

Dhumketu Apartments is impossible to find. After making the cab driver take three U-turns, I decide to find the apartment on foot. When I still fail, I call Daksh who tells me to wait wherever

I am. Daksh sounds even better on the phone. His voice has a low husky tone, like he's speaking into a microphone. He has one of those podcaster voices—borderline hypnotic.

'Aanchal?' a voice calls out, a woman's voice that's heavy and deep. 'I'm Zeenath. Daksh sent me to find you. A lot of people can't find the address.' She stops speaking, comes close, squints and says, 'Wow, you are as beautiful as he tells us.'

Zeenath is tiny. Just over 5 feet or maybe not, she looks like a child but speaks with the authority of a powerful, ageing matriarch. And though what she says is a compliment, she delivers it as if it's an insult. As if she's angry with me.

'Ummm. Thanks?' I say. 'So are you.'

'Whatever,' she says, confirming that she doesn't like me.

I wonder what Daksh might have told her about me apart from the 'beautiful' thing (which makes me blush a little).

'Is it, like, a big party?' I ask her.

She shakes her head. 'Just family. That's why we are surprised you're here. I asked them not to call you.'

She's walking far ahead of me and yet I can feel her anger radiate to me. I wonder if she has a crush on Daksh and sees me as a threat. She makes me jump a fence next to the petrol pump. On the other side is an abandoned plot infested with weeds and overgrown bushes.

'Before we go on,' she stops and turns towards me. In a stern voice, she says, 'You need to know something. Daksh hasn't told you because he didn't want you to freak out or something, but . . . Daksh's mother is dead. She's been dead for three years. Where you're going, there's plenty of sadness so don't be shocked, okay? I know you saw him last when he was rich or whatever, but things have changed now. It has taken Jagath and me a lot of to fix him a little, so don't break him, okay?'

She says everything so matter-of-factly, like telling someone to keep their shoes outside the house before entering, that the words don't register at first.

'What?'

'Daksh's mother is dead. I don't know much clearer can I be. She's dead. Do I need to repeat it?'

The words knock my breath out. 'Dead?' I whisper.

Zeenath rolls her eyes impatiently. She takes out her phone from her pocket. I see her typing 'Accident, Ras Al Khaimah Road, Four Dead'. She gives the phone to me.

4 Killed, 4 Injured in RAK Accident

Four men were killed after the vehicle they were travelling in collided with an SUV. Police said the SUV was travelling at high speed when the driver lost control at Emirates Ring Road in the Emirate on Wednesday afternoon.

Police patrols and ambulances hurried to the scene where four men were pronounced dead. One more passenger is critically injured.

Police experts are investigating the incident to determine its cause.

'She was the driver,' explains Zeenath.

My throat goes dry. The words float in front of my eyes. 'But . . . it says four men died.'

'She survived the accident and died later in the hospital. That's the worst part. That she died later,' answers Zeenath and with some rage, she continues, 'Had she died on the spot, Daksh would have been in a much happier place. But what can one do, right? We should go now. Daksh must be waiting.'

'Zeenath—'

'We can't be late. And behave yourself, don't be flirty with him or anything, he's already into you. He needs no complications in his life, okay?'

She leads me to Dhumketu Apartments. At the entrance, I
see Daksh's scooter. There are two unicorn stickers on it. This
is not his bachelor's pad. It's where he lives now. He, his father
and Rabbani.

He opens the door. 'Welcome!' he says and his voice trails
off. The shock on my face would have been easy to read because
he adds, 'Did Zeenath tell you?'

'Of course I did!' says Zeenath and barges into the apartment
ahead of me. 'If you can invite strangers into the house, I can tell
them everything too.'

13.

Aanchal Madan

The walls are crumbling, the windows are tiny and the house
smells damp. The floor beneath is cracked, but there's no
mess. Things are symmetrically kept; it's clean, organized,
bare. It's not much bigger than the room I grew up in. I have
been trying unsuccessfully to keep a smile on my face like
the others.

Rabbani and a guy are already waiting with a Ludo board,
waving at us.

'Jagath,' says the guy. 'I'm Daksh's best friend. Zeenath there
is also his best friend. But in all truthfulness, it's me.'

'Fuck off,' glowers Zeenath who is helping Daksh in the
kitchen, pressing half-cut oranges against a juicer. The kitchen is
just a slab in a corner of the room.

Daksh grumbles at Zeenath's language. He is in his black
T-shirt again. It fits him snugly and his biceps strain against it as
he pushes down the oranges against the juicer. In the open racks
that serve as the cupboard, I see five more of the same T-shirt.

'We are sorry for Zeenath,' apologizes Jagath. 'She gets like this every time someone new comes into this circle of four. Five, if you include Uncle.'

Then Jagath points at the skeletal, lifeless body on the bed next to the kitchen slab. He continues in his low, soothing voice, 'We know you remember him differently.'

Daksh's father looks a far cry from the salt-and-pepper corporate person I remember him as. Cheeks sunken, eyes surrounded by black moons, bones sticking out like a famine-stricken cow. He looks more dead than alive.

I walk towards his bed to touch his feet. His lower body is covered with a blanket. There's only one of them and I'm ashamed that his disability makes me flinch. Uncle looks at me unblinkingly. Then, with a groan, he turns and faces the wall.

'Baba's tired,' says Rabbani. 'Should we play?' She holds up the Ludo board.

For two hours, Rabbani, Daksh, Jagath and I play Ludo over helpings of namkeen and tea. We keep playing over the sound of their father's heavy breathing echoing in the room. It seems like someone's stepping on his rib cage, crushing his lungs, killing him slowly. Zeenath's warning hadn't prepared me for anything like this. The smiles and the laughs on everyone's faces seem out of place in a house that's collapsing on itself.

Daksh's eyes flit to the clock.

'We should cut the cake,' he tells Rabbani. 'You've got to sleep on time. I don't want to spend one more morning being scolded by your Archana ma'am.'

Rabbani sighs theatrically. 'Okay, only because it's your birthday,' she says. She folds up the Ludo board.

Zeenath excitedly gets the cake box. Jagath brings a knife. Daksh brings out a few paper hats. He's more excited than a guy his age should be about his birthday. I'm surprised he has found a way to be happy. As he makes me wear a hat, he notices the surprise in my eyes.

'Don't look at me like that, it's tradition!' he says excitedly. 'I have always celebrated my birthday.'

'Why?'

'They aren't life-changing events, they are life-giving events. You should maintain the sanctity of a few things.'

I remember the tattoo on his chest—Rabbani's birthday.

He walks to his father and gently wakes him up. He props him up against a few pillows. Uncle looks blankly at us as if he's confused about where he is. His eyes are glassy. The words from the newspaper clipping ring in my head: *Driver lost control. Four men dead.* If the writer were here, he would have added more details. *The driver's family has now moved to Mumbai, where the husband is now a husk of a person, having lost happiness and a part of his leg. The driver's son is now taking care of his six-year-old sister.*

Zeenath pushes her elbow into me. 'Smile! If Daksh can smile, so can you.'

Daksh drags a small table near Uncle's bed and puts the cake on it. 'You guys have got to sing or I'm not cutting the cake,' he tells us.

His joy on his birthday seems almost comical in the midst of all the sadness this house is submerged in. As he closes his eyes before he blows on the imaginary candles, I can't help wondering what he's wishing for. We sing a muted, awkward 'Happy Birthday', and he feeds Rabbani, Uncle, Jagath, Zeenath and me in that order.

'Are we getting that thank-you speech?' asks Zeenath.

'What is the thank-you speech—'

Before I can finish my question, Daksh interrupts me with a laugh. 'Thank-you speeches are essential, Aanchal. To look back and feel that there were some things that made the year worth it. Like a highlight reel, if you will. And I do this thank-you speech for people who mean the most to me. So here it is.'

He rubs his hands excitedly. With a huge, gorgeous smile, he begins, 'First of all, Rabbani Dey.'

Rabbani squeals in delight.

'Thank you, Rabbu, for being you. You're the cutest cute person I have ever seen, the cutest button, a piece of my heart, like a small *chhotto* momo. I have checked God's register of cute babies in descending order and it starts with you, and it ends with you. You're the funnest, most incredibly well-behaved, kind and awesome kid in the entire world! I don't know what I would be without you. You're amazing and I'm the luckiest Dada in the whole wide world and beyond!'

'Dada is best!'

He turns to Uncle. 'Thank you, Baba.'

Uncle doesn't look up at him.

Daksh continues nonetheless. 'Thank you, Baba, for bringing me into this world and taking care of us while you could. There was a lot of love in your silences and now I recognize that. We have been through a lot, but I am sure there are many years in the future that will be easier than the ones gone by. You're my Baba, and I will always love you.'

He turns to Jagath.

'Thank you Jagath, my first best friend, who gives meaning to the words "best friend", for being my rock and my ship-builder, for steadying me, for always being there. In the world of SIPs and stock options, you're my fixed deposit. And thank you for saving all that money by catching the Deal of the Days and what not.'

He turns to Zeenath.

'Thank you, Zeenath, my second-best friend, for being my truth, and for being a flame in the darkness that I find myself, to remind me that all grief is temporary, and some grief can be replaced with anger. And a special thank you for making the only five T-shirts I own smell and look amazing every day.'

He turns to me. My heart flutters, my body is pure nervousness. His deep, black eyes rest on me. It must have been for a second, but it feels like my body's been on fire for ages.

'Thank you, Aanchal, for this coincidence. I haven't told you this but you're probably the most beautiful woman I have ever seen.'

'A little shallow,' remarks Zeenath.

'Don't interrupt him,' I say.

'Thank you for existing, thank you for that strawberry ice cream, that frown in the Cellular Jail, the anger at my privilege, and for the Cornettos we shared. You were my last untarnished memory, and one that I hold dear.'

Everyone chuckles. I only manage a weak smile because my insides are now mush.

He continues, 'The past year has been kind to me despite what it looks like. I'm trying my best to be happy and content, and I'm getting there. Though I do wish the next year would be easier. Thank you for this year, and I will see you next year.'

We all clap.

Daksh pulls all of us into a bear hug, where I'm not the only one fighting back tears.

Zeenath speaks. 'Let's all pretend that a thank-you speech isn't weird.'

'Always pick weird over being just like everyone else,' I tell Daksh, who smiles sweetly.

At that moment, he does look like an innocent boy deserving of many birthday parties, not just one.

14.

Aanchal Madan

Daksh goes around and fixes a plate of biryani for each of us. He sits next to Uncle and Rabbani and makes sure they are finishing their portions. His own plate is untouched as of now. Jagath, Zeenath and I sit at the fold-out table with our plates. I finally ask them the questions that have been niggling at me. This house. The crumbling building. The broken-down Activa.

'You said Daksh's mother survived the accident, then died later,' I whisper to the two of them. 'Did her hospital bills wipe out their savings?'

'Look who's being sharp,' sniggers Zeenath. 'But no, you're not that smart.'

'I'm confused about why you are snapping at me,' I tell Zeenath.

'Because—'

Jagath nudges Zeenath into silence. I'm still confused by her dislike towards me when it's clear that she likes Jagath and not Daksh. I have noticed how she looks at him. It's quite obvious. But it looks like Jagath, with his obvious intelligence, doesn't know this.

'Four men died in the accident caused by his mother,' whispers Jagath. 'Because she was driving with an expired licence, the UAE courts put her through a trial. And what happens in the UAE is that if you kill someone, even accidentally, you have to pay blood money to the family of the person you kill. Or you're sent to jail.'

'How much?' I ask.

'5,00,000 dirhams for each death.'

'Over four crore rupees? For the four men dead?' I calculate.

'She's good at math,' scoffs Zeenath. 'They sold everything, borrowed, took loans.'

The number is making my head spin.

'Can we be quieter?' scolds Jagath softly. He lowers his voice. 'She was brain-dead already when they put her on trial. She was alive, but she didn't regain consciousness even once after the accident. They paid to keep her out of jail, but she was dead anyway.'

'They paid to keep a corpse out of jail,' scoffs Zeenath.

My heart aches for the nineteen-year-old Daksh who would have been in a cold hospital room with a brain-dead mother, a father in surgery, trying to explain to a three-year-old what they were doing there or why they didn't have a house any more.

Numerous questions ripple through my mind.

'Zeenath? You said her dying later was the worst part. Do you mean that if she had died too in the accident, they wouldn't have to pay the families of the dead?' I ask.

'Daksh told us you're very smart with choices in life,' rasped Zeenath. She nodded.

'Daksh had the choice,' explains Jagath. 'He could have taken her off the ventilator as the doctors suggested. There was a 2 per cent chance of her coming back. He refused to do that.'

'Had he done that, he wouldn't have had to lose all their money. Because he's stupid or whatever,' says Zeenath. 'No trial for a dead person, no money to be given.'

'Even Uncle asked him to do it,' adds Jagath. 'His mother was dead anyway.'

'He wanted to pay the families,' I guess.

'Correct, but stupidest decision ever,' snarled Zeenath. 'Had he taken her off life support, he would have been in a much better place. What did he get by being noble? Nothing. Bullshit he got.'

Jagath rolls his eyes. 'He has never complained about his decision, you have,' reprimands Jagath.

Zeenath rolls her eyes and then says, 'He's looking.'

'Not at us,' corrects Jagath. 'He's looking at you, Aanchal.'

'He called you beautiful again today,' says Zeenath.

'He keeps doing that, doesn't he?' adds Jagath. 'He never looks away from Rabbani, and he's doing that.'

'This biryani is great,' I butt in.

'Good deflect,' says Zeenath. 'Look at you blush. Don't you have a boyfriend or something?'

'I do,' I respond.

'Then why are you here?' hisses Zeenath.

'Don't mind her, but we wanted to talk to you about something,' interrupts Jagath.

'Zeenath warned me already.'

Jagath continues, 'So, you know, Daksh is in an emotionally vulnerable place. You can see that. It's a miracle he's holding up. We have seen his bad days.'

I turn and see Daksh changing Rabbani's clothes and putting her to bed.

Jagath continues, 'He keeps referring to you as his crush and that's absolutely untrue. You're not *just* a crush. We got to know about the depth of what he feels only a couple of days ago. When we asked him why he is calling you to this party, he told us you were a source of strength for him.'

'We don't hang out with anyone else,' gloated Zeenath. 'We were pretty pissed off, but he didn't listen.'

Jagath continues, 'When we asked him, he said he used to look at your LinkedIn profile and your success and tell himself that he too could emerge from his sadness. Essentially, he was turning to you in his weakest moments.'

Zeenath's piercing gaze makes me uncomfortable. 'Even though the circumstances of both of you were entirely different.'

'He didn't tell me this,' I stutter.

'Neither did he tell us this,' snaps Zeenath.

'Both of you are making me feel as though I'm at fault somehow when I have done nothing.'

'You haven't, that's true,' Jagath says. He pushes Daksh's phone towards me. 'Do you want to guess the lock code?'

The answer comes to me quickly. 'Rabbani's birthday?' I ask.

'Used to be,' says Zeenath sharply. 'But Rabbani figured that out or whatever, so he changed it. Then he put our birthdays, but Rabbani figured those out too. So he changed it again.'

'To what?' I ask.

'Jagath and I wondered what date it was and then we kind of figured it out.'

'It's my birthday?' I say unsurely.

'It's the day he met you,' snorts Zeenath.

'But . . . but . . . why would he do that?'

Jagath unlocks Daksh's phone. He opens the browser history. He keeps swiping up and stopping. Every time he stops, he points to my name. Every couple of months, there's a search for 'Aanchal Madan SRCC' and a visit to my LinkedIn profile. Then there are searches with my number too, once every few months. I feel my stomach churn thinking of this hurt boy searching for me. He could have called me, but he didn't. Then why was he tracking me?

Jagath continues as though he has pondered about this question as well, 'You were his coping mechanism of some sort. That's what we are thinking. The searches are too far and few for him to be a stalker.'

I nod. 'He never called. Despite having every reason to do so,' I mumble. 'My brother stole his Nintendo.'

'Look, Aanchal,' Zeenath says. 'You're a nice girl and all, I'm sure. But Daksh is fragile. Don't lead him on if you're serious about whoever you're dating.'

'I'm sure she won't,' says Jagath. 'Daksh won't be able to take it.'

15.

Aanchal Madan

I can't concentrate for the rest of the evening. My mind flits between two realities.

One in which Daksh calls me and confesses that he's thinking of me. He tells me of the accident, of his family being torn apart, of him being crushed by an avalanche of grief. And then him finding succour in talking to me. Of him finding a shoulder to lean on in me.

And then there's the realistic version of what could have happened. What really could have happened.

Vicky—who has always been logged into my Gmail, LinkedIn, and has all my passwords, controls who I follow and who I don't, whose pictures I can like, whose I can't—would have read his message. He would have grilled me and my parents about him. He would have gripped my arm until I had bruises.

How could I explain why a guy from Dubai was sending me a message that read, 'Do you remember me? We ate ice cream together in the Andamans. Had coconut water on the beach.' He would have raised his hand and then stopped and said, 'Had it been anyone else, he would have hit you.' But the gentle and generous Vicky doesn't hit me. When he's angry, he punishes me in other ways. When we are alone, he doesn't kiss me. He just thrusts his dick into my mouth. He holds me by my head, pulls at my hair and comes in my mouth. He likes to pretend that I like it too. Then he watches YouTube videos while I gargle. At other times, when he can't get hard because of all the hate he carries for me, he grips me tightly, spits and slaps me lightly as if it's all part of the sexual act when I know it's not. But I'm glad he doesn't kiss me that often. Because that's what I hate the most.

Jagath and Zeenath start to yawn as the night progresses. When they get up to leave, they look at me. They want me to leave as well.

'I have nothing to do,' I tell Daksh. 'I can stay for a bit.'

'Thank god someone's excited about my birthday,' says Daksh brightly.

Zeenath sniggers. 'Your birthday is over. It's past twelve.'

Jagath and Zeenath leave, knowing that I won't budge. When they are gone, I put the gift I got for him on the table.

'You didn't have to do this,' he says. Then he winks and adds, 'But I'm glad you did it because gifts are the best part.'

He unwraps the *gift*. It's a Nintendo, the same model Gaurav flicked from him. He starts to laugh.

'So it's not really a gift then, just returning me my stuff,' he chuckles, cradling it in his hands, pushing the buttons. He looks straight up at me. 'Thank you. I love it.'

'You don't play any more, do you?'

'How does that matter? You thought and gave me something meaningful. Now every time I look at this, it will remind me of our story. That's what gifts are. Remembrances of what we share with someone.'

'You do take birthdays quite seriously.'

He laughs and then falls silent.

For the first time this evening, I see the smile drop from his face. The sadness Jagath and Zeenath talked about brims to his face. In an instant, it feels like all the happiness in the room has been sucked up.

'I'm sorry about . . . Aunty,' I say.

'It's okay.' He smiles sadly. After a long pause, he says, 'I could hear you guys talk. Good to know that my friends have no boundaries and they can break into my phone.'

He knows that I know. And somehow I see no hesitation in his eyes. Neither do I feel I need to hide or cover up anything in front of him. He meets my eye. His gaze has the quality of making me want to be the truest version of myself. With all the flaws, imperfections.

'You never reached out to me. Despite all the searches—'

He leans forward. The space between our faces is not a lot.

'Aanchal. You had a possessive boyfriend. I had nothing to offer at first. And then, only grief, only baggage,' he says.

'Zeenath said you made a mistake by giving them the money.'

He shakes his head. 'It was the easiest decision I ever made,' he counters. 'What was the decision? To kill my mother sooner to avoid paying the families who had lost their people? How could I have possibly done that? Every time we went to the court, we could see them right in front of our eyes. Kids hardly older than Rabbani, women without their husbands, primary breadwinners. I couldn't have chosen to live with the guilt.'

'So you chose this,' I mumble.

'God spared us,' he says sternly. 'All four died in the other car. In ours, only the driver's side was damaged. Baba, Rabbani, me, we were all sitting on the other side. It would have been ungrateful to . . . only Mumma . . .'

The way he pronounces Mumma breaks my heart. Maa and Mumma mean the same but feel entirely different. Maa is to address a benevolent, protective figure; Mumma is accepting your own vulnerability. Maa is when you give power to your mother, Mumma is when you accept the child in you.

He composes himself.

His voice is so low now it's barely a whisper. 'I feel bad for Rabbani. She never got to know Mumma. And with Baba too . . .' His voice trails. 'Baba doesn't speak to us for days. He's experiencing a lot of phantom limb pain.'

'What's that?'

'His brain can't process that the leg's not there. And the medication for the pain wipes his brain.'

He tells me his father can go on groaning for months. They had paid for the prosthetic limb, but every time he tests it, he screams in pain. It's as if his leg—the one that doesn't exist any more—is getting mashed, bones grinding to dust, flesh pulverized. Daksh looks at Rabbani, sleeping peacefully as only children can.

'She needs him.'

'And you?'

He pulls back his tears. I wonder if he ever allows himself to cry.

'Why did you move to Mumbai?' I ask him, wondering if he would have called had he moved to Delhi. 'Why not Delhi?'

'We had no time to think. This apartment was the only investment we had left. Baba's friend here found me a job and that's it,' he explains. 'I started college online, Rabbani started school, and we stopped waiting for Baba to get well.' He looks down at the Nintendo, then packs it back in its box. 'We thought Baba would fight it, take care of us. That's what fathers do, but . . . yes, that's what it is.'

'He will, I'm sure he will.'

'Do you want chai?' he asks. 'If you're not getting late, that is.'

I wonder if anyone says no to the politest guy of all time. Armies will walk towards certain death if Daksh asks them politely. 'Who doesn't like chai after biryani?'

He stations the home camera towards Rabbani. As he's doing it, the car accident materializes in front of my eyes. I imagine the moment of their ruin. Aunty slumped over. Uncle screaming in pain, his leg pinned, blood dripping. Daksh dazed, Rabbani's crying drowned in the commotion. Then, something strikes me.

'Daksh?'

'Yes?'

'My cousin's wife died in a car accident a few years ago. I didn't know her, but I heard about the accident,' I say.

'I'm sorry to hear that—'

'My cousin was driving, his wife was in the passenger seat. My cousin swerved the car to save himself. The truck crashed into the passenger's side.'

'Okay, hmm.'

'The investigation said that it was because of driver's instinct. It happens with drivers all the time. They steer to save themselves. The passengers sitting directly behind the driver are usually safe.'

'Why are you telling me this?'

'With your accident, the opposite happened. You said only the driver's side of the car was damaged, your mother's side, right? The passenger side, and where you were sitting, right behind your father, were undamaged. Would that mean Aunty would have steered the opposite way? Put herself in the accident? She put herself in the crash,' I hypothesize.

He goes silent. I can see his eyes, he's no longer here. He's visualizing the accident.

'She . . . she might have saved you guys. I don't know . . . just feels like that.'

16.

Daksh Dey

They told us Mumma had to be extracted from the car using metal cutters. The nurses told me they used a craniotome to cut a part of her skull. The doctors informed me that there was pressure building up from her brain bleed. The staff told us that though her body was broken in multiple places, it was her mind they cared about. Statistics were thrown about, CAT scans were shown, alternatives were discussed, second and third opinions were taken, lawyers were engaged, the police were informed. We were told if we didn't pay and Mumma regained consciousness, she would be put in jail. Grief counsellors were appointed, end-of-life plans explained to us, but none of them said there was a chance that it wasn't pure luck that the rest of us survived.

They didn't tell us she could have swerved to *save* us.

They didn't tell us we were alive because of Mumma.

'Another one,' Aanchal says and shows me another accident where the driver swerved to save themselves. The driver survived, the passengers died.

Aanchal's doing this to help. Her eyes are bright, her face flushed, and I can't find the heart to tell her she's making me relive the accident.

'You can send me the links later.'

She gets the point.

'But thank you,' I say.

'Don't embarrass me by saying thank you. It's nothing.'

'It's everything. Because someday I will have to explain the accident to Rabbani, and who Mumma was. And I have always feared that all she will remember about her is that she caused the death of four people. Now, I have something. She saved us. That's going to be Mumma's story,' I say. 'By the way, how's the tea?'

'Too much sugar,' she remarks. 'I like it. This is how it should be.'

The sugary tea at the signal was at one time unpalatable. Now it's part of my routine. We are all capable of doing things we once thought impossible.

'How are your parents?' I ask her, remembering how cute the two of them were.

'They are good,' she answers like she's hiding something. She continues, 'They keep finding some reason or the other to stress about.'

'That's what parents do, right?' I say. 'And how's Gaurav, *choro ka raja*, Daniel Ocean, heist expert?'

I watch her face fall.

'Hey? Hey? I'm joking. I'm glad he stole it. It was high time I stopped playing anyway. I was pretty shit at it.'

'You're not the only person he stole from,' she says glumly. 'He . . . he stole from us, dropped out of college. Then he ran away and came here, to Mumbai, but . . . it's tricky, he's . . .'

'Drugs?'

'Games,' she answers. '*DotA*, *Counter-Strike*. He wants to be a gamer.'

'You're not serious!'

'It's nothing to be happy about,' she retorts. 'My parents and Gaurav haven't talked in seven months. It's just so stressful. And if he doesn't report back to college, he will waste three years. He's going to be a twelfth pass all his life.'

'I remember he was incredible at it, a lot of potential,' I say. 'I think he will do very well. He was a natural.'

She glowers at me. 'It's stupid. He's throwing his life away. The least he could have done is finished his degree. That's literally just one year.'

'And lose out on a year of competing? In gaming terms, that's suicide. You need to be young to compete. Your reflexes get duller as you grow older.'

'What will he do when's forty? Keep playing games?'

Aanchal sounds like an old person now. I want to tell her that even her job at DeliverFood will look very different when she's forty. She will be replaced by AI, the delivery executive by the next version of drones.

'All he needs to do is win one major tournament. He plays *DotA*, right? The prize money is in millions. Even *Fortnite* or *Counter-Strike*. He can chill or pivot or be a tester. Options are plenty.'

She doesn't look convinced. 'You sound exactly like him,' she grumbles.

'I'm guessing you will meet him and pester him to go back?'

'My friend will,' she answers. 'He doesn't talk to me any more. Just to a friend of mine. He has a crush on her so she's going to try and knock some sense into him.'

'Honey trapping your own brother, nice,' I say. 'It's your brother, but my suggestion is to let him do what he wants to do. He's not stupid that he took a decision that big. That itself should tell you about his seriousness.'

'*Woh gadha hai,*' she says. 'Anyway. I don't want to talk about it. Even at home, we talk about him most of the time. Tell me about you. Apart from . . . you're not dating?'

I wonder if I should tell her about the daydreams I have had about our dates.

'I have tried,' I answer. 'But when I tell someone the full extent of my history, trauma, quirks, they run away. As they should.'

'You're handsome enough for that not to matter.'

He turns to look at me. There's surprise on his face.

'Wait . . . are you . . . is this the first time . . . are you . . . are you flirting with me? Is this the first time Aanchal Madan is flirting with me?'

'You're not naïve, you know I have flirted with you before,' she says. She blinks, and her eyelashes come down in a dramatic wave. 'If sitting behind you on a scooter and sharing an ice cream cone with you isn't flirting, I don't know what is.'

'Good to know I wasn't imagining it. Oh, by the way, you look . . . I am just going to repeat myself. But you look like a movie star. Like an empress who has taken a night off royal duties to hang out with the common people.'

'You say all these things, Daksh, and then go missing for four years.'

'As opposed to what? Being in touch and watching you with someone else? No, thank you.'

She smiles and sips her tea.

Today, she is in a black–and–gold salwar suit that seems like it's made just for her. When I saw her at the door earlier this evening, I felt a part of me that was long dead come alive again.

As if the air around me was now charged, electric.

Throughout the evening, I have had to tear myself away from fixating on her lips and what I want to do to them. I look at her slender hands and wonder what it would be like to hold them.

Her phone beeps.

For the past couple of hours, I have seen texts appear on Aanchal's phone panel. She replies, then swipes it away.

'How's Vicky?'

Aanchal knows what I'm asking. I don't care about Vicky. I want to know if Vicky and Aanchal are still going strong. More than that, I am hoping they are not.

I continue, 'Are you wondering if you should answer that?'

'I'm thinking how unfair it would be to complain about life after what you have told me . . . after what has happened.'

'C'mon. The last time we met, I bitched and complained about Sameeksha when your life was hanging in the balance. All problems are relative. You can start complaining, I won't mind.'

She looks at her tea and exhales deeply. Crease lines form on her forehead and she looks deeply unhappy.

'I don't want to be with Vicky any more. But I can't break up with him. That's what is going on with him . . . Anyway, there's nothing left in that relationship but anger.'

I see a window of opportunity. I want to smash through it and take her away from Vicky.

'Why are you together then?'

'. . . because he still loves me as much as he hates me. He would never let it end.'

'Aanchal, you're the smartest person I know, but this is a dumb thing. You can leave anyone at any time. Who's stopping you? Just walk out. People break up all the time.'

She shakes her head like it's not even an option. It makes me furious.

'I'm not putting Maa through it,' she says. 'Gaurav's doing whatever he's doing and then me. It would be too much for them.'

'So? You will get married to him eventually because you can't tell your parents that you want to leave him? Say that sentence in your head and see how crazy it is.'

She waves me away. 'How bad can it be? People are in loveless marriages all the time. It's pretty much the hallmark of marriage: unhappiness,' she says.

'I disagree. Getting married to someone is the holiest thing you can do. It's a promise like none other,' I tell her. 'And how you're dealing with this is the worst possible way.'

She shrugs as if it's no big deal. 'It's a piece of paper.'

'It's a life together,' I respond, shocked at her nonchalance. 'Whoever you're thinking will judge you or your parents for breaking up doesn't matter. The world moves on, Aanchal. They don't care what we do in our lives. And those who truly care, they won't mind.'

'I'm trying to make him break up with me.'

'What did he do?'

She catches my gaze. 'Why could it not be something I did?'

I know Aanchal can do no wrong. 'You would be forgiven for everything.'

'I cheated on him.'

I want to ask her who she cheated with, but that's none of my business. I am jealous but also angry with both Vicky and the nameless guy with whom she cheated. How could they have ruined the opportunity of being with her?

'Again,' I ask her, 'what did he do?'

'He did what guys do,' she says with finality. 'It is what it is. I don't have the luxury to leave. He's not going to be my entire life, just a small part of it. Anyway, I won't be the first person to get married to someone they don't like. Big deal.'

'That's just nonsense.'

'You wouldn't get it.'

'Of course, how would I get what's really important in life?'

'I didn't mean it like that.'

'I'm sorry, I didn't mean to snap.'

She touches my arm. 'Daksh, I didn't tell you this so you could solve it for me. That you listened is enough. We should stop talking about it now. I will manage, it's not a big deal.'

'No—'

'Hey, maybe Vicky will break up,' she says with a smile. 'I torture him a lot. It's only a matter of time before he realizes he's with the world's worst girlfriend.'

'You should be with a nice guy.'

She catches my eye. After a pause that seems like an eternity, she says, 'Like you?'

My heart thumps. Her words wrap around my heart like a blanket on a chilly morning. My body warms.

'I'm hardly a nice guy.'

'Of course you're not, Daksh. You're the worst guy ever.'

'And you're the world's worst girlfriend,' I announce. 'We are a match made in heaven.'

Just then, there's a call on her phone. It's Vicky.

'I will go now and video-call him from the hotel or he will go mad,' she says.

The thought of Vicky and her being held hostage in a dead relationship makes my entire body revolt.

'Aanchal. I thought the point was to make him mad enough to leave. I should pick up and tell him that his girlfriend is with me, in my house. I should tell him that we just had the most incredible kiss in the brief history of time.'

'What else would you tell him?' she asks, her eyes meeting mine.

I step closer to her. 'That I have had the biggest crush on his girlfriend for the longest time.'

'We can hardly call it a crush any more, Daksh.'

The lower register of her voice makes my heart race. 'I don't want to call it an obsession.'

'I'll allow obsession.'

I want to take her face in my hands, truly see if she's real. I'm obsessed with who she is, what she is, her face, her body, every inch of her, every moment of her existence.

'He will call my parents and tell them what you tell him.'

'He really needs to meet my fist.'

'My cab's two minutes away, Daksh.'

'I want to drop you to the hotel,' I say.

'Can you?'

'Rabbani.'

'It's a good thing you can't, Daksh. I don't want you to,' she sighs.

'Why?'

'Because I am alone in my room and my room is just a one-minute walk from the cab drop-off,' she says.

'You're giving me reasons why I should drop you, not why I shouldn't.'

'Things are already too complicated.'

The invitation and rejection rolled in one makes my heart pound against my insides. I feel a stirring within. A desire I haven't ever felt before. We stand there, looking at each other, and for a brief moment, we are the only ones at that traffic signal, beneath the yellow glow of the streetlights, and the universe has melted into nothing.

She breaks my reverie. 'Rabbani's cute. She's growing up to be quite smart.'

I am yanked into the present. Into a reality where she has a boyfriend and I have a broken life.

'You still hate kids, don't you?'

'Even more now,' she says. 'Three DeliverFood VPs have gone on maternity leave. They will lose out on so much growth. It's stupid. We try to say ya, nothing matters, but the guys at the same level will zoom ahead.'

A conversation that's not about us feels unnecessary, empty words to fill time. A white Dzire comes to a stop next to her.

'Will I see you tomorrow, Aanchal?'

'I hope so,' she tells me.

'And what will happen tomorrow?'

'We will torture ourselves again with a changed past and a future that doesn't exist,' she says.

'So we will torture ourselves with possibilities?' I say. 'Cool. I am used to that.'

I step forward to hug her, my face within breathing distance of hers. She looks up to catch my gaze. In her eyes, I see hesitance, eagerness, rage, love.

'Do I get a hug?'

As she wraps her arms around me, I feel her body lose its composition and melt into mine. I grip her tighter. I'm made of nerve endings. I feel everything. A deep hunger for her body uncoils within me. I want to keep holding her. I want her clothes to be gone, I want to feel her skin against mine, my tongue against hers. I want her to be mine.

I let her go.

She gets into the cab.

'You're right about that. It is torture,' I admit.

'I will think about you, Daksh.'

The driver asks for the OTP. He puts the car in gear. She waves at me. I keep waving till she looks away from the rear-view mirror. It feels like my heart's being ripped out of my chest.

Back home, I slip next to Rabbani in bed. She snuggles up to me. I hear Baba turn sides. When I look at him, his eyes are open. I assume the worst.

'Baba?'

He blinks. He's alive.

And then, he smiles. He doesn't turn away.

'Sleep, Daksh,' he tells me before closing his eyes.

Yeah, right.

17.

Aanchal Madan

My body's on fire.

I can still feel his hands on my body. His fingers burned through the fabric, and I could feel them on my skin. When his body pressed against mine, I felt naked. Every ridge of his body against mine was like it was always meant to be. I felt every inch of him against me and every inch of me blazed with thirst. He pressed against me and every fibre of my being wanted to meld into him. Every time I have been touched before, shame flooded me. The shame of doing something wrong, the shame of being with someone wrong. But today, I felt none of it.

My body was no longer mine, but his.

Had he pushed himself into me, I would have let him. If he would have slipped his hands inside, let his fingers run over the small of my back, I would have encouraged him. If he would have breathed heavily near my ear, I would have moaned and asked him to go on. If his lips rested against my neck, I would have invited him to do more. If he had pushed his bulge against me, I would have grabbed him and urged him to go further.

But he didn't.

I felt his laboured breath, I could sense his beating heart against my breasts, and yet he let me go. And when his body separated from mine, I felt like a part of my body was being severed.

I had shuddered at the thought of him coming back to the hotel with me. We wouldn't have reached the room. I would have devoured him in the lift itself. I would have . . . I . . . I didn't think my body was capable of this desire.

I want him.

I can't stop thinking about how his body felt against mine. I fail spectacularly trying to push Daksh out of my mind.

Twenty minutes have passed since he waved yearningly at me. And I still can't breathe.

'Inside?' the cab driver asks me outside the Marriott.

I nod.

Just as I get down from the car, I see two faces together that I haven't seen in the longest time. Vicky and Vanita. The lobby's echoing with their screams.

18.

Aanchal Madan

Everyone in the lobby is stunned to hear them fight. Vanita screaming her lungs out, Vicky bellowing, spit flying out of his mouth. Vanita shaking her fists, Vicky clenching his jaw. The front desk people try to calm them down. The guards try to break them apart. Someone's calling the police. Vanita and Vicky keep lobbying the same words to each other: 'LET HER COME, LET HER COME!'

They are screaming about me.

'What the fuck are you doing here!' Vanita screams at Vicky.

'WHAT THE FUCK ARE YOU DOING HERE?' Vicky screams back.

Both of them spot me at the same time. The ground trembles beneath my feet. My mind goes numb. Twenty pairs of eyes turn towards me. I, who spent the night at a random guy's birthday. Vicky, whose eyes are burning red, pounds towards me. Vanita, with her tall legs and longer strides, outpaces him and stands between him and me.

'Who was he?' he roars. 'WHO THE FUCK IS HE? *KAUN THA BEHENCHOD!*'

My mind whirrs. I feel the strength go out of my knees. My heart pounds so loudly I can't hear my own thoughts. My life's over. It's done. I might as well be dead.

'STEP BACK FROM ME, YOU BASTARD!' Vanita screams.

'You need to take this outside,' the front desk manager pleads.

'Gau . . . rav . . . I was looking for Gaurav,' I mumble.

Vicky's eyes are ablaze in rage. '*CHUTIYA HU KYA MAIN!* Call him if you were with him! CALL HIM!'

'MIND YOUR LANGUAGE!' Vanita yells over him. 'LET'S GO TO THE ROOM.'

Vicky glares at Vanita. 'Ask your randi to call Gaurav. *BOL SAALI KO!*'

'That's some real class, Vicky. There's no fucking point making a scene here,' Vanita argues. 'Let's go to the room and talk.'

'SHE'S LYING TO MY FACE! *Behen ki laudi,* I knew you would never change. MUMMY TOLD ME SLUTS LIKE YOU NEVER CHANGE!'

'Yes, she's lying,' answers Vanita, lowering her voice. 'But let's not do this here.'

'Vanita, I'm not lying—'

Vanita cuts me. 'It's done, he knows you're lying. Let's just go from here.'

'Sir, ma'am,' interrupts the hapless manager. 'You people need to go.'

Vicky stares at me and in a low grumble says, 'Randi, *chalein?* Or should I stuff some money down your bra? Or your mother's?'

'Enough!' warns Vanita.

'I KNEW it, Aanchal, I knew you wouldn't—'

'Not here,' Vanita shuts Vicky down.

'I have lost the key card,' I mutter.

Vanita holds my hand and takes me to the front desk. The girl there looks at my face with pity and confusion and gives us the room's key card. We take the lift to my room. Vanita's holding me by my shoulders as we walk slowly towards the room. At the door, Vicky stops Vanita from entering.

'This is between us. What are you doing here?' commands Vicky.

'I'm not going anywhere. Whatever you guys talk about will happen right in front of me,' snaps back Vanita. 'And Vicky, you touch me one more time, I will make another Sanjog out of you.'

Vicky steps away from Vanita. His face hardens.

'Why? Why in front of you? Who are you?' he spits back. 'Oye Aanchal, ask her to leave or—'

'Or what? What will you do? Tell me, what?'

My throat's dry, the world spins lightly. No words come from my mouth.

It feels like an out-of-body experience. I'm not here. My body is all that's here, and I'm watching it from above. My real self is in the future. We are in Vicky's house, where Vicky is telling Maa–Papa how I was having sex with random men in Mumbai. Maa is telling Baba that she wished she had died in childbirth. Vanita swipes the card. The room opens. I walk to a corner of the room. I can't bear to look at Vicky. He looks like he can do . . . anything.

'Who was he? Don't you dare lie to me,' growls Vicky.

I try to talk but I can't form the words.

'*BATAEGI* RANDI or will you just keep looking at your feet?'

'It doesn't matter who he was,' answers Vanita. 'We all know you're going to say whatever you feel like to her parents.'

'I'm asking you!' thunders Vicky. 'HAVE YOU GONE DEAF NOW? DID HE FUCK YOU IN THE EAR TOO?!'

'Daksh . . .' Vanita says. 'He's the guy she met in the Andamans.'

I look at Vanita, horrified. It's time to beg, not fight. Ask for his forgiveness. That's what works with Vicky. When I look up, I find Vicky marching towards me. His face is inches away from me. I flinch backwards. His bad breath wafts towards me. Rivulets of saliva hang from his canine teeth like a rabid dog. A strange fear takes root in me.

'Who's he? What did you do with him!? DID YOU FUCK HIM? TELL ME!'

Vanita comes and stands next to me. 'You don't have to answer that,' repeats Vanita. 'He's going to say shit anyway. So what's the difference? Don't say anything, Aanchal!'

'MADARCHOD!' he screams and walks away.

He paces around in tight circles. He picks up the fruit plate from the table and throws it to the ground. The glass shatters. Little shards strike Vanita and me.

He turns to us, 'BEHENCHOD! Have you guys gone crazy?' He picks up another plate. 'TELL ME OR THE NEXT ONE WILL BE ON YOUR FACE!'

Vanita stands between me and him.

'OYE!' he explodes.

'DON'T OYE ME,' warns Vanita. 'YOU'RE A FUCKING NOBODY!'

'Stop it, Vanita, please stop speaking,' I finally mumble. 'You're making it worse. Please, please go. I will manage.'

'Listen to her, this is between the two of us!'

'Oh, please!' says Vanita. 'Listen, Vicky. This had to happen. She had to sleep with someone.'

'*Chup kar,* BEHEN KI LAUDI!' shouts Vicky. 'No one's talking to you!'

Vanita throws her hands up in the air. 'She loves you, but the sex between the two of you was horrible. She told me everything about it.'

'Vanita!' I squeal.

Vicky turns to look at me, eyes bloodshot. 'What did you tell her?'

'Everything, she told me everything, Vicky,' answers Vanita. 'That you just make her give you blowjobs! That sometimes you don't get hard and just slap her around.'

'IT'S NOTHING LIKE THAT!'

I feel light-headed. I sit on the bed.

Vanita laughs and continues while pointing at Vicky's crotch, 'She told me Rajat was better, thicker! She lies to you that Rajat had a small dick, but let me tell you, she has shared pictures and it's HUGE!'

'WHAT THE HELL ARE YOU SAYING!' roared Vicky.

'Stop it, Vanita!' I cry out.

'Tell her to leave!' growls Vicky.

Vanita waves me down. 'And you're tiny, Vicky, she told me! She told me that's why you don't get hard.'

'BEHENCHOD!' screams Vicky. '*BATAU TUJHE KISKA CHHOTA HAI.* WILL FUCK YOU AND YOUR ENTIRE FAMILY!'

'Of course she went for a dick!' says Vanita with a laugh.

Vicky, face streaked with tears, looks at me. There's a rage in him I haven't seen before. He clenches his fist.

'STEP BACK FROM ME, VICKY!' warns Vanita.

'*Kyun?* What will you do? *Haan?* YOU WILL FIGHT ME? *MAA CHOD DUNGA TERI!*'

'Fuck you,' says Vanita, calmly. 'You limp-dicked asshole.'

Vicky charges at Vanita. A silent scream escapes my mouth. He raises his hand. The plate's in the air, in his hand, and it's coming slowly, painfully towards Vanita's face. I scream.

'NO!'

He crashes the plate against Vanita's head who brings her arm up just in time. Dread races through my body. Something breaks deep inside of me. It's as if my brain, my heart, all of me is being crushed, broken, blended and I'm being put together again.

There's overwhelming pain . . . but there's anger too.

Vanita bleeds from her arm. And I freeze for a few seconds before snapping out of it. I am on my feet again. Vanita's buckled over. I run to her but before I reach her, Vicky grabs me from behind and flings me towards the wall.

'VICKY!' I scream.

I know at this moment that no matter what the cost, Vicky had to go.

I scramble to my feet. I want to take him down, kill the bastard. I charge, teeth bared, wanting to rip him apart with my bare hands, fucking just kill him, but Vicky's too quick. He lunges and his fist lands against my jaw. I feel my teeth shatter, my brain buzzes and I fall to the ground. I open my eyes and can see only Vicky's foot, inches away from smashing into my face.

Then, he's jerked back. Vanita's arms are locked around his waist.

'ENOUGH!' she bellows like it's a war cry.

Vanita throws Vicky against the wall. His shoulder smashes into it. A nasty crunch echoes in the room. An inhuman wail escapes Vicky's mouth. Vanita brings her foot down on his shoulder and rams down on it. Once, twice, thrice. Thud. Thud. Thud. Her strength against his body. The blows are quick and decisive. Vicky's wails fill the room. He tries to get up but sits back down. He clutches his shoulder which moves disturbingly in its socket.

He cries out in pain.

Vanita slams her foot down again on his broken shoulder.

'Don't try to get up, Vicky,' threatens Vanita. 'You can't fight me with both shoulders working so don't try it with one!'

'BEHENCHOD!' he screams in pain.

Vanita rolls her eyes. 'What's with you guys and swearing? One broken shoulder is not enough or what?'

'I will destroy you!' he threatens me.

He will. I am sure of that. This is the last day I will truly feel any kind of happiness. But seeing him helpless and in pain gives me a strange feeling. I examine it in my scared heart and know what it is: it's revenge.

It feels good.

Vanita laughs at Vicky. 'You sound like a bad villain, Vicky. You're going to do nothing of that sort.'

She walks across the room to pick up her phone, which has been standing upright on a table facing us. She shows it to Vicky and then me.

She continues, 'You assaulted us. And I have proof. It's done. You're done.'

'WHO THE HELL CARES!' he says, his words melding into agonizing wails.

'Your employers will care, the police will care, my parents will definitely care,' says Vanita, matter-of-factly. 'You think I would really let you smash that plate against my head? I can take down guys your size in my sleep, Vicky. I'm going to repeat it, Vicky. You're *nothing*.'

'But you . . .' he protests angrily, trying to get up again and failing.

Vanita shrugs and mock-wipes her hands. 'It's over, Vicky.'

The gravity of what just happened sinks in. This is it. This is freedom. Vicky realizes it too.

'IT'S NOT FAIR!' he thunders.

Vanita laughs. 'That's cute.'

I scramble to my feet. Blood rushes to all parts of my body. Relief floods me. It feels like I'm reborn.

'Vicky.'

Vicky turns to look at me.

I continue, 'What you were doing with me wasn't fair. Nothing about us was fair. Sanjog, going to my parents, throwing away everything we had. It wasn't fair.'

'Look who finally has a voice.' squeals Vanita, clapping in delight. 'Finally. I thought I would have to wait till afternoon.'

'Shut up, Vanita,' I say.

I walk to where Vicky has slumped down.

'Don't come near me,' he says, like a scared, hurt animal.

I sit next to him. He flinches when I reach out for his shoulder. I touch it softly. 'Does it hurt?' I ask him.

He nods, tears and pain flooding him. 'Of course it hurts,' he growls.

The anger, the rage, the shame, the regret—I feel it all leave my body. It's just him—the boy I had met in school, the boy I fell in love with. And it's me. *How can that have changed so much? How has it come to this?* All my life I have wanted to grow up, be an adult, take hold of my own life . . . now I realize it's all a bit overstated.

I look into his eyes. 'Jaan, look at me, please,' I tell Vicky. 'You know what has just happened. It's over. What we had, it's done, it's just over.'

Vicky looks away from me. I gently hold his face and make him look at me. He's in tears. After a long time, I feel bad for him.

'Did you guys plan this?' he asks, his voice and spirit broken. 'How did you know I would come? How did you plan this?'

'We didn't know you would come.'

'I came to surprise you.' Tears streak down his face. 'It can't be over,' he stammers like a lost puppy.

In his brokenness, I find the most love I have felt for him in the longest time.

'I made a mistake with Rajat,' I admit. 'And I'm really, really sorry about it. Because I hurt the boy I liked the most, the boy who was my jaan. But you made your mistakes too, Vicky. You have to see that, jaan. It was . . . you . . . you broke us first.'

'I'm not your—'

'Vicky, Vicky, Vicky, please look at me. Listen to me,' I take his hand into mine. It's the last time I will ever be holding him.

'No.'

'Please, make this easy for all of us. If it makes it any easier, I didn't touch any guy other than Rajat. But I have lied to you, I have broken your heart, and you have broken mine. We have disrespected each other. That's worse than sleeping with someone, jaan.'

For the first time in months, he looks at me without hate. 'What do you want us to do?'

Vanita throws up her hands in frustration. 'Isn't it obvious?'

'I'm sorry,' mumbles Vicky.

'Jaan,' I say to Vicky. And then I say the last lie I will ever tell Vicky. 'Truthfully, you have the biggest dick I have ever seen. The biggest of all time.'

Vanita rolls her eyes, but Vicky . . . Vicky smiles from behind his tears.

19.

Daksh Dey

'No more talking,' I warn Rabbani. 'Finish your sandwich. And if you don't finish your lunch, then just see what I will do.'

'What will you do?' asks Rabbani, her eyes glinting.

'Please just eat it. I don't get up in the morning for nothing,' I answer, realizing I'm mouthing the same sentences Mumma used to say.

'Dada?'

'Stop talking and eat, Rabbu.'

She pulls at my sleeve.

'No,' I tell her.

She pulls at my sleeve again.

'What?' I snap.

'There! Baba!' she says and points in Baba's direction.

Baba's sitting up in the bed.

He's not cursing or groaning.

He's trying to push himself towards the edge of the bed. I am about to get up when he looks at me and raises his hand. He will do it on his own, he gestures.

Something has changed.

His eyes, his mind, it's all there. It's been some time since his last painkiller. I realize I missed the last dose. Usually, it's in the middle of the night when the pain wakes him up.

He picks up his crutch. With a painful groan, he helps himself up. It's the first time in months that he hasn't required any help from me, Jagath or Zeenath. He hobbles towards us with small, painful steps.

'Morning,' he says to us. He pulls out a chair. 'You two shouldn't have sandwiches every day. Indian bodies aren't made to have processed flour.'

It's the longest sentence he has spoken to us in over a year. And what else would a father pick as his first words in months but feedback?

Rabbani takes Baba's hand into hers and kisses it. Baba caresses Rabbani's face and she melts into a little puddle in his hand. How uncomplicated Rabbani is! Like a puppy. She forgets every disappointment and erases all the past's complaints on receiving a little love from her father.

Baba looks at me. When he smiles, deep ridges form on his forehead. He nods. His nod is his apology. Even the seven staggered steps he took to reach me were an apology. And it's enough for me. Maybe I'm not that different from Rabbani.

'I'm here now,' he says, his voice sure and deep.

His tone used to strike deep fear within me when I was Rabbani's age. Now it comes as a sense of relief. The rasp and the surety in his voice tell me the truth of the situation. He is the parent again. I am the child. These are the roles we need to step back into.

'Dak—' His words are cut off by the pain.

'Do you want the medicines, Baba?'

He shakes his head. 'I have had enough of those, haven't I? I will throw them out today. Along with the prescriptions.'

'Does it hurt, Baba?' asks Rabbani.

He holds Rabbani's face in his hands. 'It does, Rabbu, but not so much.' He looks at me. 'I'm hungry.'

Before I can get up, Rabbani does. Together, we bring him a bowl of milk and cornflakes. He forces down one spoonful with a grimace. Then another. He gags but goes on. His muscles tense, but he keeps eating. His pain and struggle seep into us; it clouds the air, stains the wall. It's the darkness before the light. He doesn't stop till he finishes the bowl.

Then he smiles. A smile without pain. He looks at Rabbani. 'I will drop you at school today.'

'Baba—'

He interrupts me. 'You need to concentrate on work, Daksh, nothing else,' he commands me.

I shrink as sons do in front of their fathers. With every moment that passes between us, it feels like he's becoming bigger, taller, stronger. Baba takes the space I was occupying. I shrink.

I shrink because I don't have to be everywhere, do everything. I feel light. Like I can float again. It's as if Baba is not having breakfast, but he's taking a hacksaw to the shackles on my feet which have left deep, festering wounds.

'Daksh,' he scolds. 'You've lost weight. You look thirty.'

The irony makes me smile. My father, who once had a thick paunch and is now only stretched skin on bones and half-dead, is calling me thin and old.

'You have lost weight too,' I point to his missing leg.

'You will get slapped now,' he retorts.

I don't apologize. He doesn't apologize either. Among the things fathers and sons can't do is apologize. To their wives, to their children. Their apologies come in actions, in little acts of kindness.

Baba gets up to wash his face. This time, he lets me help him.

'Daksh,' he says. 'Your Mumma . . . don't blame her.'

'I never did, Baba,' I lie.

'She tried to save us,' he mumbles. 'Isn't that what the girl said yesterday? Aanchal, that's her name, right? Let's believe her.'

It's as if I have a choice. If she says it's night in the middle of the day, I would believe it.

20.

Daksh Dey

It's odd to think of Gaurav as a grown person, as a twenty-year-old. He was sixteen when I first met him, only two years younger than me, but to me he was a shrimp, half a man. To think he's old enough to run away from his home to pursue a career in gaming is nuts. I'm outside an old apartment building in the suburbs of Mumbai, which is where he's reportedly living. Finding him was easy. I searched Mumbai gaming Reddit threads to find a guy who staked his degree to join the gaming community in Mumbai. I found not only his address but also learnt that he's seen as a strange but talented gamer in those circles.

I ring the bell.

I hear footsteps. A young, short boy, not more than sixteen, in a tattered T-shirt and shorts, opens the door.

'Yes?'

'You're not Gaurav unless you have grown smaller.'

'I'm Sameer, Gaurav's teammate,' he answers. 'Are you here with the food we ordered?'

'I'm here for Gaurav,' I tell him.

'Gaurav!' shouts the boy.

Gaurav walks into the living room. He's wearing an old grey T-shirt that's been washed way too many times and shorts. Headphones hang around his neck. He's taller now but even skinnier. Most of his face is hidden behind an unkempt, sparse beard. He's pale as if he has never been out in the sun. He looks like a famine survivor. He has a buzz cut, and golden, round-framed spectacles rest on his nose. He looks like Harry Potter was locked in Azkaban, and a few Dementors let loose on him.

'Who are you?' he asks, fixing his specs. His voice is an ugly rasp as if someone has stepped on his trachea. Like his voice started to break and then stopped midway.

'Daksh,' I say. 'I met you in the Andamans four years ago. You stole my Nintendo. Ring a bell?'

There's recognition in his eyes.

I continue, 'Aanchal's looking for you.'

He looks confused and angry.

'I don't want anything to do with them. You can leave,' he tells me sharply.

'Unfortunately, that would require me to disappoint your sister and there's no way in hell I'm doing that.'

'Whatever, dude. Just leave.'

'Don't call me "dude".'

'Did you hear what he just said?' threatens the younger one, Sameer, the little boy. 'Now leave!'

It makes me laugh.

'Dude, please leave,' says Gaurav. 'I don't want anything to do with that family. I told them that a hundred times. They need to leave me alone.'

'You mean the family who raised you, made sacrifices for you? You have to think this through, Gaurav. Just call Aanchal.'

He rolls his eyes at me and responds angrily. 'That's such a cliché, Daksh. Which family doesn't make sacrifices? Literally, everyone. They couldn't have left me on the side of the road, could they? Big deal. And what are you doing here?'

'Because I have a crush on your sister, always had. So if you are making her unhappy, that's a less-than-ideal situation for me.'

'You still have a crush on her?'

'Do you have a problem with that?'

'Vicky might have. She's still with him.'

'That doesn't change anything,' I say. 'But on a side note, I do think what you're doing is pretty cool. According to Reddit, the way you manipulate creep equilibrium and adapt your item builds is top-tier DotA play. So yeah, congrats on that'

'You . . . you think what I'm doing is cool?'

'I'm a gamer without talent, Gaurav. So, of course, I think what you do is cool.'

I show him the screenshots of the best comments on his gameplay on various Reddit threads. 'Reddit thinks you're the next big thing, but I was the one who spotted you, remember?' I point out. 'I remember how you rocked Elastico in FIFA like it was child's play. And you were a child.'

His face softens. 'Even if I meet Didi, they wouldn't get it.'

'Did you hear that?' Sameer butts in. 'Now get out, Uncle—'

I turn towards him and bend down to meet his eye. 'I'm going to break your arm and shove it up your asshole. Good luck gaming with one hand.'

'Sameer, go home,' Gaurav instructs him and he scurries away, grumbling.

I step towards Gaurav. 'Look Gaurav, running away is not an option. They don't care that you stole. Even I didn't care that you stole. You know why? Because you deserved that Nintendo more than I did. Now, all you need to do is show them you can make something out of gaming. That it's worth it.'

He shakes his head. 'They won't—'

'Stop being negative,' I cut him. 'And don't kill my vibe. My one-legged, clinically depressed father got up this morning, smiled and is taking his daughter to school, so literally anything can happen today. So now, show me your set-up and what you're doing to make this a legitimate thing.'

Gaurav leads me to the bedroom that he has converted into a gaming hub. Multiple glowing PCs are stacked, cables are managed neatly, screens beam images of games, tutorials. Gaurav is the team leader of their gaming group, Phoenix Rising, a gaming team that specializes in *War of Worlds*—a multiplayer RPG, *DotA* and *Counter-Strike*. Unlike what I had imagined—he would be living in filth—it's like an organized military bunker.

There's no TV. No filth.

'You own the team?'

'Daksh—'

'You call me Daksh or dude or bro one more time and I am going to throttle you. Call me Bhaiya.'

He shrinks and nods dutifully. 'Bhaiya, I own the equipment, the house rental is in my name. My team members can't afford these . . .' he points at the set-up. 'So they come here and we train here.'

'Is your team any good? Because in the games you're playing, you're only as good as your team.'

'Bhaiya, I can't afford good players. They will take too much out of the winnings if we win any,' he explains. 'So I'm training them to be good. They will get there.'

'Smart,' I tell him. 'Never thought I would use that word for you.'

'You don't even know me.'

'I know that you dive-tackled a lot in FIFA when you last played. Dribbled too much, played the same plays . . . That's not an experience problem, that's a gamer problem. I hope you have fixed that,' I tell him. 'Do you have a YouTube channel?'

Gaurav shakes his head.

'You need to have a YouTube channel, multiple social media accounts and their back-ups, a company on paper where you're the owner. You need to register that name too. How can you not know all of this?'

He nods distractedly. I notice he's elsewhere. 'How's Didi?' he asks softly. All the bravado about not caring about his family is now gone. I can see he misses them terribly.

'We're going to see her. We will go see her and then get her here to see you're serious about this stuff.'

21.

Aanchal Madan

It hasn't even been a year and yet it feels like Gaurav was lost at sea and is returning to me after a decade. He looks skinnier, haggard, but happier than the last time I saw him. He was probably the only person who wasn't happy on his first day of college. He carried that morose expression and funereal gloom through the three years he studied there. Deep dark circles appeared behind his spectacles, and he spoke less and less. He never scored well, talked little and spent most of his time on his laptop. And yet, his running away came as a shock to us. I never thought he had it in him. He was just . . . my little brother. Sometimes there's a very fine line between courage and foolishness.

Vanita and I are in the auto following Daksh's scooter to where Gaurav lives now. It's strange and borderline terrifying to know that he lives all on his own. All these years, he had needed us for everything.

'I can't believe Daksh found Gaurav quicker than I did,' grumbles Vanita. 'Guess sex is a greater motivator than friendship.'

'That argument goes against you. The only reason Gaurav was talking to you was . . . well,' I point out. 'And in Daksh's case, he's not getting sex. He didn't go find him because . . . you know . . . sex.'

'After what you have been through, you should be fucking every hot guy between here and Delhi,' she says, winking. 'But tell me something, between Daksh finding Gaurav for you and me getting rid of Vicky, what would you rate higher?'

'If you murder someone, I have to come and help you chop the body up.'

Vanita laughs. 'But did you hear Gaurav call me Vanita? It's the weirdest thing, him being in love with me.'

'It's the weirdest thing him being in love with anyone. I thought he wasn't into . . . people.'

Vanita chuckles. 'But speaking of sex . . .'

'We are not speaking of sex.'

'You've got to thank him somehow. And after what he has gone through, I mean, the least he deserves is sex with someone he has literally worshipped for four years!'

'Are we going to be those people who talk about nothing but boys?'

'First of all, Daksh is not a boy and—'

'And second of all,' I interrupt. 'You know when Vicky hit you with that plate, I just . . . just . . . had this epiphany, a realization. It just struck deep in my heart.'

'By the way, he could never have hurt me unless I allowed it,' says Vanita. 'We needed that for the video.'

'That doesn't matter. I just saw what was at stake. I . . . I . . . couldn't believe that I could get myself in a situation like that, that I could accept living like that. You getting hurt, me living my entire life with no freedom and just . . . hate. I just knew that was the end of it.'

'End of what?'

'I'm never, ever giving up my freedom again,' I declare.

'What does that even mean?'

'Boys or men or whatever, I'm done with it. I can't do this any more. Never again, I swear to god. There's no chance!'

'Everyone says that at the end of a bad relationship. It will pass.'

'It wasn't a bad relationship. It felt as if I had left my life to be someone else. So many years just lost, Vanita. Can you imagine all that I could have done had he not controlled all that I did?'

'I kept telling you this,' says Vanita. 'You were stuck.'

'And this is the end of it. Decided, 100 per cent. I want to control every aspect of my life. I'm never making this mistake again.'

'But if you keep painting the world in the same shade of someone toxic, you will never connect with anyone.'

'You can say whatever, but this is, what I feel right now, I can't even describe it to you. It feels like someone had stepped on my chest, and finally, I have gotten rid of that foot.'

'That foot was gangrene, you have cut it off. Not everyone—'

'I can finally take a deep breath. It's been, like what, four years that I have been walking on eggshells, constantly thinking about what's going on in Vicky's mind. What will Vicky think if

I do this? Will he get angry? Is his mood off? Why is he talking like this? I just obsessed over every mood of his and . . . and I tired myself out. I kept trying to control what I couldn't control. How could I control Vicky's emotions when he couldn't do it? I gave myself so much anxiety just obsessing and being scared over his future reactions. It was horrible. Even now I'm thinking, I'm in this auto, I should tell him so that he doesn't create a scene later. I have aged just doing all this for years. There's no way I can do this again. I can't spend any more time being angry or anxious about someone. I don't have the capacity to do this. I just want to be me for a while.'

Vanita hugs me. 'I feel you,' she says as she separates. '. . . but all I'm saying is I saw Daksh's face light up like a Christmas tree when we told him you have broken up with Vicky.'

'Did you see how angry he got when we told him about what happened?'

'Scary. He could have popped a blood vessel in his eye,' says Vanita. 'You shouldn't encourage him if you have planned to you know . . . not consider any guys.'

We reach Gaurav's place.

'This is where I live, Didi,' he says nervously as he opens the door.

He fidgets with his spectacles, waiting for me to react. An hour ago, Daksh came to me with Gaurav in tow and insisted we see how Gaurav is living and what he's trying to build. I always thought I would scream at Gaurav when I saw him. But the moment I did, my heart melted. I forgave him for everything, but how could I have shown it to him? I didn't want him to destroy his life playing games. And so, I maintained my anger.

'Hmmm.'

I put up an angry front when all I want to do is hug him.

His apartment is a lot cleaner than I imagined it would be. There are no Old Monk bottles rolling about, no plastic containers with dried food, no Coke cans. The room is a far cry from how he used to live back home—like an animal. He's a changed boy.

The room is lit up in RGB lights from CPUs and keyboards. There's a dull hum around.

'It was hard to live like that, Didi,' he mumbles.

'When has it not been hard for us, Gaurav?' I scold him. 'Our lives have been a hurdles race, just one thing after another and just when we were at the finish line, you ran in the opposite direction. You could have stayed.'

'Aanchal,' Daksh interrupts, 'maybe he shouldn't have run away. But I can give it to you in writing that none of his classmates are as serious as he is about his career.'

'You mean his classmates who will have a college degree within a year?'

'He's driven, Aanchal. Surely, you can recognize that. He's like a horse with blinkers on, like you were. Who cares if his finish line is different from his classmates?'

'Does this . . .' Vanita waves at all the PCs on the table. 'Can you earn money from this?'

'A lot of money, Vanita,' answers Gaurav shyly.

He hasn't been able to meet Vanita's eyes even once. It's also the first time he's not addressing Vanita as *Didi*. It's weird.

Daksh cuts in. 'It's a serious attempt.'

Daksh takes Gaurav's phone from his hand and hands it over to me.

'Check his phone. The alarm is set for 6 a.m. That's when he gets up to train. No social media, nothing, just relentless gaming. All he needs to do is play his cards right. A streaming channel, a mysterious persona, some merchandise, an active but managed social-media presence. With his work ethic, he can really make something out of this. All I'm saying is, take him to Delhi and tell your parents that it's going to work out for him. He will need all the support. Shouldn't he get that from you guys? His family? Where else would he turn?'

I turn to look at Gaurav. He has teared up. My heart breaks a little to see my little brother helpless, lost at sea, alone. He looks at me, hopeful.

'Oye *buddhu*,' I tell Gaurav. 'I have a flight in four hours. I will see you at the airport. Let's tell Maa–Papa their son is a . . . gamer.'

22.

Daksh Dey

'Tell me what Uncle–Aunty say,' says Vanita, getting into a cab. 'And thanks, Daksh. Next time be less oversmart and let me do things for her.'

'If it's coming down to how far you will go for Aanchal, you will never beat me,' I tell Vanita.

'Boys and their overconfidence,' she smirks. 'We will see.'

'Can you guys stop?' asks Aanchal.

'No.'

'No.'

'I love you,' Aanchal tells Vanita.

'I should go now,' says Vanita and gets into the cab.

She waves as her cab leaves the hotel porch. Aanchal and I come back to the hotel. Inside the lobby, there are long lines again. Everyone who came for the conference is now checking out.

'I should be leaving too,' says Aanchal. 'I'm late.'

'Yes, you should. I don't want you to though. I just . . . don't.'

'Will you make me wait four years for a call?'

'I won't.'

She steps forward for a hug. I know I wouldn't want to leave her if I take her in my arms. When I do, I feel a rush of energy course through me. After all, that bastard Vicky's gone, that chapter is over. Between last night and now, the possibilities have brightened. I don't want to rush her, but of course, I want to rush her because it's been four long years. I feel like I'm one of those rishis who meditate and pray for what they want for so long that tree roots wrap themselves around their bodies. So yes, I feel like rushing her.

'Thank you, Daksh,' she says with a bright smile. 'You still are my lucky charm.'

'Glad to be of service.'

'I will have to go now.'

'If you have to.'

She turns and walks towards the lift. I turn towards the exit. Every yard between us feels like a physical ache. I watch her disappear inside the lift. I'm at the hotel entrance, phone in my hand, the cab application open. I can't get myself to book a cab.

I can't deceive myself any more. She's not a crush. How can she be when she was the beacon of hope while I was drowning? When all seemed lost?

It's fucking corny but she's my faith, she's my truth.

I look at her and it feels as if I'm in the house of God. It may seem dramatic, but she makes me feel that way. Every part of me surrenders to her. I'm helpless, powerless, and all I want to do is please her. She makes me want to rip out every part of my life and lay it at her feet.

It's like she's the reason for my being.

Every smile is like a solar flare, and every frown brings with it dark clouds, doubt, despair. She's the one holding my strings, my heart is in her palm. It's like I'm a limp tattoo doll in her hand. Even if she chooses to destroy me, I'd accept that fate happily. None of what I feel is rational. It's nuts. My feelings can't coexist with reason and logic. As I stand here, in the hotel, I want the world around us to burn down so we are stuck here, in this hotel, to live out an eternity. I don't want to go, I don't want her to leave.

My phone beeps.

Aanchal
Where are you?

Daksh
Still at the hotel.

Aanchal
Why?

Daksh
Couldn't get myself to leave. You done with the packing?

Aanchal
Coming down now. Don't leave.

Daksh
How can I?

She emerges from the lift, toting a laptop bag, lugging a suitcase. I run to help her.

'I'm glad you didn't leave,' she says, a smile on her face, sweat on her brow.

We get into the check-out line. We are fourth. As we step forward, she steps closer to me. The proximity of her body to mine makes my throat dry. There are things I want to tell her, but words swirl around in my mind, making it impossible for me to construct a sentence.

She's no longer Vicky's. She could be . . . mine? Her body could be . . . mine?

I watch the rise and fall of her chest, her lips parting and closing. And a deep desire for her unfurls inside of me. As the line moves forward, I tap her waist to make her move, but I cannot take my hand away. I let it rest on her back. She looks up, blinks and lets it rest there.

Fuck.

My hand against her waist, only a flimsy T-shirt separating us. From a touch, I ever so slightly press my fingers against her waist. She catches my eye and says nothing.

Either stop me now or don't stop me at all.

She steps closer to me, her leg brushes against mine, her eyes meet mine in affirmation.

We move another spot ahead in the line. She moves even closer to me. My hand moves to the far side of her waist. She pushes into me, her soft body against mine. When she looks up, we are breathing the same air. Another spot moves up. We are at the counter. The front desk person asks for a key.

She turns to me. 'It's in my back pocket,' she says softly.

No.

I take my hand off her waist and push it down the back pocket of her jeans. She pushes her ass out to meet my hand. I slowly take out the key. I can barely hear the front desk girl over my own laboured breathing.

'The hotel transport is waiting outside,' the girl says.

As we move out of the line, I take my hand off her. I'm no longer touching her and it makes me furious. How dare her body not be touching mine?

'Mezzanine floor,' I tell her.

'Take me.'

23.

Daksh Dey

I walk towards the lift. She follows. She presses the lift button. A stream of people exits. We enter the lift and slam the close button.

It's just us.

She turns, I march towards her. Our bodies meet with the fever of a thousand suns. I hold her by the neck. Her eyes are pure thirst.

The lift door opens to the mezzanine floor. I hold her hand, she clutches mine tightly. Time is our enemy. I want her, and I want her now. We walk towards the washrooms no one uses. We enter the Men's and close the door behind us.

She's facing me now. She steps a few paces away. What's in the air is electric. It's terrifying. It's like realizing only you have something that the world wants.

'Take off your shirt,' she orders.

I start to unbutton it.

As I do, she takes a few steps forward. And then unbuttons the last of them impatiently. Our breaths echo in the empty, quiet washroom. She traces her fingers on my chest, sending jolts down my spine. I hold her face, she grips me. I draw her close and her lips touch mine. At that moment, I feel I'm losing myself in her. Her lips envelop mine and mine hers, and in the warmth and the wetness, the world around me disappears. It's like her lips are the last refuge and I will spend the rest of eternity here. She slips the shirt off me. I can't let go of her lips. We get hungrier. I let my hands drop to her waist.

'I hate your clothes, get rid of them,' I whisper. 'Get naked.'

'I thought you'd never say that,' she moans.

I slip her T-shirt off. She unsnaps her bra and it's now lying on the floor. Her nakedness sends shivers down my entire body. I grab at the button of her jeans and she grabs mine. I unbutton her, unzip. She struggles with mine. Her touch electrifies my entire being. And then instead, she lets her hand slip down. She grabs my dick and starts rubbing it through my jeans. I pull her jeans down. She steps away from me. She looks at me, eyes aflame, and starts to wiggle out of her jeans.

'I want to see your dick,' she groans.

I unbutton, unzip.

We are both naked.

I take in all of her. The curve of her breasts, the flatness of her stomach, the shape of her legs, the slenderness of her fingers as she traces down to her wetness and touches herself. Her eyes half-close. When they open she meets my eyes and then her gaze falls to my dick, which is throbbing.

'I like that,' she says.

'It's yours.'

I step forward. She grabs me by my hardness and pulls me closer. She kisses me sloppily and then pushes me down. My tongue traces her ridges and curves. I'm blinded by my want of her body. I want it all. I take one breast into my mouth, licking, circling and flicking her nipple with my tongue. Her moans encourage me.

'Do you want me to be gentle?' I ask.

She's pulling at my hair, she's pulling at my erection.

'Be the opposite of gentle, Daksh,' she says.

My jaw tightens around her nipple. She moans harder. I kiss her again, this time she's even hungrier.

'I fucking want all of you,' I tell her.

She looks at me. 'All of me is yours,' she responds. 'Take all of me.'

I pick her up. Her arms are around my neck, her legs wrapped around me, my erection rubbing against her wetness. I carry her to the sink. She sits there. The mirrors in the bathroom reflect our nakedness, our craving, back at us.

'I didn't know I wanted this,' she whispers.

I pry her legs apart. She watches in the mirror as I disappear between her thighs. My tongue touches her. She's soaking wet. I bite her thighs. She groans, her body shudders. As my tongue enters her, as I taste her, I hear her gasp. In the mirror, I watch as she grabs her breasts. She grabs at my hair when I flick her. She crosses her legs around my face. I feel them tighten and clasp. I feel them shudder.

Fuck, she mumbles.

She unclenches her feet. She pulls my face away from her. She pushes me away, a smile on her face.

'I thought you were a nice guy, Daksh,' she says with an impish smile. 'I'm so happy you're not.'

'My niceness is selective,' I rasp.

'I want you,' she says and drops down on her knees. She takes my erection and looks at me. 'Choke me,' she orders. 'Don't be nice.'

She opens her mouth. I watch myself disappear in her mouth. Slow at first, and then deeper. I hold her head and push her into me. I feel her tongue all over me. My grip becomes tighter. I look down at her and she's still looking at me with her seductive eyes. She takes me out, wet and sloppy.

'I want to be inside you,' I tell her.

She wipes her mouth and with a smile says, 'That's a surprise.'

'I will wipe that smile right off your face,' I point out.

'I'm counting on that,' she says.

She grabs me and pulls me closer. I grab her thigh and hike her leg up, rubbing against her. *Fuck*, she moans as I guide myself inside. Her warm wetness surrounds me. My brain explodes. I thrust and our breaths become ragged.

'Daksh—'

Her moan is rudely interrupted.

We hear a loud bang. And then one more. The banging of the door is now loud and is echoing in the bathroom.

'Fuck,' I say.

I step away from her.

'WHO IS THERE?' a loud voice booms from the outside.

I run, grab hold of Aanchal's clothes and throw them to her. 'That stall,' I instruct.

'OPEN THE DOOR!'

24.

Aanchal Madan

We are in the office of the managing director of the Marriott, BKC.

'I thought it would be bigger,' I tell Daksh.

Daksh frowns. 'I'm going to pretend I didn't hear that.'

'Not you,' I correct myself. 'This office. I thought a managing director's office would be bigger. You're . . . just the right size.'

'Thank god for natural selection, then,' he says.

'Should we be more nervous about the police coming?' I ask him because I feel none of the nervousness.

My mind is still in that washroom, still wondering what could have happened had that stupid front desk manager not banged at the door. My body is burning with what we left halfway. If we weren't waiting for the police to decide what to do with us, I would ask Daksh to throw me to the ground and take me right here.

Daksh shrugs. 'Why should I be nervous? I'm going to tell them the truth. That you're a slut who seduced me.'

At this moment, anything Daksh says makes my body react in ways I didn't think was possible.

'I like being a slut to you,' I answer.

And I can see the effect of my words on him. He wants to step away from his chair and take me again. Finish what we started.

'You should treat me like one,' I egg him on. I point to the table in front of us. 'You should push me against this table and ram into me. You should pull my hair—'

'Stop it, Aanchal.'

'Would you not want to grab my breasts as I part my legs and invite you even deeper?'

'Please, stop,' he says, his breath ragged.

I stop not because he wants me to stop. I like him like this: a bit out of control. I stop because I can't be this much out of control. My body feels as if it's his to take: wherever, whenever, however.

'We should stop talking,' he orders.

And I listen. He closes his eyes and tries to calm down. It doesn't help. I can see his bulge from where I'm sitting. I close my eyes because I don't want to struggle for breath any more. We sit in silence for ten minutes or more. I feel the air a little less charged, my body more in the present, my mind a little rested. When I open my eyes, he's looking at me.

'Aanchal.'

'Daksh.'

'What are we going to be?' he asks, his voice deeper than I have ever heard before.

'What do you mean?'

'What will we be now?'

It's not an empty question. When I look at him closely, I realize he has the answer to the question. I let the question rest in the air. I hope it will dissipate on its own. The kind of question that doesn't need an answer. But Daksh's eyes are resting on me, waiting. Like he has always been waiting.

'What do you mean by that, Daksh?' I ask, a part of me scared at the depth of his sincerity.

He turns his chair towards me and leans forward. 'What I feel for you is not a crush, maybe not even love but something far greater.'

'Daksh . . . I . . . do we really need to talk about this?'

'I know what it is.'

'Is all this . . . too early? I just . . .'

'It's been four years, and I know I will spend every single moment of my life obsessing over you. I don't think I have ever wanted anything else in my life as much as I have wanted you.'

'You don't even know me, Daksh.'

'I know enough. And everything I have done, everything I have been through, it ends with you. It all led me to you. As cheesy as it might sound to you, and trust me, it sounds the same to me, but you're the destination, you're the home I had been looking for. I have been made for Aanchal. You're . . . you're my purpose.'

'Daksh, that's a bit—'

'Aanchal, I love you.'

'Daksh—'

He reads in my eyes what I haven't said yet. He knows what's in my heart.

'Aanchal, I really do.'

'Daksh,' I mumble. 'You know I can't. I . . . I can't.'

'Aanchal.'

'Daksh, I'm sorry. I can't give you what you're looking for. I . . . just can't.'

Just then, the door opens and the managing director walks in with two constables. I watch the sadness on Daksh's face reappear once more. But I know this time my heart won't rule my mind.

I can't.

PART 3
THREE YEARS LATER

1.

Daksh Dey

'Bhaiya, yaar,' Gaurav protests. 'Why are you not coming?'

I ignore the question just as I have for the last twenty times he has asked me.

'Both Aanchal's and your clothes are marked according to the functions—cocktail, wedding, reception,' I remind him. 'Give me a couple of picture options. And, of course, don't tear them, drop anything on them or lose them. We have to give them all back.'

'Bhaiya, please come, no. We will both travel first class. My treat!'

Gaurav's immaturity seems to grow with each passing year. He's becoming more like the thirteen-year-old mad fans who idolize him. I ignore his wasteful and unaffordable offer, knowing that if I let him loose with his credit card, he'd quickly amass a debt larger than some small island nation's.

'Listen to me, Gaurav. You're allowed to lose everything but your passport. There are a bunch of events lined up and you can't afford to be stuck there. There's team practice too. There are radical changes in the new Fortnite. I have made a list of pain points.'

He nods distractedly. Then, his face contorts into a pathetic, sad-puppy expression he has been making since the day Vanita announced her wedding.

'I can't believe I'm going to watch Vanita get married to that bastard!'

'It's absolutely believable because you're an idiot. And don't give me shit about closure. You guys had nothing. All this drama for nothing. You can still choose not to go.'

'It's not—'

There's only so long you can argue with a wall. 'Don't get too drunk or kiss someone in public. It's all illegal there and you can't bribe your way out of jail,' I warn him.

Gaurav has just started to drink occasionally, often without my permission, hidden from me, breaking our pact. Gamers expire young. By the age of twenty-four, reaction time dulls, rendering them uncompetitive. Alcohol and drugs speed up that process. To counter that, we crafted for Gaurav a social-media persona so he could extend his career and didn't have to rely on championship wins. But even then, he needs to be sharp and game as if his life depends on it.

'That's why you should come with me, Bhaiya,' he pleads. 'Listen, Bhaiya, we will be at our hotel. You don't have to meet Didi. I won't even tell her you're there. Please, Bhaiya.'

I ask the porter to start walking with Gaurav's trolley.

'I will miss you, Bhaiya.'

'Get a fucking haircut.'

He's convinced man-buns are cool thanks to his Instagram fans. One of these days I'm going to take garden shears to it. Gaurav hugs me. It's still as weird and squirmy as the first time. It was right after our team, Phoenix Rising, won its first major gaming convention, which put us on the map as the rising stars in the Asian gaming scene.

'I love you, Bhaiya.'

I love him, too, but of course, I'm not going to scream it out at an airport.

'Do you want me to say something to Didi?' he asks me with a wink.

And because he knows what I'm going to say, he slaps his big headphones over his ears.

'Ask her to fuck off,' I tell Gaurav. 'Tell your sister that she's the worst person in all of history and I hope every day of her existence is the pure definition of torture.'

He waves and follows his porter into Delhi International Airport. A group of adoring fans, none of them older than twenty, spot him and flock around him, showering him with praises. They whip out their phones for pictures. He obliges everyone with a smile and a hug. Apart from his gaming skills— unmatched in Asia—it's also his way with his fans that make him as popular as he is. Within minutes, his Discord group comes alive.

Gaurav Madan spotted at Delhi Airport!

My phone explodes with notifications from Gaurav's social-media accounts. The DMs pour in, begging for autographs, meetups and offers to give Gaurav blowjobs. Gaurav remains oblivious, having been absent from Instagram for over a year.

The last thing he needs is distraction. He's prone to getting addicted to the siren calls of social media, spending hours on it if it's on his phone. We made an executive decision to cut him off, cold turkey.

As team principal and part owner of Phoenix Rising Gaming, it's up to me to manage his—and the team's—online presence.

At the gaming conferences overseas, other team managers tell me I have done a great job building the team into a recognizable brand. Gaurav likes to credit his success to me as well, which is an overstatement because, at the end of the day, he's the one with the keyboard and the game plans.

But there's one person who thinks I'm a parasite, a bloodsucking leech sucking on Gaurav's flesh.

Aanchal.

Aanchal argues that Gaurav, the premier gaming prodigy, can throw a stone in a crowd and find someone who can manage the team. But then again, no one will take her accusation of me being selfish seriously after what she did to me and to us. She's quite literally the most selfish person ever.

* * *

The office of Phoenix Rising Gaming—of which Gaurav and I are part-owners—is situated in Netaji Subash Place, on the seventh floor of Mata Rani Building. On most days, the elevator is out of order, and we're forced to trudge up seven flights of stairs to reach our damp, windowless office. We have three people in accounts, two in post-production, not including the four team members of Phoenix Rising, and myself. We skimped on the rest of the office so we could splurge on the gaming room, the centrepiece of our office where Gaurav and his team spend up to sixteen hours a day honing their skills on top-of-the-line gaming equipment and recording live streams for the online channels. The rest of us sit at a long table facing the gaming room. It's a cramped, no-frills office that would never win the Best Workplace Award, but it works for us. Right next to the gaming room, we have a tiny podcast studio which we rent out to podcasters. It's a small but steady revenue source.

As I arrive at the office, Amruta Thakur is already in the podcast studio hooking up podcast microphones to her laptop. She's in a zipped-up black Nike windcheater and black tights. Inside the windcheater, I know she's wearing a black sports bra. She calls it her 'uniform to tackle the day'. She owns multiple, all bought in sales. She owns nothing else except three dresses, one dangerously small for an occasional wild night, one that's business-like and one that's perfect for a red carpet, all in black. She insists that wearing black is the only defence against stains. As a mother of two boys, she knows about stains. Her eight-year-old twin sons, Naman and Nishant, two of the most well-behaved, sincere, obedient boys I have ever come across, now copy her, refusing to wear anything but black Nike athleisure.

I had stumbled on Amruta's podcast six years ago when I had first moved to Mumbai with Rabbani and my depressed father.

The connect was instant.

Amruta Thakur was a twenty-one-year-old with one-year-old twin(!) boys(!) whose husband unexpectedly died of a heart attack. She was living with her parents, two bawling kids and a shattered view of the future. She had recorded her first podcast on her phone as a way to vent about life, about her husband who ate and drank too much and died too soon.

Her podcast was at once heartbreaking and funny and relatable. Her voice, a gentle balm on my frustrations of having to raise Rabbani. It was as if she was whispering in my ears, 'It's okay, everyone fucks up.' 'You forgot to pack her lunch? It's okay! Everyone fucks up.' 'You shouted at your child, it's fine, everyone fucks up, but don't do it again.'

Then, suddenly, she stopped doing the podcast.

A year ago, when we added the podcast studio in our office to get more out of the post-production guys we had hired, Amruta was the first person I contacted despite her having not recorded a single podcast in three years. I found her teaching history as an assistant professor, and she was confused as to who I was and why I would want her to get back into podcasting.

'No one listened to my podcast, except my kids,' she told me when I met her in her tiny office where there was only space for her table and books. 'They listened to it and they were like "Stop complaining about us!" So yes, there's no chance of me doing it again.'

It took me three months to convince her to get back into podcasting. It took her three months to convince me that I should be part of the podcast too.

'Ready?' Amruta asks me.

I check the levels on her laptop, adjust the gain and pull the microphone towards myself.

'Welcome back guys! I'm Daksh . . .'

'. . . and I'm Amruta! And welcome to our podcast, *Kids Raising Kids*! Where two accidental parents discuss their parenting goof-ups and hope you do better!'

She reaches out for my hand. I hold hers and feel the warmth radiate through me. It's been eight years since her husband died. When I first met her, her skin was lighter where there had once been a wedding band. Time has filled colour in it. As I caress her finger, I wonder if I should put a ring on it.

2.

Aanchal Madan

'WHERE ARE YOU!' Vanita screams right into the phone.

'I'm on the airport floor, bleeding from my ear.'

'I'm outside! Come quickly! I can't be picking up people at my own wedding.'

'I told you I will take a cab,' I protest. 'And I'm not coming out without getting alcohol. If you're really going through with this wedding, I'm not watching it sober.'

'Stop wasting my time and run, Aanchal! Everyone has already brought alcohol, yaar.'

'I'm buying gin and a little vodka. Is there anyone for whisky?'

Vanita sighs heavily into the phone. 'Bring a bit of everything,' she concedes. 'So, there will be a signboard saying Dubai Airport Taxi Stand . . . I am on the road next to it. Quick, quick, run faster. Bye!'

My work phone vibrates in my pocket. Despite a three-week notice for this holiday and multiple warnings, my team is escalating everything to me like little kids. Some of the hires are my fault—I recruited them straight out of management schools thinking they would be skilful. All they have is a degree. Looking at them makes me happy that I didn't waste two years in a management college learning marketing jargon that is as useless as climate change protests in China. I record a voice note for the office messaging group.

'YOU GUYS ARE ONE MORE MESSAGE AWAY FROM SHITTY APPRAISALS! NO. MORE. MESSAGES!'

Last week, I received a stern e-mail from HR. Apparently, I was being 'too friendly with the juniors', and that 'can backfire if one of them complains'. I delete the voice note even though I don't have to. I'm on my notice period after five amazing years at the start-up. In the last five years, DeliverFood has given me everything: fast-track success, but stress so bad I don't remember what it's like not to have a headache; bosses who have grabbed my ass at off-sites but other bosses who have picked up my slack and taught me everything I know; some friends, some assholes, experience, a rich CV, hair fall and a ton of savings. In the spirit of gratitude, I instead send the team a mail. Because I need one last favour from DeliverFood: a glowing letter of recommendation.

> Dear Team,
> As you would appreciate, I'm on leave and unable to respond to any work calls. I will prioritize all concerns the day I'm back.
> Regards
> Aanchal Madan
> VP, Marketing, DeliverFood

'LATE!' screams Vanita happily as she hugs me.

She's gotten fitter for the wedding, which is saying something because she's anyway always been all muscle and no jiggle. It's like hugging a granite sculpture of her and not her. I can't help but feel a twinge of envy and motivation all at once. She takes my suitcase and tosses it on the backseat of a rented Mustang with ease, as if it's a plush toy and not luggage.

'You shouldn't be allowed to drive,' I tell Vanita as she zips dangerously through the impossibly wide Dubai roads and incredibly fast traffic. '. . . and all this . . . this is reckless.'

'I can drive with my eyes closed, hands tied behind my back. I have been driving since I was twelve.'

'First of all, that's bad parenting,' I point out. 'Your parents should be ashamed of themselves. And I'm not talking about driving, but your marriage. Who gets married at twenty-five?!'

She rolls her eyes. 'If you pull up all-India statistics, literally every girl in India gets married by twenty-five!'

'Girls with careers, I meant. Of all the girls in our class, how can you be the first one to get married? At twenty-five! Twenty-five!'

'To be honest, mentally I feel like I'm twenty-three.'

If getting married at this age is her first mistake, having the wedding in the peak season in Dubai is her second. I had told her she was better off setting a pile of cash ablaze. She called me Uncle Scrooge, who would die clutching wads of cash.

'We are going to make a quick stop at the tailor's, some last-minute adjustments to my *lehenga*.'

'Are you making more space for your abs to fit it?' I ask her.

'Soon I'm going to have a married-lady paunch,' she tells me.

The tailor tells us to wait for another half hour. We step out of the shop and make our way to the nearest restaurant. I reach into my bag and pull out two cans of gin and tonic from the stash I bought from the airport and wave them in front of her eyes.

'. . . and you're drinking both of them,' she points to the can. 'I have long days, can't be drunk all the time. It's my wedding, I don't want to black out and not remember anything.'

'BORING! You're already getting old!' I protest, my can already half-empty. 'Who cares if you black out? We will have videos!'

I'm not an alcoholic even though my weekend enthusiasm might lead someone to mistake me for one. But I would never drink a) alone and b) on weekdays.

But on weekends, in those fleeting moments of tipsiness, all the stress and worries dissolve into nothingness, leaving only happiness and lowered inhibitions. And I have never experienced a hangover that can't be cured with an eight-hour sleep and some spicy Maggi. My boss tells me that it's only a matter of time before age catches up and makes hangovers so bad that I will swear off alcohol entirely.

'Aditya's the handsomest guy I have ever met,' says Vanita, as if to explain this ridiculous wedding.

I have seen their pictures. Vanita looks like the hot, young sister of an uncle-ish-looking boy who works in LIC or some equally drab job.

'He's 3 inches shorter than you are and has a moustache,' I remind her. 'Hardly someone you would throw away your life for.'

'Aditya has a big, veiny dick 3 inches too long, loves me and loves his job. And stop saying I'm throwing my life away! I want to give five years to the family, have two kids quickly, then get back into corporate life.'

'I'm trying to imagine a company that would want a mother with no experience and two kids, and that company doesn't exist. This is professional hara-kiri.'

Vanita shrugs as if different rules apply to her. 'We will see about that,' she challenges. 'And if you have such a clear view of the future, where will you be after five years?'

'I could be anywhere, I could do anything. That's the best part about not getting married to some random guy,' I answer.

'One thing I know for sure, I don't want to change diapers and wait for a guy to come home to give me some attention and then crib to me about how difficult his work is.'

Vanita looks at me and smiles as if she knows some secret about life that I don't. Every person about to make a very stupid decision thinks they have cracked it.

'Aanchal, I want precisely that. Every word of what you just said. I want to hear Aditya complain. I want to crib to him about our kids whom we will call Ariana or some fancy-ass name like that. I want to talk about his work, gossip about someone in his office or my friends' circle, watch a Netflix show and then go to sleep. I want us to plan family trips, and then scream at Aditya for not having packed enough chargers, and listen to him yell at me for letting the kids play in the water for too long. We will grow fat, hate our bodies, then grow thin again. We will give each other love and anxiety and sadness and anger issues. We will want to kill each other but also love each other to death.'

Her idea of her future makes my skin crawl. I always saw Vanita as a globe-trotting, joke-cracking, dance-floor-tearing-up CEO.

'How can you want that? It sounds like you want to put your hand into a blender because you like the colour red!'

'How can you want to be a VP in Singapore? Or the US? Or Australia?' she snaps back. 'It's like God gave you 7 billion people and you choose to be alone.'

It's a faulty argument. I have people for everything—Kanika to go watch movies with, Rajat for general hangouts, Smita for shopping and Arunima for window shopping. Why would I want only one person to do everything with me?

'You're going to regret it,' I warn her. 'When you're forty and you realize your kids are spoilt teenagers who never look up from their screens and snap at you for being uncool, when your husband thinks you're no longer hot, you're going to want to go back and change everything.'

Vanita looks at me, horrified. 'You think I won't be hot at forty? C'mon.'

'That part I got wrong.'

We have been through this argument before, and it ends exactly where we started. In disagreement. And the changing of topics.

I check the time. 'Another hour and Gaurav will land. To be honest, I'm way more excited about the clothes he's getting me than your wedding.'

Vanita's eyes light up. 'All of Aditya's friends will die looking at you!' chirps Vanita. 'I can't believe you're going to wear better clothes than I will at my wedding. That's like stabbing me in the back and then twisting the knife for good measure.'

I am wearing Satya Paul, Sabyasachi and Manish Malhotra for the wedding. Gaurav, my stupid but famous brother, made that happen.

'Why aren't you my size?' she complains and exhales deeply. 'Should have got married to Gaurav, then I would be leveraging his contacts.'

'I'm surprised he's even coming to the wedding,' I confess. 'That dumbo has watched too many movies and is expecting you to cancel the wedding at the last moment and run away with him. You should have seen how much he cried when you announced the wedding. He cursed me as if it was my job to make you fall in love with him.'

She chuckles. 'Cute. But well, at least he's famous. He's coming alone, right? Daksh is not coming.'

This morning when Gaurav had confirmed that he would arrive solo, a wave of relief washed over me. The mere thought of facing Daksh one more time had filled me with dread, and I had become consumed by the fear that he would somehow ruin my dear friend's wedding. In my desperation, I resorted to my tried-and-tested coping mechanism. Days ago, I had scrawled 'Jai Shree Ram' on to my palm, determined not to let it fade until I received word that he wouldn't be attending.

'Thank God he's not coming,' I say.

'He's much better than that Rajat guy. And don't give me that nonsense that he's your best friend or whatever,' grouses Vanita. 'Two people who have had sex can never be friends.'

I open the second can of gin. I can sense the beginnings of tipsiness in my body. Vanita can believe that two people who've known each other for only six months can get married and spend the next fifty years together, but people can't be friends after having sex for a sum total of six times.

'How many times do I have to tell you that Rajat has a girlfriend? Nandini,' I tell her irritably.

Vanita swats me away like I'm some housefly buzzing around her ears. 'One has to be blind not to see how much he's into you. For the last time, Aanchal, one can't be friends with people they have had sex with.'

'Rajat's going to marry Nandini. He's just looking for the right opportunity to ask her.'

Rajat's decision is more prudent than Vanita's. Nandini, already twenty-eight, feels the weight of her parents' concern as she approaches the dreaded age for Indian women. Both Rajat and Nandini boast of an IIT education and successful careers in software, comfortably situated within the same social sphere. Unlike Vanita, neither of them has to sacrifice their ambitions in the name of matrimony.

Vanita's not convinced. 'Even if they find Nandini and Rajat's skeletons cuddling in their grave centuries from now, I'd still know he's head over heels in love with you. I bet he's picturing you when he's deep inside Nandini.'

'I think you're jealous that I have a best friend besides you.'

'I'm jealous, but I'm also sad for him.'

'Be sad for yourself. Putting all your eggs in one basket,' I remark.

'Technically, he will be putting something of his into a basket of my eggs.'

'. . .'

'My uterus, my eggs, he will be putting—'

'I got what you're saying!'

'I'm in love, Aanchal. You wouldn't know.'

I let out an exasperated sigh, my eyes rolling so far back that my pupils seem to penetrate my cerebrum. 'Been there, absolutely not recommended. Love is a trap.'

'Keep believing that and one day you will end up alone and lonely.'

'People can be in marriages, in relationships, and still be lonely. At least I will only blame myself. Anyway, I would have my best friend with me,' I say and put my arm around her. 'Who will be so sick and tired of her husband and spoilt kids, she would spend all her time with me. But . . .'

'But?'

'You will have to get a US visa for it.'

'What?'

'It's true,' I say. 'Just got the employment letter last week.'

'Don't tell me!' Vanita clasps her hands around her mouth. Then throws her arms around me. 'Bottoms up for that! Wow! I love you! I'm so happy for you!'

3.

Aanchal Madan

Aditya's waiting in the porch of the ridiculously huge Atlantis, Dubai. The ocean-themed resort—made in the colours of sand

and perched right at the beach—is teeming with people. The last I checked online, all of the resort's 1544 rooms were fully booked. Which corroborated my point about Vanita's peak-season destination wedding. Such a waste!

Aditya oozes warmth and charisma, that much is clear. He whisks my suitcase away from me, tells me when Maa–Papa arrive they will be given the room next to mine and that he's eager to introduce me to his gang—all eagerly anticipating the arrival of Vanita's stunning friend.

'We are all waiting for your brother too,' Aditya says excitedly. 'We have a PlayStation hooked up in one of the rooms. We are hoping he could teach us some of his tricks in FIFA.'

'No one cares about my wedding, apparently,' complains Vanita.

I have always felt strange about people coming to me with requests to meet Gaurav. His fan meet-and-greets are bonkers. Hundreds of people mob him and he ends up signing everything from gaming controllers to T-shirts to people's hands.

'I can never get used to people thinking that Gaurav's anything but a bumbling idiot,' I tell Aditya.

Aditya brushes me away as if he knows my brother better than I do. 'He's a star!' Aditya insists. 'His gameplay is incredible.'

'If you ask your fiancée, she will tell you that Gaurav has absolutely no game.'

Vanita chuckles.

'If I were Vanita,' muses Aditya. 'I would get married to Gaurav a hundred times over instead. Can you imagine being married to someone who games for a living?'

'You can still do that,' butts in Vanita. 'He's coming, shoot your shot.'

Aditya is relentless in his fan-boying. 'But it's not just his gameplay, which is legit out of this world. He's a funny guy. Quite sharp. Reddit threads are alight about what he says during the game streams. Absolute top stuff.'

The comments section says the same thing about Gaurav Madan in different words: you play well, but we like who you are more. He's the only gamer from the community who's followed widely by people who aren't into games. Girls who don't game call him sensitive and bright. Guys call him aspirational, crafty and an alpha. Anyone who spends some time on Gaurav Madan's online profiles comes to the same realization that he's not the usual charmless gamer with a half-developed personality of a frog in a well. Instead, he's witty, whip-smart, sensitive, aware of the world, eloquent enough to have an informed and balanced opinion on everything. On his game streams, he talks about the developing political situation in the Eastern bloc, Kashmir and Latin America with the same competence he brings to the discussion about the graphics of the new Warcraft game.

'I don't see how you guys don't see how smart he is,' mumbles Aditya disappointedly. 'He's like a freaking all-knowing Yoda in the skin of a gamer.'

Vanita and I exchange a knowing glance, for we both know the truth behind Gaurav's online personality. Gaurav hasn't morphed into a different person than he was earlier. He's driven, hardworking, courageous, but he's not even close to what his online persona shows.

That's all fake.

That persona of Gaurav Madan that his followers have fallen in love with is not the truth.

The persona isn't his.

It's borrowed.

It's constructed.

It's Daksh Dey's persona.

* * *

Every time I read a tweet, listen to Gaurav's witty remark over a game stream or see an insightful caption of his post, I am acutely aware that each and every word belongs to Daksh. Every joke, every idea, every observation is his. Gaurav is a gifted gamer, but Daksh has packaged him like an exciting product that people lapped up and loved. If I'm wearing lehengas made by Manish Malhotra, it's because Daksh made him likeable enough for hundreds of thousands of people to follow him.

We get into one of the dozens of steel and glass lifts. I don't want to talk about Gaurav any more because if you talk about him, you have to talk about Daksh. The two of them have been conjoined twins since they started working together three years ago.

I steer the conversation in a different direction.

'I don't like you,' I tell Aditya. 'She's throwing away her life by getting married to you.'

Vanita mumbles a soft 'aw' and kisses Aditya's forehead.

Aditya laughs. 'Vanita told me that. Trust me, I have tried to tell her that we should wait for a bit. But your friend wants to do all of this right away.'

'You must have brainwashed my friend. Just good sex doesn't mean a relationship will last.'

Aditya's eyes light up like a little child's. He turns to Vanita. 'You told her we have good sex?'

'No, I told her I'm getting married to a guy I have horrible sex with.'

Aditya seems to grow 3 inches taller.

We turn towards my room. I can hear the revelry that only comes from a place where a wedding party is shacking. There are shouts and laughter and teasing. Vanita swipes my room card. Aditya pulls my suitcase inside the room.

'Listen, we are all going to the poolside for drinks. You have fifteen minutes,' says Vanita.

I hand over the clanging bag of Dubai Duty-Free to Aditya. 'Then you will need this.'

Aditya peers into the bag. His face breaks into a huge smile. 'And here I thought you were serious about hating me. You're now our best friend! Now all we need to do is find a boy for you!'

4.

Daksh Dey

Amruta and I record a three-hour episode on 'How to Deal with Kids When They Swear and How to Make Them Stop,' an interesting topic, because both of us believe swear words, such as 'fucking', 'behenchod' and 'madarchod', have practical use in daily life. Most of the advice we give on our podcast is stolen from articles, books and what we hear in other podcasts. We can't be trusted with our own advice and we warn our listeners multiple times in each podcast that we are 'accidental parents'. Sometimes, we are so unoriginal that we think we are fraudsters earning money by summarizing various sources.

'You're very funny during the recording. I hate it when you're funny,' complains Amruta. 'Now our mail ID will be full of Daksh! *You're so cute*! messages from women with unhelpful husbands.'

'Look who's talking,' I respond. 'You have the most number of marriage proposals per mail. You can choose to be married to a thousand men at the same time.'

'A legitimate nightmare,' she says with a chuckle.

Almost every mail in our podcast-only-mail is addressed to Amruta and comes from a very specific type of man. We have narrowed down the profile. A mid-forties divorced (very occasionally widowed), polished man, with plenty of money that has been earned from a management job/software, father of at least one kid, a wife who's no longer in the picture.

Amruta has a deep, husky voice and sounds like someone in her early forties, or at least in her mid-thirties. Despite her reminding everyone that she had her kids early, everyone tends to forget she's only twenty-six. Sometimes, even I forget she's only twenty-six. She doesn't look a day over nineteen. That she's 5'1" and has a round face makes her look even younger.

Sometimes I, too, forget I'm twenty-five.

But *we feel old* when we look at others our age. People our age are still doubled over in front of clubs, vomiting their insides out while we are ironing the kids' uniforms for the next morning. Amruta and I did a two-part podcast about 'The FOMO of Young Parents' and came to the very obvious conclusion that we want to do everything: be with the kids but also party, read books but also go on long drives, stay at home but also go on impromptu jaunts, go on solo vacations but also go on family trips, watch a kid's movie but also party with people our age. It's because of these fairly obvious, unintelligent pieces of advice that we caution our listeners not to take us seriously.

'You're getting the mathematics homework done today, okay?' Amruta warns me the third time in the past few hours.

'I . . . fine,' I mumble. 'I . . . just can't believe that they are still struggling with subtraction. How can someone—'

'Don't shame our kids,' she cuts me with a laugh.

She feels exactly the same as I do about our kids' ineptitude with numbers.

Both of us are extremely impatient teachers of math. It's unbelievable how bad Rabbani, nine, and Amruta's sons, Naman and Nishant, eight, are at mathematics. We like to tell ourselves that by the time they grow up, technology will make mathematics-related jobs obsolete and it's not going to matter. Every couple of months during the parents-teachers' meeting, Amruta and I spend twenty humiliating minutes in front of the worried class teacher of 3B, Bal Bharati School, listening to her tell us how badly Rabbani, Naman and Nishant are doing in math. The same worried class teacher gossips in her staffroom about whether something is going on between Amruta and me.

The class teacher's right.

There's something between Amruta and me. We just don't know what it is. Our lives fit in like a complex jigsaw puzzle, a tall Jenga tower. Rabbani and her sons are in the same class, we both live in Gurgaon, we both have flexible day jobs, this tiny podcast and a mid-twenties life that's not shared by a lot.

And we are both scared.

If we fit in the last piece of the puzzle and get our lives intertwined, we would be taking a decision for too many people. Her parents, my father and the kids. And that scares the living daylights out of us.

My phone rings.

'Hello . . . what . . . nonsense . . . you serious? . . . no way . . . I will see what I can do . . .'

I cut the call. Instinctively, I open up MakeMyTrip and check the next flight to Dubai. It leaves in two hours.

'Is everything okay?' asks Amruta.

'The airlines forgot to load Gaurav's luggage,' I answer. 'The next flight is in the night. If the clothes need to get there then—'

She cuts me before I can finish. 'I'm not teaching the kids, absolutely not!' she protests. 'I will let the kids fail rather than teach them subtraction,' she says.

'I would rather have an aircraft run over me than teach them.'

'I would rather walk into a turbine than teach them.'

'I would rather sit in a cargo hold and freeze to death than teach them.'

She laughs. 'We should say all of this in the podcast. Go now, leave. I will see you tomorrow.'

The immigration officer at Dubai Airport looks at me, then at my passport and then back at me. 'Used to be a resident, habibi?' he asks me in his thick Arabic accent when he spots my old residence visa.

'It took everything away from me,' I respond to him with a smile.

'Hope it's better this time. Welcome to Dubai!' he tells me and stamps my passport.

The dry air of Dubai at once feels familiar. I load Gaurav's suitcases in the boot of the taxi. 'Atlantis,' I tell the driver. 'I will come back to the airport so don't stop the trip once I get there.'

The roads of Dubai come into view. The city that chased us away.

My phone beeps.

Amruta
Are you okay?

Me
The city has changed. Thank god for that.
Every city transforms in five years. New buildings obscure the older ones. Roads are widened. More cars spill on to the road. Dubai does that faster than any city. I pass by landmarks I recognize, but most of what I remember has been painted over, built over, broken and rebuilt. It's a small kindness that this city no longer looks like the city that wrested everything away from me.

The closer I get to the Atlantis, the more uncomfortable I feel. The last thing I want is to bump into that oversmart, cold, heartless person I was once in love with. Until now I didn't realize the visceral hate I still feel for that self-centred woman. I feel it rattling in my bones.

'Don't stop the trip,' I repeat to the driver as I pull out the suitcase outside of the Atlantis. It's 6 p.m. so there's still plenty of time for the cocktails function to start.

The front desk has a long serpentine queue with tourists lugging their carry-on bags and checking if they've lost their passports.

'I'm here to drop off Gaurav Madan's luggage,' I tell the lady managing the check-ins.

'Do you know the room number, sir?' she asks.

I call Gaurav. And, as usual, he doesn't pick up the call.

'Listen, he's not taking my call. Can you call his room and inform him?'

She looks at the line behind me and is about to protest.

'They're wedding clothes, or I wouldn't waste your time,' I inform her.

She checks the room number and makes the call. She shakes her head and puts the receiver down.

'Sir, no answer,' she says. 'You can keep the luggage here and go check in the open area. Maybe you will find the guest there. That's the best I can do for you.'

'Perfect,' I tell her.

Except that it's not perfect. I should have been in my taxi, going away from this city. Not towards her, the reason I spent a couple of years in absolute misery.

After wandering through the multiple corridors, I spot the cocktail venue. *Vanita weds Aditya.* The stage is set, the lights have been turned on, the harried staff is running around shifting chairs, arranging flowers, testing the sound system. The wedding planners in black T-shirts bark instructions over their walkie-talkies. White people look on, wondering what's happening. Faint sounds of Hindi songs are in the air. I turn back and walk towards the reception.

That's when I see *her*.

Aanchal fucking Madan.

My biggest regret. The World's Worst Girlfriend.

A wave of hatred crashes upon me. I am consumed by it. It engulfs me entirely. My body sears with the heat of my loathing.

My first instinct is to turn away, to avoid her presence altogether. But I feel compelled to confront her, to release the pent-up fury that threatens to tear me apart. I want to remind her of the pain she left behind. I want to grab her and demand answers. I want to know if she regrets what she did. Was the shattering of my heart simply another task on her endless to-do list?

The receptionist is showing her the suitcases. She spots me as she's talking to Aanchal.

'There he is!' the receptionist points towards me. And then addresses me excitedly. 'I found her! I found you guys!'

Yeah, you fucking did.

Aanchal turns to look at me.

The correct course of action would be to walk towards her, point at the suitcases, nod and then walk away from her, pretending as if the weight of our history isn't suddenly weighing down on my back and breaking it.

I should remind myself that she's now a rotten, forgettable part of my life I have buried and gotten over. It's taken a part of my soul and then some to heal myself from Aanchal's rejection. If I love myself even a little, I should walk away from her. If I don't want to spend one more minute trying to ascertain what I did wrong and what I didn't have, I should run away from her. I should walk away from her, get into the taxi whose meter is still on, fly back to Amruta and complain about her mathematics teaching skills.

But my feet take me to Aanchal.

'I have your baggage,' I snarl. My entire body burns with anger. 'Take it.'

I finally muster some control and turn away from her. I walk away from her: from all the hurt and rage I brought upon myself by falling in love with her. I hear her jog behind me. I want to stop her. Ask her to go back to her life. A life I have made painstaking efforts to stay away from. I don't want to hear her, pick at the scab left by the wound she caused.

'Daksh?'

I don't answer.

'Daksh?'

My strides get longer, my chest heaves.

'It's not a race,' she tells me.

That's when I snap. I stop, turn and with the force of a thousand suns, scream right into her face. 'FUCK YOU!'

A satisfying sense of relief runs through my body. *Nice.*

'FUCK YOU,' I seethe again.

I regret not having done this earlier, when she had my heart in her palms and she had crushed it without a second thought.

'YOU ARE THE WORST FUCKING GIRLFRIEND IN THE WORLD!' I shout.

It's like therapy. Watching her eyebrows curl into a frown comforts my heart. It reminds me of all the times she gave me excuses, explanations, and I tried to find some understanding in her eyes and found garbage.

'GET THE FUCK OUT OF MY LIFE!'

She meets my eye. I try to find regret in them. I find only coldness.

'Daksh, don't leave,' she mumbles.

My eyes turn into furious pools of wetness. 'No! Aanchal, you can't do this to me.' I step closer to her. 'You can't! I can't waste another moment on you.'

'And yet here you are.' Her voice is cold and calculative. Like she's enjoying this exchange. As if she likes seeing me torn up, hurt.

My mind's raging, pure lava. 'I can't believe you. And fucking presumptuous of you to think I'm here for you. I'm here for Gaurav.'

'And why are you still with Gaurav?' I ask.

'It's my work. I would never abandon it.'

She stares into my eyes. 'You know that's a lie. Gaurav's your tenuous link to me, Daksh. If you don't work with him, our link would break,' she says with a seductive note in her voice, something she has learnt over time to add to her arsenal to make people do what she wants them to.

Her audacity doesn't surprise me any more. 'It's nothing more than work,' I growl.

I have met a fair share of selfish people in the world, but she beats all of them by a mile. I remind her of what's most important to her. 'You will never abandon your work. You will sacrifice whatever it takes for your work!'

I think she's smiling. She scoffs, 'You say it like it's an insult, Daksh. And yes, you're right. I will never abandon it.'

'Great then, fuck you, fuck your work, best of luck for your life.' I flash her two middle fingers as if I'm a high-schooler and she's my school crush. 'Fuck you, Aanchal.'

'HEY!'

A loud voice boomed from the side. We both turn. I don't see them at first with all the crowd that's gathered around us. Three policemen are marching towards us, their hands on the holsters of their guns. Before I can react, they are surrounding me and spouting angrily, 'You can't do that in here, habibi!' says a tall, bulky policeman as he grabs hold of my arm. 'You can't swear in public. You have to come with us.'

'She deserves it,' I hear myself mumble.

5.

Daksh Dey

Aanchal and I sit on opposite sides of a small glass table in a room in the hotel's business centre. I have the choicest of slurs sloshing about in my brain. The uniformed police officers are telling me that swearing in public in the UAE is a jailable offence. Unless of course, the hurt party grants pardon. I want to tell the policemen that Aanchal is indeed deserving of all the expletives I can think of and she's not the *hurt* party. If they knew our story, they would agree with me as well. They are men too. I stay quiet. My brush with UAE law has taught me that, king or pauper, the rules don't bend.

Actually, they do bend. But only for the literal king of the UAE.

Aanchal asks the policemen to wait outside. Reluctantly, with their hands on their holsters, they move outside.

'Just tell them I apologized and we can get out of each other's way,' I demand Aanchal.

She looks at me unmoved. 'I'm not going to lie,' she answers with a straight face. 'You need to apologize, Daksh. That's the only way it ends. That's what the law is.'

It's mind-boggling how big a piece of shit she is. 'Don't waste my time, Aanchal. I have had enough of these fucking games.'

'Careful, you're swearing again,' she warns me. 'And your client is in Dubai. Where do you have to go that's so important?'

'You call your brother my client rather than Gaurav? It's not syntax, it's a window to your shitty soul. Everything is a transaction.'

For the first time, I see signs of anger on her face.

'And you're the noblest boy in the world, Daksh Dey, aren't you? Step off your high horse and for once see things from other people's perspective.'

People like her don't change. Who does she think she is?

'You still have pig-headed confidence that you're right!' I try to rein in my fury. 'Listen, Aanchal. We can trade insults all night long, but I don't have the time and you have a wedding to attend.'

Leaning into her chair, she gives out a weary sigh deeply. 'Why can't you see that I had to do what I had to do? Can you please see that for once?'

My heart races like a runaway train. The policeman outside sees the anger in my eyes and steps closer to the glass.

'Aanchal, I don't want to talk to you, see you, be around you. You're a fucking stranger to me. I wish you always were a stranger.'

'Don't say that.'

I know what I'm going to say is a lie but I want to hurt her, see her cry.

'I regret the moment I met you. I would do anything to forget you and everything about you. If I could, I would burn every reminder of your existence from my life.'

She stiffens. She says with a shrug, 'Fine, then just go to jail. Then you will certainly remember me.'

'What part of "I hate everything about you" don't you get, Aanchal?'

'The part where what happened wasn't my fault.'

'How can you be so fucking dense? You broke my heart . . .' My voice trails. I could feel my heart pounding in my ears. I was choking on my own breath. 'You were all I wanted. Everything I needed in my life, you just took away. You just fucking had to ruin everything, didn't you?'

She exhales long and wearily as if it's me who ripped her soul apart and shattered her spirit. 'It's been three years, Daksh.'

'And yet it feels like my wound is as fresh as yesterday, rotting and eating everything about me. You left me a shell of who I was, Aanchal.'

'It was just a month, Daksh,' she insists, her voice now slowly rising. 'It was just a month! How are you feeling my problem!'

I force back my sadness as I promised myself I would if I'd see her any day. 'First, it was forty-three days. And if I can string together the fragments of happiness I felt in those forty-three days, they look like an eternity to me. So don't tell me that our love was governed by fucking time.'

I have imagined this conversation multiple times over the last three years. I didn't know until this moment that I wouldn't stop loving her. The sight of her is still painful, like all beautiful things are.

'We wanted different things,' she says, bringing all the hurt back instantly.

I shake my head. We didn't want different things. Her decision was based on what she wanted. There was no discussion, no chance of a compromise. She was a boulder rolling down a hill and she crushed me. I was supposed to just say yes, that's it.

'That's bullshit.'

'Daksh,' she says, her voice serious. 'I had just broken up with Vicky. I was just coming out of a four-year-old relationship which was just . . . toxic. You can't even imagine what I went through.'

'With a guy you shouldn't have been with in the first place,' I argue.

'I needed time. I couldn't get into something so quickly. Don't I have the right to freak out?'

I feel all my wounds slowly reopen. 'And I clearly told you that I would be there every step of the way. Did I or did I not tell you? I begged and fell at your feet to give us a chance and you just . . . I had been in love with you for years, and you trampled on all of it. Just like that.'

'I needed to figure out what I wanted for myself.'

'And how's that self-discovery going?'

She leans forward and fixes her gaze on me. 'Daksh, it was too much for me. I just wanted to be . . . free. I just wanted to be Aanchal for a while.'

I gather myself and fortify my heart against any more pain that she can inflict. And she can. Even after all these years, I'm a slave to her love. Even now, with every passing moment, Aanchal becomes more radiant, a flower that keeps on blossoming. But how am I to forget what's inside of her, what she did to me, what she did to us?

'You broke up, I respected that.'

She interrupts me. 'You broke up, Daksh, I didn't.'

I restrain myself. 'Who took the decision was immaterial. You pushed me to do it. You think after what you did, how you did it, I would stay with you?'

She gives a mournful chuckle as if I have said something funny.

'There was a difference between you and me, Daksh. I never promised you anything. That was all you. You always loved to say all those fancy things about forevers and sacrifices and what-not. You used to say that you would be with me no matter what. You promised you would go to hell and back with me. I never even wanted to be in a relationship! But you said you will make everything all right. That you would hold my hand, guide me out of the sadness Vicky had left me in and whatever. That was all a big lie. So, if there's one person to blame in all of this, it's you, Daksh!'

My blood pumps furiously at her accusation. She leans back in her chair. As if the executioner can be blamed for the crime. I might have ended the relationship, but she forced my hand. *She* made it impossible to be with her any more.

I concede. 'It's me. I was the problem. Fine, I agree. Can we get over this charade of a conversation and get on with our lives?'

'Our lives as in Amruta and her kids?' she asks me. 'Nice podcast by the way—'

I interrupt her. 'I don't want you in my life. I told you, no calls, no messages, nothing. I stuck to that. There's nothing between us.'

'It doesn't need to be this caustic. The least you could have done is pick up—'

'We were over. What did you want me to say after picking up your calls? That I moved on? Of course I hadn't moved on. Why would I lie just so you could be okay with your decision? You wanted to find yourself, no? Then go, fucking find yourself!'

Her eyes burn with disappointment. 'This is who you are, Daksh. Not the one who you pretended to be—the perfect, all-accepting, nice guy. You, too, made promises you couldn't keep. What's the difference between—'

'Don't compare me with Vicky.'

'I didn't want us to be anything!' she exclaims. She bends forward. 'You told me you were different from him. But you lied.'

I have reached my breaking point with her. I get up. 'I can't waste any more time with you. I'm done. So now, show some grace for once, tell those policemen about the apology and let's fuck off from each other's lives. I have lived three years without you, what's another thirty?'

She rolls her eyes. 'You were unfair then, you're unfair now.'

I let the words wash over me. 'Fine.'

But she continues with a disgusted look, 'You make yourself out to be the victim, but I was the victim because you said you were in love but you weren't. I went through years of trauma with Vicky and you did the same to me. You made me swear off love forever. Do you ever think about that?'

'I was willing to do everything.'

She tosses her head back in frustration.

'So generous, Daksh, so fucking generous. You were willing to do everything that was okay by you, not me. You wanted to be my knight in shining armour but I didn't need all that. I needed a guy who would love me the way he said he would. So with all due respect, fuck off, Daksh. You can leave.'

6.

Aanchal Madan

Up on the top floor of the Atlantis, Vanita and Aditya's presidential suite is a chaos of colour and movement. Vanita's walk-in wardrobe has turned into a makeshift beauty salon, with a squad of people fussing over her hair, make-up and outfit, and they have all made Vanita look amazing.

And despite the whirlwind of activity around me, my mind rests with him. The memories of Daksh's betrayal flood my mind and overwhelm me. I'm paralysed just thinking about them. Sometimes things so bad happen to you that once you heal, you wonder how you even bore the pain.

'Oye?' calls out Vanita. 'Get your make-up done. Only fabulous people in my wedding video.' She motions one of her girls towards my suitcase. 'Hey, can you get her clothes out and iron them carefully?'

'I will do it myself.'

'No way,' cuts in Vanita. 'You have other duties. Call in-room dining and order us some ice and set up the drinking station. I'm not reminding you again that it's my wedding. And whatever your deal with Daksh is, it can wait till later,' she says. 'But on a side note, has he gotten hotter?'

'Vanita—'

She swivels in her chair to look at me. 'I'm just saying. He looked like one of those boys who grow into men and not uncles. Did he apologize for what he did and ask you out again?'

'He told me that he hates me and would like to keep it that way,' I answer.

A girl named Parul makes me sit on the sofa and asks me to close my eyes. Then she opens her make-up kit and pumps foundation out on her palm. But to Vanita's question—did he become hotter?—unfortunately, yes. He was in a black polo T-shirt and black trousers that fit him snugly and was wearing white sneakers. That's what he wears these days. It is the attire of a coddled spoilt brat, perhaps, the kind that plays leisurely games of golf or indulges in extravagant brunches with his equally spoilt friends.

'And you? Do you still hate him?' asks Vanita. 'I need to know because I will behave with him accordingly.'

'Please hate him.'

This question has haunted me for three long years. Every time I delve into my brief relationship with Daksh, I find a new answer. But as I continue to examine those forty-three days we spent together, two things become increasingly clear.

First, I didn't fall in love with Daksh when we were together. I fell in love with Daksh after he turned his back on me and left me. Even then, I didn't fall in love with the complete version of him, but the aspects I wanted to cherry-pick. Not the whole of him, but parts of him. When we were together, despite the happiness he brought into my life, I was still too broken from my past to truly love him.

Second, our break-up was not my fault—it was his. He might claim victimhood, but the blame rests entirely on him.

'I never got to start loving him properly. He broke my heart, Vanita. After knowing everything, he . . .' I explain myself.

The make-up person carries on. I wonder how many secrets make-up people and cab drivers know about their clients.

'See, I stand by whatever you do. I also feel he's too intense, I agree,' says Vanita. 'He's not for everyone.'

'I can't believe it was just forty-three days. It just . . . seemed longer.'

'How often do you think of Daksh?' asks Vanita.

'Every day,' I say, without a second thought.

Vanita waves off the hovering make-up brush. 'Every day? For three years?'

The presence or the absence of Daksh in my life is like an interesting scar. You touch it every day, but it doesn't mean anything any more.

'Don't you think there's something there?' asks Vanita.

'Whatever is there, Vanita, I don't want it,' I say. 'You really think he would have changed now? Have you not heard his podcast with that woman?'

'You're jealous of her.'

She glances in my direction and I wave her off dismissively.

'He's obsessed about family, raising kids and what not. I don't find myself fitting in there. It was a red flag even then, I don't know how I missed it. He's twenty-six, not forty! He's too much of a . . . man.'

'Some people would say it's a massive green flag,' she argues. 'His podcast . . . is . . . sorry, not bad.'

Rajat has said the same thing about his podcast. Despite being on my side of the rink, the fact that they listen to it isn't acceptable to me.

'I'm not some people,' I remind Vanita. 'I don't want the same things you guys want. And it wasn't just that. There was Rabbani in the picture too. And his father was still recovering. How could I have wrapped myself up in the visions of his future? I mean, even now, Rabbani's just nine. He was literally a father. Being with him would have meant being like a proxy mother to Rabbani who was like . . . six.'

'He wouldn't have asked you to do that.'

'Who knows, Vanita? Who knows how boys turn out? All I know is that I should have stuck to my decision in that hotel manager's office. But no, what did I do? I let him charm me into saying yes to being in a relationship and see what happened . . . do you not see it? I was back in a relationship within . . . like . . . twelve hours of ending one!'

'Gaurav was telling me Daksh's father's now a VP in an engineering consulting firm,' says Vanita.

'Whatever, Vanita. I just don't feel I'm mature enough to do anything other than take care of myself. Not a girlfriend, not a wife, not a mother any time soon. It seems like a burden. Even you being in this bridal outfit is insane to me. I can't do it. I want to be alone.'

She looks at me as though it's a sad thing to want. But why can't I be happy on my own? Why should I have to want someone else to be completely happy? I truly am completely happy. I have freedom, I have a career, my parents are happy, my brother's doing well. Why would I throw a guy in the mix—no matter how good—and spoil it all?

'Don't you feel like sharing your life with someone?' she asks.

Every time I have been asked this question, the tone's one of pity. As if I'm missing out on something.

'I wake up, I make my tea, I spend some time with my parents, then go to work where I have the best time. I come back home or go out with office people or acquaintances, watch TV and go to sleep. I like this, Vanita. I know this is not your idea of happiness, but it's mine. I like this uncomplicatedness.'

Vanita nods, like all committed people do. And I know for a fact that every committed person wonders what it would be like to be single again.

'If that's what you wish for,' she says with a resigned sigh. 'But don't you think about how life would have been if, you know . . . you know . . .'

Vanita can't even bring herself to say it. She, too, behaves like I'm a murderer of some kind. Like Daksh does, or I'm guessing even Amruta does. When push comes to shove, everyone's minds are still stuck in the 1970s.

Even hard science won't convince them that it was not murder.

That's how I convinced myself that what I did was not only morally acceptable but also the best choice I could have made.

At thirty-five days, the only sign of a pregnancy is a 2 mm embryo inside you. It's smaller than the length of the nail of my index finger. It's a tube-like structure with blood flowing in it. It's like an artery, one extra vessel of blood.

That's it.

Even coronary arteries are bigger and thicker than this tube-like structure. I didn't want this growth in me. On the thirty-fifth day, I took a tablet just four days after I missed my period. The medicine blocked progesterone, the lack of which broke down my uterus walls. A day later, I took another medicine that helped me expel the uterus lining. The pain and the blood were not more than or less than a period which I should have gotten five days ago. It was no less clinical than getting rid of a back pain.

It was not a baby. It was not even a foetus. It was not murder. It was science.

And yet Vanita can't say it.

'Had I not got the abortion done? Just say what it was,' I tell Vanita irritably.

'I—'

'Don't you understand that I would have been miserable? Married to Daksh, with a crying two-year-old who I would have hated, and a nine-year-old Rabbani. My career would have been destroyed. Why would I want a life like that?'

7.

Daksh Dey

'I'm staying,' I inform Gaurav as I turn away from the window in his room.

'Are you serious, Bhaiya? Are you sure you're going to be able to handle it?'

I glare at him.

'Fine, fine, it's just that it's already a stressful environment with Vanita getting married and then my best friend and my sister—'

'I'm not your best friend, Gaurav.'

'C'mon! Jagath and Zeenath?' he argues. 'You can't be friends with married people! They keep telling you the same stories. They are boring as fuck.'

'Take that *kurta* off, I'm wearing that to the *sangeet*. You're wearing something else. '

I had picked for Gaurav the black *kurta-pyjama* he's wearing at the moment. We take showers, blast hot air into our hair, pat them down with wax, shave and are ready in fifteen. Gaurav's pleading all this while to drink.

'Only three drinks,' I allow him, just to make him shut up.

At his third Absolut-Red Bull, he gets chatty, irritating, and I'm already regretting my decision to allow him to drink.

'Why are you staying? What's the real reason to stay?' he asks with a stupid smile that I want to smack off his face.

Just then, the bell rings. Aditya's guy friends come streaming in, drunk, loud and full of hugs and energy. I realize I'm not drunk enough for this. For this wedding, for this happiness, for facing Aanchal. Big fans, they tell Gaurav effusively. Gaurav, who's now happy-tipsy, hugs them warmly and accepts their invitation to play FIFA after the sangeet ends. Then one guy asks, 'Hey? Do you want to join in the dance performance?'

Gaurav turns to me to ask. 'Should we?'

'Is her friend dancing? The one from Delhi, the good-looking one?' I ask Aditya's friends.

'Aanchal!' two of them squeal. 'She is!'

I see that she still has the same effect on men as she used to.

'Then we've got to beat them, don't we?' I tell them. 'Do we have enough alcohol?'

An hour later, we are in their room practising the dance moves. The more drunk they get, the better they move. I have tweaked their choreography a little, borrowing from the dance routine from Jagath and Zeenath's performance last year. I concoct a lethal shot of a third Jägermeister, a third Chivas and a third tequila and pass it around. I can see their eyes cloud over in real time. Two of the boys have named me their new best friend, 'bhai for life'. One of them has vomited, has had a fresh lime soda and is drinking again. Empty bottles of Black Label, Absolut and beer litter the tables. Everyone's remembering the girls who have broken their hearts.

'And to think of it, you weren't even coming!' says Aditya, who's on the cusp of getting too drunk for his own function.

I warn him that Aditya has had the last drink of the evening. After one final shot of Jägermeister for everyone else but him and Gaurav, we make our way to the venue.

I don't know if it's the alcohol in my system or if it's genuine, but I'm startled by how beautiful the venue is. But then again, Vanita's taste has always been impeccable. The sangeet venue—dressed in black and gold like all of us, lit up in glittering fairy lights—is small, but its elegance is beyond question. I look around trying to spot Aanchal. I relished the frustration on her face when I'd met her earlier. In that, I'd found relief.

I spot her at a distance.

She's with Vanita's friends at the bar where the bartender is tossing bottles into the air and whipping up strange-looking drinks that everyone tastes and crinkles their noses at.

Aanchal's black lehenga shimmers with gold. She looks better than I had imagined she would when I packed it in the suitcases. She has little or no make-up, or make-up that fools you that there is no make-up. She does this intentionally because she's a rank narcissist and wants to shove her raw beauty in other people's heavily made-up, Botox-ed faces. My gaze drifts to her exposed back and the tiny knot that secures her shimmering *choli* in place. Emotions of anger mix with a strange want in me. What was I thinking? That I could be with her? So what if I could love her like no one else could? There's nothing good that can come out of beauty like hers. Only pain. As her lips move while talking to a girl, all I want to do is push her against one of the fake pillars and shut her up with a kiss and let the past obliterate itself.

We walk towards the bar.

For years, I've been tormenting myself with daydreams of Aanchal and me getting married. In my mind, we've been through it all—the grand weddings in different destinations, the little *varmala* games, the stunning lehengas, the happy tears, the wild dance parties, the post-wedding orgasms and naked afternoons spent in the plunge pools in expensive honeymoon hotels. I've imagined taking her hand and promising to be with her forever, again and again, in this life and the next.

But now, seeing her like this, it's tearing me apart.

Our eyes meet, and all my anger melts away, replaced by a rush of love that I know will never be reciprocated. Loving Aanchal is like stabbing myself in the heart, over and over. It's a constant act of self-inflicting pain. Like in a cheap Bollywood flick, I want to grab her hand, take her to the *mandap*, drop a flaming lighter into the *havankund*, stride through the seven pheras, then take her to the wedding suite and take her.

The guys with me place their orders with the bartender.

'Last drink,' I warn Gaurav who walks away from his sister and me.

Aanchal notices me when she turns. The laughter dies. 'You stayed back?'

'Is it difficult for you to imagine that someone sticks around?'

'That's not a very smart clapback, Daksh. Maybe it's a good thing our relationship ended because you would have given me such weak replies all my life.'

'You don't deserve the best of me. By the way, you look stunning. It's as if I have a crush on you again like old times, but the only difference is that you're also a horrible person.'

She laughs. 'I would take you seriously, Daksh, but by now I know to take nothing you say seriously. You're clearly not a man of your word.'

I point to a girl who's at the *chaat* counter. 'That's Vanita's friend Tejal, right?' I ask Aanchal. 'The one in green? What do you think of her?'

She throws her head back in annoyance. 'Daksh, we are not seventeen. Let's not play this game of making each other jealous. Yes, she's Tejal, and if something does happen between the two of you, I will be quite happy,' she says. 'But just don't drag her into this mandap and ask her to marry you tomorrow morning. '

Talking to Aanchal is like this. Every moment is like getting my heart ripped out.

'And for the record, I'm very happy about Rajat and you too,' I tell her.

She eyes me with disgust. 'We are friends.'

'Your definition of friends is rather broad. So Rajat, apart from being the guy with whom you cheated on Vicky, is also the guy who helped you get the abortion pills because . . . let me guess . . . he also wants to sleep with you again?'

The disgust in her eyes changes to rage. 'You're a hypocrite, Daksh. Rajat, as a friend, did what you couldn't, even while saying you loved me.'

'I think I have had enough,' I say with a chuckle. 'Just wanted to hurt you a little. I quite like the anger in your voice. Nice.'

I walk away from her.

Later, when it's time for us to dance, the *ladkawalas* (people from the groom's side) knock it out of the park. Aanchal's face is as white as snow when we steal the limelight from their performance, which was middling at best.

8.

Aanchal Madan

'THIS IS AMAZING!' I scream into Vanita's ears. Vanita smiles widely.

It's 11 p.m. and we have been dancing since 8 p.m. The DJ knows everyone's drunk so the only music he shuffles is popular Punjabi music and none of the techno-EDM stuff that everyone has to pretend to like. There are a bunch of *dholwalas* who drum like their life depends on it. And like us, they are soaked in sweat and Vanita's parents have rained dirham notes on them. A couple of aunties have even hit on them seeing their vigour, quite telling of the state of their marriages.

Every now and then, Daksh and I collide into each other on the dance floor. But both he and I are too drunk to mind it. I even welcome it. When his hand touches mine, it feels electric. When I twirl and his fingers brush against my bare back, little jolts run down my spine. Every time he looks at me, I'm sharply reminded of the hunger with which he used to take me. It's as if my body crumbled and melted with his touch. Of the times we did it, in rented bedrooms, hotels, cars, empty movie halls, it never felt like the sedate term *making love*. It was always dirty, we always came out of it bruised and battered, our souls imprinted with each other, the experience etched in our minds. It was a duel in which we both were always winners. No, we didn't make love, he fucked me, and I fucked him. Long after we were done, I could feel the little tremors in my body just thinking about it. Long after we broke up, I would read his sexts, about what he would do to me. They were never the childish 'I would do you so hard, and it will be the best sex you have ever had' but used to be paragraphs detailing every lingering touch.

Even after I hated him, I longed for his body to touch me again and to be fucked like that again.

When we do dance together, one of the aunties circulates a couple of currency notes over our heads and then throws them in the air for the dholwalas to gather them up. The guys who were hitting on me now don't. I can almost hear them murmur, 'She will be in his room tonight.' And I wish, just for this night, he wasn't him, and he was just a guy I'd met at a wedding in a black kurta, beads of sweat running down his hair, dancing like there's no tomorrow. The girls who were hitting on Daksh have also backed off.

Every time we—or anyone on the dance floor—comes close to sobering up, Daksh pours a fresh batch of shots for everyone. With everyone else, he holds their face in his hand and pours the drink straight down their throats. Except for Gaurav, whom he has barred from drinking any more. And with me, he hands the shots over. Despite his betrayal, I want him to hold me by my throat.

'Do you want something?' I ask Vanita.

'WATER!' she screams. 'I WILL COME WITH YOU!'

We slip out of our heels, she hooks her arm through mine and we totter into the hotel. The lobby is a cool oasis of silence, but the beats of the music still thump in our ears and our feet can't help but tap at the rhythm. We find a couple of water bottles and an empty couch. As we plop down, it's as if all the exhaustion from our lives has finally caught up with us. We sink into the cushions, feeling like we've never rested before.

'Too bad you can only get married once . . . actually you can get married multiple times, but can only truly have a big wedding once . . . otherwise you look crazy,' grouses Vanita. 'I would want to do this once every year!' Her make-up is now streaked with sweat. She looks at her watch. 'Uncle–Aunty must have landed, right?'

'They are on their way,' I tell her. 'I think I have had my last drink.'

Vanita has a mischievous glint in her eye. 'Unless, of course, Daksh asks you to have another one.'

'It's not like he's holding my face and pouring it down my throat,' I say.

I can already feel the regret bubbling up inside me, knowing that the words about to spill out of my mouth are going to give Vanita endless ammunition for teasing, but I say them nonetheless.

'I really want him.'

Vanita chuckles. 'You think we don't see that? The way you two are dancing and looking at each other . . . if I keep that in the video, it's going to be vulgar.'

'I . . .'

'Everyone's drunk. No one minds. At least it's better than your brother. So much for being in love with me,' says Vanita.

I don't remember noticing Gaurav. My eyes have only been on Daksh.

Vanita explains. 'He was kissing Tejal, it looked as if he was going to eat up her entire mouth! Aditya's friends were pretty impressed he could pull her in.'

I would rather have my retinas burnt off than see Gaurav being intimate with a girl. 'That's what Daksh was doing, setting him up with that girl.'

She nudges me. 'He still loves you.'

'He likes playing the lover boy. And this is a wedding. The perfect place to play that role.'

She wraps her arm around me, letting me know she gets it. 'We are all twisted in our own ways. Guess we are looking for people who can accept us with that twistedness.'

'And you have found that person.'

She heaves a sigh and hugs me tightly.

'My parents are going to be after my life now that you're married,' I complain sadly. 'It's all going to be your fault. When everyone around was getting married, I kept telling them I will get married when Vanita does, and then you stabbed me in the back. If you had held out, I could have said, "See! Even she's not married."'

She rubs my hand. 'You will find someone. Who knows, you might just find someone in the US. Though I expect you to come back here, okay? Don't become a US citizen or something. Do a *Swades,* earn some money and come back.'

'That's the plan. Will be there for a few years,' I say. 'Also, Maa–Papa won't be able to put pressure to get married.'

'Good plan.'

'My body is now itching to dance again.'

I make her get up. She clasps my hand. 'I'm glad you're here.'

9.

Aanchal Madan

As the cab pulls up to the front of the Atlantis, Daksh and Gaurav are ready and waiting. I piece together what must have happened. Daksh would have asked Gaurav to go to his room, but an inebriated Gaurav would have insisted on coming to meet Maa–Papa. And so he's here, eyes rolling, slightly swaying, smiling stupidly. Gaurav rushes to open the door while Daksh heads to the trunk of the cab.

When I hug Maa–Papa, it doesn't feel like I have been away for just a few hours. Gaurav's hug lasts longer. He spends less time at home and more at his office and his own flat. Since last year, when Gaurav bought his own two-bedroom apartment near his office, he keeps asking them—and me—to move in with him. I keep telling him that our parents will not move out of the house

I paid for. I am the elder kid, after all. But that's only part of the reason. The other reason is that Daksh lives in the same building as Gaurav and I didn't want to bump into him. Worse still, I didn't want my parents to get more reasons to like him. Like right now, he has touched their feet, asked them about their flight, his voice rich with empathy, told them not to worry about their luggage, already has the key to their room and has chai waiting in the room.

So needy.

'I am so happy to see you here, beta,' says Maa, cradling Daksh's face with a gentle touch, as if he's a precious piece of her own flesh and blood. 'I will see you in the morning?'

'Aunty, you have my number. If you need anything, just let me know,' he answers, as if he's not a wedding crasher but a wedding planner. 'And you know I never miss breakfast. Who knows who I might meet there?'

Maa–Papa laugh at this often-recounted joke. I hate it when they do that. Treat Daksh as one of us.

'We are also here only,' I remind Maa, hooking my arm into hers and walking away from Daksh and Papa.

Gaurav interlocks his arm with Maa from the other side.

As we walk towards the room, I overhear Daksh and Papa talking animatedly about the weather, the last test match between Pakistan and India, and how petrol prices have risen again since they last spoke. Papa talks to Daksh more often than Gaurav. Papa believes Gaurav would be in the wilderness, lost and struggling, without Daksh's guidance. Blah. If Daksh is so good at taking care of Gaurav, why isn't he whisking him away from Maa–Papa who have literally shrunk at the stench of vodka coming from Gaurav and frowned at his wasted, unsteady steps?

Daksh leaves us at the room door wishing all of us good night. Gaurav turns away from us and pulls Daksh into a long embrace. I think Daksh gets a kick out of my family loving him more than they love me.

'I will see you in the room,' Daksh tells Gaurav and walks away.

'Drink only as much as you can handle!' Papa scolds Gaurav.

Papa is the only one among us who has remained unimpressed by Gaurav's newfound success and all the flashy trappings that came along with it. I know, in Papa's heart, he wants him to put on a white shirt, a blazer, a tie and go manage a small team of people in a bank or an FMCG company. He's proud of him, but he doesn't understand it. Just like he doesn't understand why his twenty-five-year-old daughter refuses to even start meeting boys for marriage. I have lost count of the times Papa has slyly tried to put the idea of Daksh and me together.

As we settle them into the room, memories flood back of our first stay in a hotel like this seven years ago.

Just then, the bell rings and Vanita walks in. She has changed into her pyjamas, her make-up's all smeared. Normally, Maa–Papa wouldn't bother showing up for the wedding of any of my other friends. But Vanita is a different story. They love her and keep telling me to be more like her.

'Aunty! You should've come earlier!' complains Vanita, pulling Maa into a hug.

She touches Papa's feet.

Papa touches her head lightly. 'Where's Aditya?'

'He's still making some last-minute arrangements,' says Vanita without a crease on her brow, when we both know Aditya's probably vomiting from all the fancy cocktails Daksh has been whipping out for him.

Maa makes Vanita sit on the bed next to her. 'Look at you, so beautiful. And your *mehendi*! Such nice colour.'

'I know, right,' slurs Gaurav from the corner of the room. He points at Vanita. 'She's the best! Look at her! She could have been . . .'

Maa glares at Gaurav. Papa grumbles from his side of the room.

'I don't mind him,' says Vanita with a giggle. 'I'm so glad you're here.'

'Ask your best friend also to get married, *na*,' pleads Maa. 'She doesn't even see the profiles Papa sends her. I don't know what she wants.'

'Aunty, she will do it when she feels it's the right time. For me, the right time is now, maybe not for her.'

Maa lets out a long, sad exhale as if the burden of the entire universe rests on her shoulders. 'I don't know when the right time will come for her. She keeps saying career is important, it's important, don't we know that. You are also getting married, na? So? What's the big deal?'

Gaurav's drunk giggle cuts through the room. 'What . . . I was . . . what . . . she should have gotten married to Bhaiya only when he asked you!' says Gaurav playfully, in a jumble of slurred words. 'It would have—'

'Gaurav, shut up!' I cut him. ' Maa, please tell him not to drink so much if he can't handle it. Gaurav, just go and come back when you're sober. *Kuch bhi bolta hai.*'

Gaurav's still looking at me with the dopey grin.

I feel the weight of Maa's stare as she pivots to face me. 'Did Daksh ask you to marry you? You told us he didn't like you.'

Before I can answer, Vanita butts in, 'Not very seriously, Aunty, just in a jokey sense. Gaurav, you should go to sleep now. Come, I will take you to your room.'

Vanita gets up and walks towards Gaurav.

Maa looks at Papa and then at me. 'Why did you refuse Daksh? You were shy?' She affects a very soft tone. 'Do you want us to talk to Daksh? He will listen to us.'

'Maa, yaar!' I cut her. 'What are you saying? Gaurav's drunk, he's saying anything. Please don't talk to anyone. And when the right time—'

My words are cut by Gaurav's stupid chuckles. Vanita's now tugging at his arm, trying to get him to stand up.

'HE IS NEVER GOING TO MARRY HER!' slurs Gaurav as he stumbles on to his feet. 'He could have been my real brother . . . actually, brother-in-law . . . actually *saala* . . . wow . . . oh no . . . I would be the saala—'

'GAURAV! Please get out,' I command.

As Vanita yanks Gaurav by the arm towards the door and he staggers away from us, I feel a sense of respite wash over me. As they disappear from my line of vision, I let out my breath.

The door's just closing when Gaurav asks Vanita, 'Would . . . you tell me . . . would . . . no, you tell me . . . would . . . Aditya marry you if you aborted his child without telling him? No . . . no . . . chance, right?'

The door closes behind them.

10.

Daksh Dey

The beach at the Atlantis would have once been serene and peaceful, but that's not what you can expect during peak tourist season when they descend like locusts with their swimsuits and floral shirts. But I'm glad there are people around so I can pretend to look somewhere than into the sad and bewildered eyes of Aanchal's father.

I make a mental note of not letting Gaurav ever drink again.

'You kids think you know everything,' he mumbles softly, his voice thick with emotion. When he turns to catch my gaze again, it feels like his wrinkles have become deeper, like someone has taken a knife to it. 'What kind of career is this that she couldn't take out a few months? Wouldn't we have raised the child? She could have gone to office! Who would have stopped her?!'

'Uncle,' I respond with as much calmness as I can muster. 'It was three years ago.'

The disappointment in his voice is palpable. I can feel it in my bones. I have felt it too.

The first time Aanchal called me, it was from a clinic. She had already decided on the course of action. She knew how I was going to react, so she didn't even bother telling me. The next week, she was going to take two pills and fix her 'mistake' in just twelve hours. She asked me to come to Delhi and be by her side, saying the process wouldn't be painful but it would be comforting to have me there. Her words hit me like a freight train, two bombshells dropped in rapid succession. In one moment, she told me I was going to be a father, and in the next, she had decided that there couldn't be anything worse than raising a child at this age. She had made her decision. And she demanded support. I had begged her, grovelled, pleaded with her to think about it.

'This is not the right time for me to be a mother,' she kept telling me.

I pleaded with her not to take the pills. She kept sending me flight options to Delhi. I promised that I would stay at home, take care of the child, and she could chase her dreams.

'The child would be my responsibility,' I told her.

'It's been barely a month since Vicky,' she reminded me coldly.

For a week, we shouted and screamed and called each other cold, heartless and selfish. On the seventh day, she took the pills in the presence of Rajat.

'Go fuck yourself,' I had told her when she informed me it was done.

'Why did you not come to stop me? You just stayed in Mumbai and kept shouting on the phone!' she screamed.

'You know why!' I screamed back. 'How many fucking times do I have to tell you it was Baba's prosthetic—'

She interrupted me with a long sigh. 'I didn't want you to stop me,' she said forcefully.

'Make up your mind, Aanchal.'

'That's what you're not getting. Things are important. Baba, Rabbani, my career! This pregnancy wasn't important. Is this the time for us to get married and be a family? No! There are other important things!'

'What's the problem in having everything?!'

'You're just another . . . guy who wants things his way. You know what you should have done, Daksh? You should have supported my decision. If you truly loved me, na, that's what you would have done!'

I still feel a knot of pain when I think of it. I feel heat radiating from the pit of my stomach. I push the thoughts out of my head.

'Uncle, she didn't want to be a mother who gives birth and then goes off to work,' I lie to placate him. 'I think we should also look at her perspective.'

The pain in the bottom of my stomach rises.

Uncle shakes his head. 'Maybe it's our fault. We pushed her too hard to be successful and now that's the only thing she knows.'

'This is no one's fault,' I tell him. 'There's nothing right or wrong about this. It is what it is.'

'One day, beta, she's going to look back and regret this decision. You mark my words. She will miss a family and then all this career growth will count for nothing.'

'But she has a family, Uncle. You, Gaurav, Aunty . . . what else does she need?'

'Her own family,' cuts in Uncle.

'But things have changed, Uncle. You also know that. She has worked so hard in her life. Why shouldn't she want success? Hai na? And I've known for very long that everything she does, she also does for you. She wants to give you rest. But if you start scolding her for this, not talking to her, then she will lose all her strength. Please don't do that. We will see what the future holds. For now, don't break her hope.'

Her father exhales deeply. 'And you were okay with what she did?'

Some lies are better than truths. There's no place for idealism in happiness. If there was, Aanchal would have not done what she had done for her happiness.

So I say, 'It was her decision.'

My mind wanders off to what the future might have looked like had things been different. Aanchal and I in a one-storey rowhouse. Downstairs it would have been her and me, upstairs Rabbani and Baba. We would have had a little garden with our three-year-old kid plucking flowers, and Gaurav monkeying around with Baba's blade-runner prosthetics. These warm visions of the future hurt even worse because it was within my grasp. Gaurav's a brother, I love him more than I should. And her parents love me more than I have given them reason to. If only Aanchal . . .

The gnawing ache in my bowels intensifies.

'Are you okay, Daksh?' asks Uncle. 'You're sweating.'

'I'm fine . . .' My voice is punctured by a groan. A shooting pain rises from my lower abdominal area. 'I must have eaten . . . something bad.'

'Aunty has homeopathic—'

Before he can complete what he's saying, my knees buckle under me. The pain's unbearable.

My words slip out in a painful whisper.

'I think I need to see a doctor.'

11.

Aanchal Madan

'You should have gone with him,' Maa scolds Papa, who was sitting next to the driver, commanding him to drive faster and cut between lanes.

'How would I know he would require an operation?' Baba shoots back.

'You know nothing only. He was in so much pain and you didn't think you should go?'

Papa shakes his head. 'I thought it could be food poisoning.'

'And only he got it? No one else. You say anything. Poor Daksh,' Maa says. 'He has no one here.'

That's a bit rich because not only us, but every other person in the sangeet who was dancing and drinking with him has gone to the hospital after him. It's as if he's been spreading pheromones in the air.

Maa locks her gaze on me. 'What did Gaurav say about Daksh? Is he okay?'

'He said they will operate on him in an hour,' I answer.

Maa nods.

No one speaks another word in the car, which is a relief. Gaurav's damning revelation should have triggered a torrent of judgement and vitriol from my parents, yet it has been remarkably restrained. Maa refused to speak to me and Papa, and instead of speaking to me, she wanted to talk to Daksh.

But Daksh distracted everyone by doubling over on the beach. Suddenly, the wedding party, which had been too drunk to even remember their own names, descended to the lobby, called an ambulance and then took a fleet of taxis to the hospital. While I am indebted to him for this timely distraction, I am surprised at the degree of affection these strangers have for a guy they met only hours ago. It's not the first time that this has happened. Time and again, I have seen people at Gaurav's events—the shrewd marketers, the ambitious brand executives—turn mellow and treat Daksh like he's one of them. Last year, I told Gaurav he was stupid to be splitting the revenue of Phoenix Rising Gaming evenly between Daksh and him when it was he who was the undisputed star gamer.

Gaurav looked at me as if I was an old, evil hag trying to poison his ears.

'You don't know where I would have been had he not been there,' Gaurav had said coldly to me.

'You would have found another way.'

'I would have lost my way. You don't know anything.'

The hospital—even the emergency section—is calmly and weirdly inviting. There's an aroma of coffee and freshly baked goodies wafting in the air from the coffee shop nearby.

We take the elevator to the third floor. Outside his room, Aditya and a bunch of his friends are waiting. Some of them are still in the suits they were wearing at the party. They all look worried, drunk and hungover at the same time.

'Are you not even going to come inside?' asks Maa as I stop at the door.

Papa holds my hand and drags me inside the room behind him. For all I know, in their minds, they have gotten me married to Daksh because he impregnated me. They would learn it the hard way. Just because Vicky has seen me naked doesn't mean he owns me, and just because Daksh got me pregnant doesn't mean I owe him something.

Despite his condition, Daksh appears to be without pain. His kurta has been removed and he now wears a flimsy hospital gown, barely held together by strings. As we enter the room, Daksh greets us with a pained smile. As he doubles over a little, I notice his strained biceps, which is a strange thing to be noticing about him. I find myself weirdly wondering if the gown is the only thing he's wearing right now.

'So many people not allowed, sir,' the nurse complains in her thick Malayali accent and schoolteacher demeanour. 'The entire wedding party can't be here.'

'This is the last thing I want too,' Daksh says and then doubles over in pain. 'Sorry Vanita, for spoiling your night.'

Vanita waves him off dismissively and clicks a picture of him. 'This is what happens when you come to a wedding without a wedding gift.'

'Nurse,' Daksh says. 'I want my appendix dipped in formaldehyde, gift-wrapped and given to this girl.'

Vanita crinkles her nose in disgust. Daksh leans back into the bed, clutching his abdomen. He has made sure not to make any eye contact with me.

Just then, Gaurav's phone rings and fills the room with its shrill sound. I see that it's a video call from Rabbani. She's much older now, nine or ten. From the little snippets Daksh shares on his Instagram profile, I have noticed she's whip-smart and is often taking down her brother with her brutal comments.

'DADA!' she squeals when he answers. 'LOOK WHO DOESN'T DO POTTY ON TIME!'

She breaks out in cute laughter.

She's not the only one. I hear two boys on the speaker too. Their laughter echoes in the room. Everyone, including the nurse, is giggling now.

'It's all the Diet Coke!' one boy says.

'And the bhujia!' the other boy says.

'Okay guys, enough!' says a lady whose voice I recognize immediately.

Amruta from *Kids Raising Kids*.

She's the kind of seemingly perfect woman who's making us all look bad by managing two kids, a career in education and a podcast irritatingly well. She has the kind of gravelly, naughty voice that's built for radio, the kind of voice that guys fall in love with over phone calls. I liked her the first time I heard her, and then hated her with a passion. Her understanding and chemistry with Daksh were unmissable. Half of their podcast is just one of them saying, 'I feel the same!' or 'I thought it was only me who thinks like this!' They are usually about things I don't think or care about—kids, family, chores, education. Their banter is natural, free-flowing, and they look as if life has brought them together. As if it's fate! I imagine if the three of us would go out, I could just walk away without informing them and they wouldn't even notice and keep talking. On their social profiles, people ask them if they are a couple. They have never answered this.

'Do you want us to come, Daksh?' she asks. 'The flights are expensive, but I'm thinking I will send the kids by cargo, and I will take a business-class ticket.'

'I'm not coming in a hundred lifetimes,' jokes an older voice, which I guess is Daksh's father. 'I have had enough of Dubai for a lifetime.'

Uncle has been on a recovery journey that's seen him heal more than anyone has the right to. From the clunky functional prosthetics, he has now graduated to the cyborg-looking blade prosthetic and leads a running group that wakes up at 4 a.m. for their runs. A few weeks ago, he had posted a shirtless picture of himself and other men in his running group, looking too fit for his age. Interspersed with his running pictures on LinkedIn are the consultancy projects he does every now and then. Sometimes I feel as if I had only imagined it all: Mumbai, his skeletal frame and his desire to embrace death and depression.

'I will be back in two days,' says Daksh.

'Does it pain, Dada?' asks Rabbani.

'You're joking? Me and pain? I eat pain for lunch.'

'Of course, you do,' chuckles Amruta. 'Listen, I'm landing in the morning. Your Baba is taking them out for the day.'

Daksh shakes his head. 'You're absolutely not leaving them with my father. I don't trust him with kids.'

'Oye!' his father says. 'I raised you!'

My own father laughs. 'Dey *ji*! This is what kids are like these days!' He walks to the bed and then waves at Daksh's father.

'*Arre*! Madan ji, long time.'

Amruta interrupts this. 'Can we have this conversation later? Daksh, I will come in the morning, okay?'

'No,' Daksh insists. 'I will come to you.'

Daksh then looks at the screen for a few seconds. His eyes grow soft and the conversation happens through subtle expression changes. It's like their own secret language. Like they know what's there in each other's hearts without needing to use words.

'Fine,' says Amruta. 'We will wait then.'

Then there's a long pause.

'I miss you, Daksh.'

I miss you.

Amruta's words make my world stop.

Suddenly I feel the air get sucked out of the room, and I am gasping for breath. The words, said with the sincerity of a monk, the seriousness of a dying person, are brimming with love.

My heart breaks.

The words make me feel small, diminished, just a blurry background in the story of Daksh and Amruta, a footnote, to be forgotten. I'm no one in Daksh's life story, just a mistake in the past.

It's not just me, the others feel it too.

Vanita turns to me with a look of pity. Maa–Papa exchange a glance tinged with a sense of sorrow. Even Gaurav catches my gaze as if to tell me that Daksh and I were a missed opportunity and I would come to rue this in the future.

And when I turn to look at Daksh, his eyes looking softly at the screen, the small curve of his lips, I feel a sharp pain piercing my heart. A pin-prick that burrows deep and fills me with an all-consuming ache. My pain is punctuated by a squealing voice.

'EW!' say the kids together. They, too, have sensed what's happening between Daksh and Amruta.

Daksh has an entire constellation circling him, and I'm alone, a dying planet.

12.

Aanchal Madan

No one moves from the waiting room till the time the doctor—whose son turns out to be a fan of Gaurav—emerges from the operation theatre, slips off his surgical gloves and tells us that the operation was a success. He adds that Daksh's last words before he was put under were that his appendix be gift-wrapped and given to Vanita, which the nurse had to respectfully decline because medical waste is not allowed to be taken outside the hospital.

'No part of him is waste,' Gaurav says, 'but you can keep it or dispose of it. But let me tell you, every bit of my friend is precious.'

Gaurav then gives the doctor a signed Nintendo Switch for his son, which he had someone send over from the hotel.

The doctor tells us Daksh will be unconscious for a while and will have to stay under observation for a day.

It's decided that everyone will go back to the hotel except Gaurav, who will move into the room with Daksh. Papa offers to switch places with him in a couple of hours.

'I'm not going anywhere,' says Gaurav rather dramatically.

Back at the hotel, everyone disappears into their rooms, to catch some sleep before the *haldi* ceremony, which Vanita had pushed by two hours.

I get into bed but sleep evades me. I toss and turn but all I can think about is Daksh. Maa–Papa talked to me on the way rather normally. As if their daughter hadn't just robbed them of a chance of a granddaughter.

'What did Daksh tell you?' I had asked them.

'Not to come between you and your dreams,' Papa had replied without any hint of anger in his voice.

It's strange Daksh is asking them to do what he couldn't. But I can't escape the undeniable truth: he said what he did to protect me. I put on my earphones and play some music to drown out my thoughts about him. It has the opposite effect—every song seems like it was written for us. Be it a love song, a heartbreak song, an item song— all I think about is how it's about us. Nothing helps. After what seems like an eternity, I sit up and reach for my phone. I dial Rajat's number and recount the entire sequence of events to him.

'You should do what you want to do,' he says.

'That's the most generic answer you can give, Rajat.'

'And that's because I'm done playing a part in life-changing decisions of yours, bro.'

'You never had a problem before,' I argue.

Rajat was the only person I could turn to when I held that pregnancy strip in my hand and the result stared back at me. I was twenty-three and pregnant. I had to end it.

I couldn't have given up my freedom.

I had just broken free of Vicky's clutches. My freedom was so new even then that I would wake up in the middle of the night in dread, thinking that Vicky was back in my life somehow. I knew my parents wouldn't understand my reasons to terminate the pregnancy. After my job started, I knew they felt an emptiness in their lives. They would have jumped at the opportunity of being grandparents. Like Daksh, they would have promised to do everything to relieve me of the pressure of raising a child.

But I couldn't have done that to myself.

Why would I rob myself of time, a successful career, romance, a married life before a child? Vanita—with her own rules and ideas about family—would have tried to convince me otherwise. And since I love her to death, I would have listened.

Rajat came along without a question. He took charge and immediately booked a hotel room for the foetus tissue to pass, and to recover from the bleeding, filled the room with snacks and made a list of shows we could watch. That day is the actual anniversary of our friendship. He—and I—both believe that was the day we saw each other as friends for life. It was forged through tears, loss and new beginnings.

'My own life-changing decisions are enough, bro,' he complains. 'Nandini has been fucking dancing on my head asking me to take the next step and that's kind of enough for me.'

'Okay.' I take a deep breath. 'Why aren't you getting married to her?'

'She thinks I still have feelings for you.'

'Which you don't.'

'I'd rather be suspended from the ceiling by my pubic hair. My parents are going to create a big scene if I tell them about Nandini. They will feel intimidated by her parents. Anyway . . .'

'You're dying to tell me what to do.'

'Run the opposite way, bro,' he says with a finality in his voice. 'It's just the rush of a new place. All of your relationship with him has been that—the Andamans, Mumbai and now this. You think you're a new person in a new place and you want to take all these risks. Real life is not a vacation. And you also know he's too good for you.'

'Good to know my friend is on his side.'

'He's good in a way guys are supposed to be good—family, love, romance and all of that. You're not like that. You're good in a way where you protect your own happiness.'

I take a deep breath. 'So, I should just ignore this little whisper in my heart.'

'Snuff it out. Murder it.'

I close my eyes and imagine what my life would look like in the US. My second international flight, my new home in a new city, so many new things to see, enjoy, worry about, get intimidated by. With the glut of emotions I am going to feel, this little flutter in my heart will be dead before I know it.

'Done,' I say, 'and you should tell your parents. They love you too much to not agree.'

We disconnect the call. The flutter is no longer merely that. It's a drum beat that's getting louder with every passing second.

13.

Daksh Dey

It takes me the better part of an hour to send Gaurav away for the wedding. The unslept, tired nurses are thankful the last person from the wedding party is out of their hair and not telling them how to do their job. The head nurse connects the Wi-fi on my iPad and I click on the Zoom link shared by Gaurav for the wedding.

'Whose wedding is it?' asks the nurse as she peers into the iPad. 'The tall girl in the lehenga, right? She's beautiful, by the way.'

I nod.

The nurse laughs and then hooks a new IV drip into my cannula. 'If they are coming, tell them to come here with some sweets, okay?'

There's finally some movement on the Zoom screen. The first few guests reach the mandap and start to appraise the decor, nodding, appreciating the niceness of it all. Then, Aditya's friends stumble in drunk and high, their eyes searching for snacks. They take pictures, throwing peace signs in the air, leaving the elderly onlookers perplexed.

I miss being there.

A few minutes later, the pandit appears on the scene and starts to arrange all the sweets and *samagri* needed to get Vanita married to Aditya. Aditya's a nice guy, I noticed that. There are some people whom you see and then think, yeah, these guys fit in like a glove. That's the vibe I get from Vanita and Aditya.

Quite the opposite of what I felt during the brief time I got to date Aanchal. From the moment we exited that washroom on the mezzanine floor, I knew my heart, my soul, everything I was given by God was no longer mine. On the way to the airport, after she rejected me once, I tried to make her understand the depth of my feelings for her. I recounted every flutter of my heart, every lost breath, every gasp I'd felt over the years. She told me later that my confession had scared her because I looked 'too sincere'. How can you be insincere about love? Love is the realest thing there is.

When she stepped out of the taxi, she was ready to give *us* a shot.

I missed her from the moment she disappeared for the security check at the airport. I wanted to Hulk-out, tear the airport apart, keep her from going away from me, breathe in the same air as hers. When her flight took off, I felt an unbearable physical pain shooting through my body. We had promised we would meet again, but it still broke my heart. Delhi didn't seem like a two-hour flight away. Instead, it seemed like centuries and alternate realities separated us. In the forty-three days we were together, I was in a haze of inexplicable joy. When I talked to her, it felt as if I was talking not only to the love of my life but also my therapist, my best friend, a little adorable puppy, an old, wise person, a giggling baby, all mashed up. When we made love or, as she liked to say it, when we fucked, the world seemed to disintegrate and splinter, like we were the singularity from which new worlds are created. Her naked body was my favourite thing in the world. She told me it was mine to take.

Many times during the day I would stop and examine this gooey feeling in my heart and wonder what it was doing there, making me feel warm and fuzzy all day long. Then it would strike me: because I was with Aanchal. People argue that the honeymoon period is heady, but I knew this was more. I wasn't so much drawn to the excitement of the newness, but the possibility of spending the rest of our lives together. I must have lived a thousand futures together. I was the Doctor Strange of love stories, sifting through every possible future for us, bending time and will. We could take a billion paths together; some would absolutely crush us, but even then, they would be paths taken together.

And then, it all came crumbling down.

Aanchal likes to paint me as a pro-life traditionalist who would make women bear children against their choice. Maybe that's how she sleeps better at night. But she couldn't understand that no one, literally no guy she would ever meet, not even she, knew more intimately what it was like to raise a child than me. I had lived it, day in, day out, as a twenty-year-old. All I had asked her for was nine months. Nine months to carry the child, to give it life, and then she could hand it over to me. Even if she birthed the child, gave the cute one wrapped up in cloth in my hands and pranced away to the airport in her hospital gown to live a life on her own terms, I wouldn't have minded in the slightest.

But she couldn't sacrifice those nine months.

She likes to argue that she was not ready for a relationship, but I know that's nonsense. I hadn't conjured up the love I felt for her in those forty-three days. She loved me. She stayed up nights, wrote me letters, sent me video confessions of her love. I could feel her love in the touch of her fingers, in the look of her eyes, in the way she lit up when we met, in the tremble of her voice, in the nimbleness of her gait. She might have raised walls around us a million miles high, but I know that caged within those walls was a heart that beat for me. I could hear it pump even beyond her fortified walls of career, ambition, future.

Was that all untrue then? Of course not.

She took a selfish decision.

Because that's what she is—a girl with no sense of sacrifice and who holds on to her own happiness like Gollum screeching, 'My precious!' Did she not know what I thought about children? About my history with Rabbani and how caring for her had saved me and given me purpose?

After I dumped her, I thought I would lose my way. And I did but it could have been far worse had I not made a friend. An unlikely one at that.

Gaurav, and his parents, think I saved Gaurav from oblivion. Far from it, it's Gaurav who saved me. Watching him play video games is, and always has been, one of my greatest joys. I have watched him play with aggressiveness, concentration and dexterity unmatched by anyone. His spatial awareness, his reflexes, are once in an era. Aanchal once asked him why he had to share his earnings with me. After all, he was the one with the talent. He could make it big on his own. And she was right. Gaurav doesn't need me. It was just dumb luck that I happened to be in the right place at the right time.

When I break out of my reverie, I see on the screen that a crowd has gathered in the mandap, and it's aglow with the sacred fire burning brightly. And in the crowd, I spot her. Dressed in a sparkling pink lehenga that hangs alluringly just below her waist, her hair cascading in dramatic curls over her shoulders, while a glittering *tikli* dangles from her forehead. Every time she moves to shower rose petals on Aditya and Vanita, my eyes flit to her bare midriff and I wonder what it would be like to touch her again. I don't know if it's the drugs in my system, but my entire body feels alive thinking of her. Every time I look at her, I feel reduced to my most basic of evolutionary biology. To find a thing a beauty, because not all beauty is conditioning—Aanchal is beautiful by any standard.

When the camera pans, I see Vanita and Aditya walking towards the mandap. I feel a sharp pang in my heart. The camera follows the two—they keep stealing glances at each other as they walk. They are showered with petals, Aditya's friends are hooting in the background, and Aanchal's piercing whistle penetrates through the loud cheers. She's encouraged by the aunties. She slips in two fingers and whistles harder.

When they sit, the light of the ceremonial fire lights up their faces. Their happiness is so complete, so pure, so palpable, I can feel its warmth all the way in this cold hospital room. The pandit starts to chant. The Sanskrit verses are unintelligible, but I can feel their power seep into the air around me. Two souls getting intertwined forever, their lives now one. It's the beginning of something magical. In a person's life, can there be a decision more powerful, more courageous, than deciding to share your life with someone? If the world is a stage, as people like to say, then you're an actor, and the one you're married to is your audience, your cheerleader, your director, your co-actor, the reason why you exist. We like to pretend that careers and personal milestones are important, but we forget it's all make-believe. Would the world be a better place with twenty-minute deliveries of daal-khichdi? Or would it be better if all of us found someone who loves us and accepts us truly as their own?

Vanita and Aditya's happiness feels bittersweet for me. When I look past them, I see Aanchal again. And for a moment, it looks like she's looking straight at me. Of course, she's not. The camera has just caught her. But she doesn't look away. Her gaze lingers as if she can look through the lens, the mysterious Internet waves and the pixels of the tablet, and then straight at me.

In the forty-three days I had spent with her all those years ago, I had learnt to recognize each of her expressions, and this one was unmistakable.

This is one of love, longing or regret.

Or all three.

14.

Aanchal Madan

I had been steeling myself not to feel anything.

Vanita's wedding, Vanita's marriage, it's her new beginning. I should just feel happy for her and not let myself get carried away in the wave of emotions. When she gets up from the mandap, Vanita seems to be a new woman. Her fingers intertwine with Aditya's, she looks powerful—the exact opposite of what I thought she would seem. Marriage is surrender. And yet she looks bolstered by it. As if now, forged in the ritual fire, she has access to Aditya's courage, strength and intelligence too.

My gaze shifts to the camera, the one that's live-streaming the wedding to all the guests who couldn't make it today. Daksh is among them. Even though the link says there are fifty-four viewers, it feels like he's the only one on the other side. I can almost hear his voice in my ear, full of love and pain. 'This could've been us,' he whispers. My heart aches at his words, but a little voice in my head whispers back, 'It could still be us.'

Every time I blink, my heart wages war against my mind. My heart conjures up an image of Daksh in a black kurta, hair perfect as it always is, his sharp jawline glistening, his eyes as watery as they can get, a small smile on his face. It's warmth and sex and comfort all rolled up into one. My heart reminds me how alive I felt, how deep was the happiness, how fuzzy the comfort, how passionate our touches.

Daksh likes to think I severed all ties with him with the coldness of a serial killer. That's how he sees me. First, I got the abortion, and then I walked away from him as if it were nothing.

But he saw none of the nights I spent crying for him. He doesn't know of the searing longing I felt for him for months on end. He knows nothing of the crushing pain I felt, the long hours I used to stare at the phone waiting for his call, the envy I used to feel looking at other couples and how my heart used to break every time he used to talk to Gaurav and all I wanted him to say was, *Hi Aanchal*.

I felt starved of his love.

It was like he got me addicted to the drug that was him and then left me to deal with the withdrawal cold turkey. After the anger of his abandonment petered out, all I felt was pain. A sharp piercing pain that wouldn't go away and became a part of my being. Every other happiness paled in comparison. Sometimes I think if Daksh didn't work with Gaurav, it would have been easier to get over him. Because now I saw Gaurav and Daksh become best friends and then brothers. I could see how much love Daksh was capable of, how much love I could have received from him but missed out on. If he could love Gaurav, a legitimate stupid person, so much, how much would he love me? Every time Daksh stayed up nights driving Gaurav from one gaming competition to another, cooked meals for him so Gaurav wouldn't get lethargic during sessions, made his bed, laundered his clothes, took care of him—it all made me burn with envy.

I could see what we could have been. He would have been perfect.

Had he come back, would I have accepted him? In a heartbeat. They say your idea of love is shaped by what your first love story teaches you. My first love story, which I know is with Daksh and not Vicky, taught me to wait. Wait for time to heal all wounds and for the love story to start.

As Vanita steps down the stage and comes to hug me—her first time as a married woman—my heart feels full to see her happy.

'Now you can have non-dirty, legitimate sex in the eyes of God,' I whisper.

'It's still going to be dirty,' she whispers back with a laugh.

The rest of the relatives swarm around her, showering her with blessings and wishes. Her mother—who anyway lives in a different city than her—still bursts into tears. Everyone knows that Vanita's not going to someone else's house where she will play the coy *bahu*, she's going to invade it and make it her own.

I find my own parents tear up when Aditya and Vanita touch their feet to get their blessings. Gaurav sulks in the corner, playing the part of the heartbroken lover as he gazes longingly and smiles sadly at them. He looks ridiculous. Then Tejal links her hand with his, and he breaks character and smiles.

When they leave the wedding venue for the hotel lobby among cheers, I feel a sudden void inside of me. Maa–Papa tell me that they are going to the room to change, get some rest and then come down for the reception dinner. Gaurav has already begun chatting with Tejal animatedly. Aditya and Vanita's friends are making their way to grab another drink. They implore me to join them, and I promise to catch up in a little while. I know I would be lonely with them. Which is strange because I have never felt lonely in my own company.

Seeing Daksh again after so many years has opened up the wound again. This time I can't slap a Band-Aid on it and hope for it to heal. No matter how far I run, this yearning that has taken root in my heart again is only going to rise. I had ripped him out of my heart once, but I know I won't be able to do it again. Back then, I had a well of anger to draw from. I felt wronged, betrayed, but now I have nothing. I just have love in my heart for him.

The residual anger I felt for him petered out the moment I saw him, his kind eyes, and sensed that he still felt a little love for me. I have found myself drowning in a sea of emotions—the love I feel for him and the love he still has for me. It's a powerful combination, and I'm not sure if I'm strong enough to handle it. But one thing is sure—seeing him again has changed everything.

Ten minutes later, I find myself in a taxi hurtling towards
the Saudi German Hospital. What do I have to lose that I haven't
lost already? I want to tell him that I want to give us another
chance. I want to propose a truce and a love story. A difficult,
long-distance love story, but a love story worth a shot. I'm going
to go down on one knee and ask him to give me one more shot. I
understand this would require an apology, that's mission-critical.
And I would give him one. Who says relationships are built on
the truth and only the complete truth? If an apology would set
things right, then why not?

I burst through the hospital doors, the frigid air blasting me
in the face. The hallway feels as though it has been dipped in ice,
sending shivers down my spine. And then I notice it, my lehenga
is not meant for the morgue-like cold. All around me, eyes are
glued to the spectacle. A girl in wedding finery, sprinting through
the halls of a hospital. I know what they must be thinking, how
crazy I must seem. But I don't care. I have to do this. I catch a
glimpse of the nurse from earlier as she exits his room. With every
step, the absurdity of my actions grows clearer. But I don't stop.
I can't stop. And then I'm there, standing in front of the nurse.

The nurse shakes her head. 'Another one? There's already a
visitor inside.'

Visitor? I wonder how Gaurav could have got to him before
I did. My heart pounding, I slowly nudge open the door and
freeze in my tracks. My breath catches in my throat as I see her.

Even with her back turned to me, I know exactly who is
sitting on Daksh's bed: Amruta Thakur. The sound of her voice,
so familiar and so detested, fills the room.

'No ceremony . . . just you and me . . .' the voice says.
'Seeing you like this, it's scary, Daksh. We shouldn't be alone,
should we? It makes sense, you and I, our kids . . . it's like we
were custom-built for each other.'

The silence between them feels like an eternity, as if time itself has frozen in place. I try to command my body to move, to run to him and stop what's about to happen. But my limbs refuse to obey me, and I am trapped. My heart beats so fast that I can barely hear myself think. With each pulse, it seems to shatter and then mend again in a never-ending cycle. I want to scream out my feelings to Daksh, but my voice is stuck in my throat, and all I can manage is a shallow breath. My feet feel like they're bolted to the ground, and I can't move, no matter how hard I try.

'We are . . . made for each other,' says Daksh.

The woman leans over and kisses my Daksh on his lips.

Is that the end?

In a world where timing is everything, one can't help but wonder—will Daksh and Aanchal ever find their moment? They've always been two halves of a perfect whole, two people whose connection runs deep. Daksh, with his passionate heart, has always been a boy and then a man in love, spellbound by Aanchal since the moment their paths crossed on the sandy beaches of the Andamans.

Drawn by her beauty, who she was made her his North Star.

Aanchal, on the other hand, always cherished Daksh's companionship. He was her one-person audience.

However, as the sands of time slipped through her fingers, she began to recognize the love that was always present in Daksh's eyes—a love she mirrored but had never noticed before, a love she felt deeply but couldn't reciprocate.

But their timing was never right.

Now, as Aanchal stands on the precipice of realizing her feelings, Daksh, weary from the years of unrequited love, has started to look elsewhere—for stability, for predictability, in Amruta.

So far, I have been straightforward with you about the story. And you must have thought, this is where it ends. I thought that too. Now, I can't help but ask—will they ever conquer the vagaries of time and find each other? Or will different versions of them in love with each other be forever out of sync?

But now is not the right time. Think about what you'd like the ending to be, and we'll find out soon . . . together . . .

When I finish writing the concluding part.

—Durjoy Datta

PART 2 OUT SOON!

You might also like

WORLD'S ~~WORST~~ BEST BOYFRIEND
DURJOY DATTA

Hate is a four-letter word.
So is love.
And, sometimes, people can't tell the difference . . .

Dhruv and Aranya spend a good part of their lives trying to figure out why they want to destroy each other; why they hurt each other so deeply. And why they can't stay away from each other.

The answer is just as difficult each time because all they've wanted is to do the worst, most miserable things to one another.

Yet, there is something that tells them: THIS IS NOT IT. If you want to know the answer to it all, read the book.